Something was wrong in their little corner of the desert...very, very wrong.

The sun hid below the horizon when Rachel walked to the main building and entered the hotel kitchen. She stood alone in the dim light, smelling the lingering sent of bleach and disinfectant. Determined to do battle with her long-eared visitors, she assembled a plate of vegetables from the walk-in, artfully arranging carrots, celery, and lettuce, humming as she worked. Her sneakers squeaked on the vinyl floor when she crossed the kitchen, hoping she could come up with a more permanent solution to their bunny problem soon, without hurting Peter Rabbit's family.

She stepped outside the back door of the kitchen and the sky greeted her with a wide band of pink on the eastern horizon. The air felt cool and delicious. A roadrunner scooted out from a cluster of olive trees with a little critter in his mouth, and darted past, surprising Rachel.

She gazed out toward the desert, scanning the area for signs of furry visitors. A pair of taupe-colored rabbits hopped out from behind some rocks near the employees' parking lot. They lifted their heads, sniffed the air, and looked in her direction.

Rachel stood statue-like for several moments before they turned and bounded toward the courtyard. Stealthily pursuing them in the dim light, she stepped through the cracked and buckled parking lot until she spotted something out of the corner of her eye.

Someone had parked a car at the edge of the lot. Rachel looked at it quizzically. She was sure the old Subaru belonged to no one who worked at the hotel. So why was it there?

Rachel approached the car, noticed something lying on the blacktop by the front tire, and smelled something bad. The dawning sun suddenly splayed over the object and Rachel froze in place like a pillar of salt. The object was a woman, her head bent at an awkward angle as if her neck were broken, her eyes and mouth open in terror. Rachel knew she was dead.

Something was wrong in their little corner of the desert…very, very wrong.

The sun hid below the horizon when Rachel walked to the main building and entered the hotel kitchen. She stood alone in the dim light, smelling the lingering sent of bleach and disinfectant. Determined to do battle with her long-eared visitors, she assembled a plate of vegetables from the walk-in, artfully arranging carrots, celery, and lettuce, humming as she worked. Her sneakers squeaked on the vinyl floor when she crossed the kitchen, hoping she could come up with a more permanent solution to their bunny problem soon, without hurting Peter Rabbit's family.

She stepped outside the back door of the kitchen and the sky greeted her with a wide band of pink on the eastern horizon. The air felt cool and delicious. A roadrunner scooted out from a cluster of olive trees with a little critter in his mouth, and darted past, surprising Rachel.

She gazed out toward the desert, scanning the area for signs of furry visitors. A pair of taupe-colored rabbits hopped out from behind some rocks near the employees' parking lot. They lifted their heads, sniffed the air, and looked in her direction.

Rachel stood statue-like for several moments before they turned and bounded toward the courtyard. Stealthily pursuing them in the dim light, she stepped through the cracked and buckled parking lot until she spotted something out of the corner of her eye.

Someone had parked a car at the edge of the lot. Rachel looked at it quizzically. She was sure the old Subaru belonged to no one who worked at the hotel. So why was it there?

Rachel approached the car, noticed something lying on the blacktop by the front tire, and smelled something bad. The dawning sun suddenly splayed over the object and Rachel froze in place like a pillar of salt. The object was a woman, her head bent at an awkward angle as if her neck were broken, her eyes and mouth open in terror. Rachel knew she was dead.

The abandoned hotel on Blood Mountain stood vacant for twelve years in the Arizona desert, shrouded in mystery and rumors, until LA playboy Buddy McCain inherits the property and decides to reopen the inn. He convinces his contractor pal, JT Carpenter, to move in and help him remodel the once-fine hotel, but then, trouble starts.

When JT's wife Heather and her dysfunctional sister, Rachel Ryan, join them in their project, the group is systematically terrorized by someone who desperately wants them out...and leaves a dead woman in the parking lot, just to make sure they get the message.

While Buddy and JT struggle to reopen the hotel, Rachel defies the orders of the local deputy sheriff and investigates the strange happenings on her own, but Blood Mountain holds tight to its secrets.

KUDOS for Blood Mountain

I thoroughly enjoyed Blood Mountain by Joanne Taylor Moore. I love old abandoned buildings that are brought back to life, so this book was just my cup of tea. The story centers on Rachel Ryan, whose sister Heather and brother-in-law JT Carpenter team up with a longtime friend Buddy McCain to restore the old hotel he inherited on Blood Mountain in the desert of Arizona. When Rachel loses her temper, and consequently her job, she has no recourse but to join the motley crew in the desert to help with the hotel. Rachel figures that she will be bored stiff from day one, but little does she know the desert is teaming with excitement: hunky men, dangerous criminals—are they one and the same?—secret caves, drug runners, and murder. The plot had so many twists and turns I couldn't put the book down until I finished it. – *Taylor Jones, reviewer*

Blood Mountain by Joanne Taylor Moore was extremely well done for a first time author. This lady has real talent. The plot was extremely complex, with so many bad guys that

I couldn't be sure who the real villain was right up until the end. The characters were delightful and totally believable. Rachel came across very well as a smart, spunky, independent lady, who was too much of a curious busybody for her own good. Despite strict instructions from *two* determined law-enforcement officers to leave well-enough alone and let them handle it, Rachel sticks her nose in where it doesn't belong and nearly gets her head taken off. And while I was screaming at her not to do the dumb thing I just *knew* she is going to do anyway, I was right there with her, rooting for her as she did it...the book is a page-turner, and I will also add that it's a keeper. – *Regan Murphy, reviewer*

Acknowledgements

I would like to thank and recognize the following people for their kind and generous help:

Fran Yackowski, Jan Lefebvre, Valarie Donnelly, Joan Stanhope and Gail Thompson for being painfully honest about my first draft; Steve Lund, and my email writer's group, especially Don G. Porter, Bill Marsik, Ivan N. Pierce, and Joan Condit—all authors themselves—for taking the time and extreme effort it took to edit my work; my Yuma writer's group, John Coultas, Robin Christensen, Ana Ferguson, and Debbie Lee, author of Journey to Jordan, all of whom were with me every inch of the way, and Rick Sanchez, Rocky Sailors, and Deann Sandry who gave me technical advice. A special thanks to our son, Kevin Moore, for his technical help and advice, and to Jack Jackson for his cover design.

May God bless you all.

Blood Mountain

Joanne Taylor Moore

A BLACK OPAL BOOKS
PUBLICATION

Black Opal Books
BECAUSE SOME STORIES JUST HAVE TO BE TOLD

Genre: Mystery/Suspense/Romantic Elements

This is a work of fiction. Names, places, characters and incidents are either the product of the author's imagination or are used fictitiously, and any resemblance to any actual persons, living or dead, businesses, organizations, events or locales is entirely coincidental

Dedication

This book is gratefully dedicated to the two men in my life, without whose help this book would never have been published: my husband and soul mate Larry Moore, and my mentor and friend, author Don G. Porter.

Prologue

The Discovery:

The crimson sky reflected on the water, turning it red, like the color of blood, as Eduardo Ruiz cautiously stepped toward the canal blockage. A stench hit his nostrils and he jerked his head back. He spotted a shotgun lying on the ditch bank; he stopped to stare at it.

It was Juan Rodriguez's old Remington. Suddenly, the hair on the back of his neck stood up. He took another step and froze, a scream stuck in his throat.

Jammed up against the gate was the twisted body of a man. Floating next to it was a head, bobbing in the current like a giant apple. It was the body and severed head of Juan Rodriguez, the night irrigator.

1

Juan:

Twilight came; heat lightening danced in the darkening sky. Juan's thick, calloused hands raised the gate of the number three ditch. He watched the canal water flow in and move along silently, seeking the portholes that led to the field of new hay.

Juan had worked this job so many nights that he could tell by the feel of air that the temperature still hovered at a hundred degrees, but the trickle of breeze was enough to dry the sweat on his face when he stood up to survey the farm in front of him. In the glimmer of twilight, only a fraction of the forty-nine-hundred acre spread lay within his line of sight.

Most men shied away from the job of night irrigator. It was a lonely, boring job, lifting gates and watching water flow. Juan loved it. Aside from the occasional snake he'd find residing in a ditch, he loved the hush and stillness of the night, the solitude and peace that came from working by himself.

Juan was a writer. While he drove the canal banks, thoughts struck him like the sharp little rocks that hit the undercarriage of his truck. He filled notebooks with his stories, with his hidden life, written under moonlight, sharing them only with the woman he loved and her young son. The boy would run to him, begging for a tale of dragons or adventurers, and he'd catch a glimpse of the boy's mother and her approving smile.

When Juan stood, he noticed a flicker of light out of the corner of his eye. It was a greenish dot on the east side of Montana de la Sangre, or Blood Mountain as the gringos called it. He jerked his head to stare at it.

Standing near the center of a long range of tall peaks, Blood Mountain rose higher and bolder than the rest, and it proved true to its name. Before twilight faded, the massive, rock-strewn mountain turned the color of blood.

Most illegals wouldn't have given the greenish light another thought, but Juan was not like most. His curiosity was strong enough to ensure that he always carried binoculars in his truck, and his common sense required he also carry his 12-gauge Remington buried under a blanket behind the seat, just in case his curiosity lead him into a situation where he needed it.

He adjusted the binoculars in time to watch the second green light appear. The two

3

green orbs floated in the darkness not far from the old Indian burial ground. Like everyone else who worked for Venkman Farms, he had heard the old ghost tales and was discouraged from checking out the area. It was private property, anyway, most of it locked up behind a chain-link fence, belonging to the owner of an old, abandoned hotel.

Yet Juan often wondered why lights would appear in a place that had been unoccupied for so many years.

He went back to his truck, dug around under the seat, and retrieved one of his cheap spiral notebooks.

In the dim light of the cab, he flipped ahead to an empty page and noted the date and time. Turning to the front, he realized he first had seen the green lights two years ago. He gazed up inquisitively at the mountain.

Juan went back to his work and finished up quickly, Montana de la Sangre now faded to a dim outline pasted on a darkened sky. He checked his watch and calculated he had two hours to kill.

He figured he'd have plenty of time to drive up the mountain, find the source of the lights, and get back to open gate number four before the water filled the field. He was dead wrong.

The Venkmans:

Franz Venkman raced the Dodge Ram over the dusty roads, crushing the chunks of clay that spilled out from the old canals. He cried out when he reached the damage, slid to a stop, and felt a knife-like pain cut through his gut.

Irrigation water had broken through an earthen dike surrounding acres of month-old romaine and quietly flowed into an adjacent field to the south, turning it into a calm, shallow lake. He stared at the disaster. Pale green seedlings floated aimlessly on the surface of the lake like tired swimmers, their roots no longer connected to the fertile soil. Forty acres of new lettuce was totally destroyed.

Franz stepped on the gas and raced again toward where Eduardo waited, all the while filling the cab with his swearing and cursing.

Otto, huddled in the passenger seat as far away as possible from his father's spewing anger, stared straight ahead, and said nothing.

The Dodge slammed to a stop next to the new Ford. The father and son jumped down onto the canal road where Eduardo Ruiz stood waiting.

"What the hell happened?" Franz screamed at the foreman. "I got forty acres of ruined lettuce out there. Do you have any idea how many thousands of dollars that means? Do you?" he demanded.

"Dad," Otto Venkman said, nudging his father on the shoulder. "Over there." He cocked his head toward the canal.

Franz turned his head toward the water. He noticed the body, muttered a curse, and let out a deep breath. "Who was he?" His eyes turned to steel and his lips pulled into a thin, tight line.

"Juan Rodriguez, a night irrigator," Ruiz answered softly.

The sun ascended over Blood Mountain, bathing everything in a golden light. The men stood silently for a few moments as moist heat rolled stealthily toward the cooler soil of the irrigated fields. They turned at the sound of an approaching truck.

"You called the sheriff?" Otto asked, recognizing the vehicle.

"*Si, señor,* right after I call you."

"For a suicide?" Otto turned to his father. "Do we need to get the law involved with this? That Tucker will be all over the place."

"Too late to worry about that," Franz answered with a dour look.

"But you know he killed himself," Otto said, his voice a notch higher. He turned to Ruiz. "He was depressed. Don't you remember, Eduardo? He'd been acting strange lately." He stared at the foreman with the same cold blue eyes his father had. "Eduardo?"

The foreman, his face brown and wrinkled from years at his job, understood. He dropped his eyes and nodded. "*Sí, señor,*" he finally said.

Chapter 1

Rachel:

Rachel Ryan balanced a corrugated box on her shoulder with one hand, unlocked the door to her apartment with the other, and kicked the door open with the pointed toe of her Manolo Blahniks. She stepped over the threshold, dropped the box on the floor with a thud, and flung her Gucci purse toward the sofa.

Kicking off her four-inch heels, Rachel sank her feet into the lambskin rug, slipped off her designer jacket and threw it behind her. She stretched her arms and straightened her back, drawing herself up to her full five-foot-eight-inch height, then shook her arms, trying to get the numbness out of them. She took a deep yoga breath. The room still smelled of the Chanel No. 5 she had sprayed on herself that morning.

The yoga breath didn't help. *You stupid twit. Now you've really done it.* She plopped down on the sofa and it sagged pitifully beneath her. *What were you thinking?* She reached over with long, slender arms and snagged the box, tugging it to her. She studied it. The box contained the personal effects she had liberated from her office on the mezzanine of the hotel where she had worked until earlier that morning.

Her gaze flowed over her tiny living area and kitchen, then again at the photos, award plaques, certificates, and artifacts that filled the box. *Where am I going to put all this junk?* The room overflowed already. The bedroom was even smaller. Perhaps she shouldn't even bother to empty the box. What if she couldn't find another job in Boston and had to move? That was a horrifying thought.

Her mood started sinking. *Don't cry, don't cry,* she admonished herself. She looked at the box again, at the photo that lay on top. Two women stood with their arms around each other, one older, one younger. Rachel and her sister. What in the world would she tell Heather?

Rachel's eyes clouded up. *Stop. Don't cry.* She jerked herself up and went to the kitchen, zombie-like, and automatically opened one of the drawers. No cigarettes. Of course…she'd quit. No wonder she had been on edge. Perhaps she could go to her boss, explain her outburst, and blame it on the stress of quitting smoking. *Oh sure, that'll work.* She opened the refrigerator. Not much there. She poked around the containers of leftover Chinese food, found part of a lime and a bottle of gin in the back. She pulled both of them out. *The trouble is, I was right. Henson was wrong, and he knows it. I just made the mistake of telling him that in a rather exuberant manner.*

She cracked open the turquoise bottle and poured some of the contents into a glass. She squeezed in a few drops of lime and took a sip. The Bombay Sapphire slid down her throat, warm, comforting. She took another Yoga breath. *Relax. Relax. You can handle this.*

She walked into the bedroom, tiny but clean. It contained a queen mattress and box spring, a lone nightstand and dresser that didn't match, and a closet crammed with designer clothes. A mirror hung on the outside of one of the doors. She yanked the bed covers down. *Why was I so stupid? I know better than to shoot my mouth off like that.* She thought about crawling in and pulling the covers over her head.

She slipped out of her skirt, hung it on a hanger, and squeezed it into the closet. She took another slow sip of gin, pressed a button on the answering machine, and walked around the bed.

"Rachel? It's me, Heather." The machine began its tinny recital of her sister's message. "I just called to see how you're doing. Please give me a call."

That was it, just her sister. No boss calling her back, no sympathetic co-workers, no other messages.

Rachel put the glass to her lips again. She couldn't talk to Heather, not today, anyway. She didn't need, didn't want, mothering.

She stared out the window at the Charles River. It looked so cold, so peaceful. A few of the trees lining the river were turning an incredible shade of salmon pink. Fall was definitely in the air in Boston.

Have I totally lost my mind? She turned away and looked at her reflection in the full-length mirror, almost expecting an answer.

She pulled the pins out of her hair and let it flow loosely over her shoulders and down her back like a river of pale champagne. She shuddered, remembering the ugly scene with her boss, and then pictured herself choking the old man until his eyes bulged out of his head.

Rachel tipped her head back and emptied the glass. Perhaps she should call Dr. Kent. She walked back around the bed to the phone and pictured him, composed, analytical, wire-framed glasses resting on his perfect Anglo-Saxon nose.

No, not just yet. Too many thoughts whirling around right now. Maybe tomorrow. She picked up the pretty turquoise bottle and poured herself another drink.

JT Carpenter, Buddy McCain:

Jackson Thomas Carpenter studied the bid that lay before him, intently scrutinizing each paragraph. Columns of figures with cross-outs and red markings stared back. He could see his company making a profit, but would it be enough?

He rubbed his hairline, an old nervous habit he had since high school. His hairline remained the same as the one he had in high school, too. A little proud of that fact, he knew it made him look much younger than his forty-five years. A few gray hairs wove their way among the dark ones on his head, but to his credit, he resisted plucking them and considered the gray above his ears to be a distinguishing characteristic.

JT, as he preferred to be called, had grown a beard once, but the gray in it made him look more his age, so he shaved it off. Except for that little sin of vanity, however, he allowed himself few others. He never cheated on his wife. He rarely lied. He didn't use bad language nor did he allow his employees to do so within his hearing, and his hearing was very good.

A loud knock broke his concentration and he spun around in his chair.

"Buddy." JT's deep voice boomed across the room.

Buddy poked his bushy head through the doorway. "Got a few minutes?"

"Sure. Where've you been? I've been trying to get a hold of you for a week."

"It's a long story," Buddy said, stretching out the word *long*. He strode into the room, arms swinging, blue eyes flashing against tanned skin and sun-streaked hair. He plopped into a black leather chair in front of the desk. "I almost don't know where to begin."

JT eyed his long-time friend and warning lights went off in his brain. Buddy never did fit the mold of a serious-minded accountant and managed to bring the term *woman trouble* to a new level. "Don't tell me you got married again," he said cautiously.

"Yeah, right. Why is it you always think it's a woman?"

"Why?" JT's eyes rolled up and he looked at the ceiling. "Let me see...I've known you, what, fifteen years?" He dropped his gaze to the man he sometimes considered to be a meat-headed younger brother. "You've been married and divorced three times, and that broken nose on your ugly mug is the result of an irate husband finding you with his wife. Think that could be it?"

"Hey, that's not fair. I never knew she was married." Buddy unconsciously rubbed his crooked nose. "Besides, you were flat-out lucky to find a wife like Heather first time out of the chute."

15

Before JT could reply, a puff of wind off the Pacific Ocean blew some papers off his desk. He caught a breath of the fresh, salty air; and with a reach of his long, muscular arms, he swung around and lowered the window over the credenza. He glanced out at the sea, less than a mile away, the waves rising and sparkling in the sun. A gull squawked loudly, sailing by the window in a deep dive.

JT walked around to the front of the massive oak desk and took the stack of papers Buddy picked up. "Okay, so tell me."

Buddy looked up at JT, dwarfed by a man the size of Smokey the Bear, and gauged his mood. "Two things, actually," he said, taking off his titanium-rimmed glasses. "The first is a surprise and the second is the offer of a ride in my new Beech Bonanza."

JT's eyes lit up. "You bought a new plane?" If he hadn't been so busy running his construction company, JT would have taken flying lessons and bought a plane himself.

Buddy just grinned and nodded. "Oh, she's a real beauty, too. Top of the line."

JT dropped his gaze to the papers in his hand and let out a reluctant breath. "Man, you know I'd love to, but I'm working on this bid for the city of Long Beach."

16

Buddy blew the dust off his glasses and scrunched up his face. "Now don't start giving me that stuff. I happen to know how much you love all that paperwork, and I'll bet that bid isn't due for a week."

JT turned his head away and studied the pile of papers littering his desk. Buddy was right.

He loathed paperwork, and the bid *wasn't* due for a week.

Furthermore, JT questioned whether he even wanted the job with the city of Long Beach.

Bureaucratic red tape was so pervasive, he was even having crazy thoughts about selling the business.

Buddy tried to contain his excitement while he watched his friend mentally debate his decision.

"Okay," he pressed, putting on his glasses. "How about if I throw in a free burrito and a bottle of Bud?"

JT thought about the offer for a few seconds and his mouth fought a crooked smile. "Make that two Buds and you're on."

Stanley Belinski:

"Mr. Templeton will see you now," said the tall brunette with the D-cup cleavage, standing up behind her desk. In her platform heels, she reached a height of six feet. She sashayed toward her boss's office, hips swaying, long legs moving like a lazy cat.

Stanley Belinski followed the trail of her perfume, head down. He brushed the wrinkles out of his suit, wishing he wasn't bulging out of his white shirt, and hoping Cyrus Templeton would cut him some slack.

"Sit down, Stanley," Templeton ordered. He spoke in a calm voice that rang with disapproval and sat behind a custom-made mahogany desk, surrounded by the aroma of expensive cigars.

Belinski trembled as he walked toward the chair. He could feel Templeton's eyes on him and heard that controlled, uninfected tone before. There would be no slack, he feared, and sweat beaded on his face.

The glare from the windows overlooking the city of Las Vegas blinded him, and Belinski waited while his eyes adjusted to his position directly in front of them. In the corner, a man the size of King Kong stood with his arms folded across his chest, the strap of his shoulder holster clearly visible. Belinski pressed his hand on his knee to keep it from twitching. He shifted his eyes back to Templeton, a short man whose beefy round head seemed attached to his body without benefit of a neck.

"I'm really disappointed in you, Stanley," Templeton finally said.

Belinski's stomach flipped over. "I can explain," he offered, eager to excuse his failure.

"The tax assessor—"

"Stop." Templeton commanded, holding up a hand. "I'm not interested in excuses. We made a deal. I agreed to forgive your quarter-million debt in exchange for getting me the deed to Blood Mountain.

"Yes, you're right. We did have a deal." Belinski looked earnestly into the dark glasses resting on Templeton's nose. "And we still do. I can get the job done, I swear. All I need is a little more time to talk to the new owner." Sweat rolled down his back and he wondered if his deodorant still worked.

The man behind the desk sat motionless like a fat wax dummy, his shaved head gleaming from the window's glare. "Time? Do you understand what's at stake here?"

"Yes, of course I do, Mr. Templeton, and let me assure you I can make it work." He pictured Templeton's bodyguard throwing him through the plate glass window, his body falling forty floors to the hot pavement. "I've sold eighty percent of the real estate in the east end of Yuma County for the last ten years," he continued. "I will deliver that property to you, regardless of what it takes."

Templeton rubbed his chin and stared out of his sunglasses with small, recessed eyes. "Regardless of what it takes?"

"Absolutely, sir. Regardless of what it takes." Belinski stared back without blinking, without moving a muscle, having no idea of what that could be.

Templeton continued to rub his chin while he considered Belinski's request. "Thirty days," he finally said. "Not a day longer."

He turned his head and pressed a button on his phone. "Raquel, you may see Mr. Belinski out now," he said, and dismissed the man with a wave of his hand.

❧❧❧

JT pushed the hangar door all the way open and admired Buddy's new acquisition. Buddy walked around the Bonanza to check it, and after lifting the cowling, he measured the oil and made sure everything was in place and secure.

Once inside the plane, Buddy set the throttle and turned the engine over until it caught with a cough. He adjusted the fuel mixture, ran the throttle up to twenty percent, and studied the instrument panel, his eyes going over every gauge.

In a way, he felt relieved that Heather had left town so he and JT could make the flight alone. He wasn't sure what Heather would think of his little surprise.

JT sat quietly, watching Buddy roll the plane down the taxiway. Although he loved to give Buddy a hard time, JT couldn't help but admire him. Eight years his junior, Buddy was a gifted CPA, a licensed pilot, and a multi-millionaire with brilliant ideas.

Then again, he could irritate you like a bird pecking on your forehead, and some of his ideas were totally wacko.

Turning onto the active runway, Buddy pulled the plane into the wind and pushed the throttle against the firewall. He grinned at the big guy next to him and pulled back on the column, feeling the plane start to rise.

"Okay, you can tell me the big secret now," JT said. "It's too late for me to escape."

"Not yet." Buddy turned his eyes back to the control panel, hit the toggle switch to retract the gear, and watched the altimeter turn steadily clockwise.

"You bought some property, didn't you," JT guessed. "That's what you're going to show me."

"Hey, stop trying to ruin my surprise," Buddy whined.

"I hate surprises."

"I know." Buddy gave him a wide, toothy grin, settling the issue.

After the Bonanza reached the desired altitude, the engine settled into a low, steady hum. Eventually the browns and tans of the Anza-Borrego desert came into view. "Beautiful plane, isn't she?" Buddy's eyes glazed over.

JT laughed. Beautiful planes and beautiful women had the same effect on his friend.

"She sure is," he answered, as the plane held a steady course on an easterly direction.

The block of stress that recently built up in JT's life diminished with every passing moment. He looked at Buddy, and for the first time, felt a tinge of envy. It surprised him. JT could easily afford the plane, so it wasn't that. The women? No, no. He studied Buddy's face. It was the suntan.

"What?" Buddy turned to him, feeling the stare.

JT shook his head. "Nothing." He turned his face away, but he couldn't remember the last time he had been outdoors long enough to get a tan. He couldn't remember the last time he hammered a nail or drove a Bobcat. He discretely squeezed the muscles on his arm. They felt loose, flabby. A wave of something flowed up from his gut. He pressed his head against the window. "Say, isn't that the Colorado River down there?"

"Sure is."

"Where are you taking me?" JT frowned, and then noticed their gradual descent.

"Mesquite, Arizona. We're almost there."

"Mesquite, Arizona? What's that?"

"Oh, it's a little town that would probably fit inside the parking lot of your business," Buddy joked.

JT squinted at him. "You bought a whole town?"

"No, and quit trying to ruin my surprise."

The older man shook his head. "I can't believe you talked me into this."

"Oh, don't be such a puss. I'll get you home before dark."

The plane banked, and JT caught a glimpse of the desert landscape spreading out below, followed by a narrow, winding river, and fields of gold and green.

"Okay, now look down," Buddy said. "See that mountain range at nine o'clock?"

The plane dropped and turned to the north, arching toward a range of rock-covered mountains. "Keep your eyes on that larger peak, the one that looks red. It's called Blood Mountain."

"Blood Mountain? Oh, that's a great name," his friend quipped, and craned his neck. "So what am I supposed to be looking for?"

"On the south side. See those buildings down from the peak? That's the Mesquite Mountain Inn." Buddy grinned. "That's it. That's the surprise. I own it."

JT gawked at the four buildings laid out in a rough square. He shook his head in disbelief, and then turned and stared at Buddy for several seconds. "Man, have you completely lost it?"

After tying down the Bonanza, Buddy and JT stood in the heat at the edge of the undersize airport, studying the somewhat battered, ten-year old Lincoln. "Is this the best you could do?" JT asked.

"Hey, be grateful this town even *has* a rental car," Buddy countered. "And an airport."

"This is an airport?"

"Oh, shut up, JT, and get in the dang car."

In spite of its age, the Continental started up and settled into a smooth purr. "See? An oldie but goodie," Buddy said.

JT buckled up and looked out through the layer of dust on the windshield. They were up on a mesa and he saw a long, fertile valley below, and beyond that, the mountain range they had viewed from the air. "Okay, Buddy. Exactly when were you planning on telling me what's going on?"

Buddy headed the car in the direction of the mountains, took a deep breath, and let it out. "You remember a couple months ago when my uncle Bryon died."

"Vaguely. You said you hardly knew him."

"True. But he liked me, no doubt due to the fact my mother named me after him."

"And he had no kids of his own."

"That, too."

"So you inherited his hotel? Is that it?" JT asked, eager to move on.

Buddy shook his head. "I hate it when you do that."

"I hate it when you take so darn long to get to the bottom line."

"Okay, okay. He left me the hotel, a few miles of mountains and a little nest egg."

JT let it sink in and let out a low whistle. "That sure was nice of him." He looked ahead at the mountains. "So tell me about the hotel. Is it in good shape?"

Buddy frowned and looked straight ahead at the cracked, pot-holed road they navigated.

"Well, not exactly."

"What's that supposed to mean?"

"Well, I uh, actually haven't been inside the place yet. It's been deserted for ten years."

"Oh, boy." JT turned his head away.

While the Continental ascended the winding road, JT pictured some of the wrecks he had flipped when he first went into the contracting business, buildings only a few years old. This would not be good.

"But the mountains are as good as new," Buddy joked, making light of his situation. "And to think, I almost lost the place."

"You almost lost the place?" JT repeated, wondering if Buddy had lost his mind. "What do you mean?"

"Well, for some unknown reason, Uncle Byron rarely paid the taxes after he closed up the hotel. When I found out about it, I flew right down and paid them off out of the nest egg he left me."

"Hmm," JT mumbled. "And how many eggs are we talking here?"

"Well, actually, all of them." Buddy kept staring straight ahead. "But it was either pay up or lose the place. I had three days before they put the property up for auction. What makes it more peculiar is that I had the feeling the tax assessor didn't want me to pay off the property."

JT turned to his friend with a puzzled look. "How so?"

"Well, first of all, he looked like he'd seen a ghost when I showed up. Then he starts telling me about all these things wrong with the place and about this guy they found near my property that blew his head off.

JT grimaced. "That doesn't sound good. But obviously, if it was a ploy, it didn't work."

"No, it didn't. Then, when I finally left the courthouse after two hours, this suit walks out behind me and gives me his card. Tells me he has a client who wants to buy the property."

"Interesting."

"I tell him I'm not selling and try to walk away, but he follows me, trying to press the deal. He offers me market value, plus the quarter mil I paid in taxes, plus twenty thousand more for my trouble."

JT frowned, wondering what kind of deal Buddy had gotten himself into. "So what kind of money are we talking here, kid?"

"About nine million total."

"Oh, boy." JT nervously rubbed his hairline, sensing something odd was going on. "People have been killed for a lot less than that."

The Lincoln crunched to a stop in front of a chain-link fence, and the two men climbed out, greeted by a stinging blast of hot air.

JT took a deep breath. The air smelled clean, tinged with something heady, like vegetation cooking in the sun. He looked around and heard something rustling through the weeds. He froze. A lizard darted out, scooted up on a pile of rocks, and stared him down. He had to laugh.

Buddy pulled out a large set of keys and starting jingling it, searching for the one to open the padlock hanging in front of him. JT pressed his face to the fence for a closer look at the Mesquite Mountain Inn.

Plywood was nailed over the windows and Mexican tile covered the roof. The slump block walls appeared to be in good shape and could last a hundred years or more. At first glance, the place didn't look as bad as he feared. Then his ears picked up the sound of an approaching vehicle.

"Don't look now, but we've got company," JT warned.

Both men watched the tan SUV screech to a stop, gravel flying, and an older man with a barrel chest and fat belly get out.

"How do, gentlemen?" the old man said, his right hand resting on the butt of the gun strapped to his hip.

Chapter 2

Heather:

Heather Carpenter hummed while she put away the groceries, arranging them on the shelves by categories and carefully folding the plastic bags. Previously, she had stocked the refrigerator with cheeses, cold cuts, and three gallons of milk, one of them chocolate. Pizza, burgers, and extra buns filled the freezer, along with six gallons of ice cream.

It was enough food for the twins for a couple of days, anyway. She laughed to herself but knew her joke was pretty close to the truth. She knew firsthand how much food two six-foot-four teenage boys could pack away.

She brushed a wisp of auburn hair away from her face and wondered if she and JT had

30

made the right decision. A stab of loneliness shot through her and she sat down at the little table in the kitchen trying to hold back the tears. Justin and Joseph's eighteenth birthdays weren't for another month, but already they were starting their sophomore year in college. After home schooling them for ten years, it felt a little scary that they were suddenly gone. No, it felt a *lot* scary; and if JT's parents weren't living on the other side of the duplex, she would never have agreed to let the boys live on their own.

Heather suspected the twin geniuses inherited their high IQ from her gifted parents. *No doubt a recessive gene,* she ruefully thought. *It certainly appeared to have skipped our generation.* That immediately made her think of her only sister.

"That Rachel Ryan has not returned a single one of my calls," she said aloud, venting her frustration at the empty kitchen. She was worried, and not without reason. Trouble followed Rachel like a lost puppy. Reaching for her cell phone, she shook the anxiety from her voice. She jabbed in Rachel's number once again, and tapped her foot while the machine on the other end repeated its spiel.

"Rachel? It's me, honey," she cooed sweetly into the phone. "I've left three messages and I'm starting to get worried about you. Please call me back."

Sheriff Dewey Tucker:

JT and Buddy stood in front of the chain link fence and watched the older man lumber toward them, his cowboy boots crunching the gravel on the road. He hiked up his pants a bit, though in no way did they cover his overhanging belly.

"Good morning, Deputy," Buddy said, noting the silver star on his shirt. "To what do we owe the honor of this visit?"

"I was just checkin' the area and was wonderin' what you gentlemen were doin' on private property," the deputy said. His eyes, hidden behind reflective lenses, scanned the two men.

Buddy's teeth glistened in a wide smile and he stuck out his hand. "I'm Buddy McCain and this is my friend, JT Carpenter. I'm the new owner of this fine establishment."

"Oh, yeah, I heard about you, Mr. McCain." The big man gripped Buddy's hand firmly, and then shook JT's. He squinted at Buddy. "And I can see you favor your uncle, too. I'm Deputy Sheriff Dewey Tucker." He smiled a big wide smile, his cheeks balling up above a long, gray mustache, reminding Buddy of a fat, happy walrus. "I'm sure sorry about Byron," he said, his smile gone. "He was a good man. I still miss him."

"Thank you. It's nice to talk to someone who knew him," Buddy said, relieved.

"A lot of folks around here knew him and liked him." Tucker stuck his hands in his pockets and rocked back on his heels, making his chest and belly look even bigger than they were. "He and Nell were really fine folks and the center of Mesquite's social life for a lot of years. Why, people came from miles around just to have dinner at the hotel." He lowered his head and shook it in a gesture of sorrow. "He never was the same after Nell died."

Buddy studied the older man. A little crusty perhaps, but sincere, and Buddy guessed the deputy and his uncle Byron had been good friends.

"What's the story on this?" he asked. He flipped his thumb toward the concertina wire and chain link. "There's enough wire here to surround San Quentin."

Tucker gazed at the long line of fencing that surrounded the buildings. "Five months after Nell's funeral, Byron had 'er all locked up. Then he left. Never came back."

The deputy paused and fixed his eyes on the large ring of keys in Buddy's hand. He dug in his pocket and pulled out a small key. "Here, why don't we try this one?"

A gust of hot wind blew dust against the men and a dried ball of tumbleweed hit the fence, scattering pale bits of weed on the ground. Tucker stepped up to the padlock and unlocked the gate. "Your uncle gave me the key before he left and asked me to check the place once in a while. So I did. But I guess I can turn it over to you now." He handed the key to Buddy and stepped back. "Are you planning on reopenin' the place?"

"That's what we're here to look at."

"Well, I reckon lots of folks might appreciate it if you do. Especially Byron and Nell, God rest their souls." He touched his hat. "Nice meetin' you both."

Tucker turned to walk back to his truck.

"Wait." A puzzled look crossed Buddy's face. "Can I ask you something, Deputy?"

Tucker turned back around. "Shoot."

"Is there any reason someone might not want me to take over this property?"

Tucker stroked his mustache and thought a moment. "See that farmland yonder?" He pointed toward the west valley below. "That's all owned by one man, Franz Venkman. He's been buyin' up land around here for over twenty years, but he got himself into a pissin' contest with your uncle Byron right after Nell died. Byron refused to sell just to spite ol' Venkman. Just closed the place down and ran this fencin' all over the property. Last I hear, Venkman was chompin' at the bit, waitin' for the county to sell it for taxes so he could snap it up for a song." He smiled that big walrus smile. "You done fixed that."

JT squinted at the deputy while the morning sun rose higher. "It doesn't sound like you like him much."

"Oh, hardly anybody likes him," the big man remarked. "It's just that everybody's afraid of him. Everybody but me, that is."

The deputy crunched his way back to the truck and Buddy and JT's eyes followed him. Gray hair sticking out beneath his Stetson testified to his age, but given his size and demeanor, Dewey Tucker still looked like a man you didn't want to mess with.

35

"Then there's the rumors, too," he called back in a rough voice when he climbed into his truck.

"Rumors? What rumors?" Buddy stepped up to the truck door and the deputy turned on the ignition.

"The hidden gold mine back in the hills." Tucker cocked his head toward the mountain west of the buildings. "Then there's the old Indian graveyard that some folks say is haunted. And the UFO sightings. Let's not forget them." Tucker smiled his walrus smile one last time and flipped up the air conditioner. "See ya, pardner."

He raised the fingers of one hand off the steering wheel in a cowboy salute and headed down the hill.

Buddy and JT looked at each other. "Let's see now," JT began. "You own a broken-down hotel in the middle of a rich man's ranch that's in the middle of nowhere that's got an old gold mine buried in it, dead Indians dancing around on it and aliens from space using it as a landing field." He pushed open the large, metal gate with a flourish. "What more could a man ask for?"

The sun perched straight overhead by the time JT completed a cursory check of the hotel and found it to be structurally sound. The Mexican tile roofs and slump block walls suffered no damage and kept out what little rain had fallen over the years. The chain link fence and concertina wire kept out everything else except the spiders and scorpions and maybe a few snakes. Even the plumbing and electricity worked.

The layout was well designed, another plus. The four units were set in a square, with the main building facing south at the front of the property. Twelve casitas sat part way up the hill at the back, parallel to it, affording the luxury suites amazing views of the valley. JT stood in front of them, gazing at the farmlands below. The air was so clear he could see machines working in the fields and the plumes of dust hovering over them.

A block of two-story guest rooms stood on his left and another on his right. He saw every room had a view of the courtyard, and he strolled through the grounds carefully, watching for snakes. He studied the patches of dried weeds around him, and imagined the colorful gardens that once flourished there. All that remained were skeletons of plants and shaggy trees. The pool and Jacuzzi were cracked and crumbling, their bottoms covered with years of blown-in dirt, a total loss. Still, the contractor in JT had to admit the place abounded with possibilities.

He strolled to the east end of the property, and stared at the southern sky. It was the color of a robin's egg, and it looked so clear he felt like he could reach up and grab it with his hand.

Lost in thought, he never heard Buddy walk up to him. "So, what do you think big guy?"

JT kept his eyes on the view. "Hear that, Buddy?"

Buddy turned his head in both directions, puzzled. "What? I can't hear anything."

"Exactly." JT grinned. "No cars, no planes, no air conditioners humming. Nothing but silence and peace, beautiful peace."

"Does that mean you like the place?"

JT turned to Buddy and the corners of his mouth twitched to turn up again. "You ready to buy me that burrito and beer? I'm inclined to give out more favorable comments on a full stomach."

Buddy drove down the twisting gravel road and through two miles of farmland before he reached the paved street with the sign announcing the town of Mesquite. They passed old mobile homes, in various states of disrepair, set up on blocks. Most of them, singlewide, with aluminum foil taped inside the windows, squatted in dirt yards that substituted for landscaping. A coin laundry followed, along with an ancient gas station that stored a broken-down truck without wheels and an old yellow school bus off to the side.

JT frowned and reassessed his opinion of the area.

Buddy looked over at his friend. "I can hear your brain clicking from here, so why don't you think out loud?"

"Man, I hate to say this, but this town looks like a big dump." JT kept staring out the window.

"It's not," Buddy insisted, "You'll see. But what about Blood Mountain? What about the hotel?"

JT scratched his hairline. "I can't believe it, Buddy, but your property is amazing." He turned to look at his friend. "You know I've always told you never to get into anything with your heart, only your brain."

"I know," Buddy agreed. "But when I found out about the inheritance, all I could think of was how awesome it felt when I came here as a kid. Until tenth grade, I spent every Christmas vacation here. Why, I remember the time—"

JT held up a hand. "Hold on. You can reminisce another time. Right now, you need to think about what you want to do with the place."

"You're right," Buddy agreed, closing the lid on his box of memories. "But that's where you come in. I need you to tell me. Is it doable?"

"Doable? For you? As in you alone want to bring it back to its former glory?"

"Well," Buddy answered sheepishly. "Not exactly."

JT turned his head away. "Oh, boy."

They passed by a John Deere store that displayed a few signature green tractors out front, followed by a gift shop painted a bright pink. "Right now I can only tell you what I think," JT said. "The place has tremendous potential. But I can't even keep up with the jobs I've already signed for, if that's what you have in mind." He kept looking out the window while they wove their way up a hill and passed a golf course on the side of the mesa. Large luxury homes surrounded its perimeter.

"This is where the good part starts," Buddy said, noting the development.

"Well, that's a relief. But where do they *eat*? I haven't seen one restaurant," JT said. Up ahead, he spotted a real estate office. "Pull in there." He pointed. "Real estate people always know where the best restaurants are. It's part of the job training."

"No cars," Buddy said, turning into the small parking lot. He pulled up in front of a building stuccoed in a dark terra cotta with a sign that read Mesquite Realty, Stanley Belinski, Realtor. A little clock on the door announced someone's return at three.

"Where the heck is everyone?" JT grumbled, looking around. "There isn't a soul on the streets. Is this the Twilight Zone or what?"

Buddy glanced at the car thermometer as he backed up the car. "It's a hundred and four degrees out there. Don't expect to see many sane people walking around right now." He pulled out onto Main Street. "Besides, I don't think a day or two of starvation will hurt you." He poked the slight paunch above JT's belt.

"Watch it," JT said, slapping Buddy's hand away, not happy to be missing a meal. "Hey, hold on." He spotted a sign set back along the pitted road ahead. "I think we've found our place."

Conspiracy:

"Where are you?" Little asked, his voice anxious.

"At Redondo Park," his partner said.

"What are you doing there?" Little's voice raised a notch higher.

"I just drove into town and needed to take a leak. That okay with you?"

"Stay there."

Little jumped into his new Dodge Ram and drove to the park near the town limits of Mesquite. He spotted his partner's truck under a ficus tree with grey elephant arms that shaded half the parking lot. Pulling up right beside it, Little rolled down his window and gestured to his partner to get out.

"Do you always have to be so paranoid?" his partner asked, moving to a nearby bench. "Nobody's gonna plant a bug in my truck."

"You never know," Little said. "We can't afford to take any more chances."

"Okay, okay. So what's the big deal?"

"It's Ezra Sample. He screwed up. Byron McCain's nephew came in and paid off the taxes. Blood Mountain is off the auction block, the hotel, everything."

"This is what you're freaking out about?" Little's partner shook his head and looked away in disgust. When he turned back, his voice softened. "We always knew that could be a possibility. It won't affect our work."

"But we *paid* Ezra," Little insisted.

"Well, that's life, ain't it, Little? Ezra's a stupid tax assessor, a government employee, with no real power."

Little narrowed his eyes. "I asked you not to call me Little."

"Okay, okay, sorry. Look, this is not that big of a deal. Get Ezra to pay you back the money, if that's what's bugging you. The fact that someone took over the property doesn't mean a whole lot. What are the chances, really, of anyone finding out about us?"

Little raised an eyebrow. "That Mexican did."

"So that's it. I thought we already talked about that. Juan is not a problem. Everyone thinks it's a suicide. End of story."

"That's what you think," Little spit out. "Our illustrious deputy sheriff, Dewey Tucker, is still nosing around about that."

"So? He's a moron. He'll never come up with anything. We covered all our tracks, believe me. There's not one speck of DNA in the truck, as if he'd ever check for that to begin with. I even burned the tarp we carried him in."

"I wish I had your confidence," Little said, looking around, making sure no others were in sight. "But I'm starting to get a real bad feeling."

Chapter 3

Rosario:

Gravel scattered when the old Continental turned into the parking lot of Pablo's Cantina. The restaurant looked small from the front, which needed work, especially at the bottom where chicken wire showed through the missing stucco. But the place was open, and a welcoming Budweiser sign glowed in the window.

A rotund, middle-aged Hispanic man, wearing what had been a white apron in a former life, waved them in. Pablo, they guessed. JT and Buddy breathed in the greasy smell of deep fried tacos, seated themselves, and picked up the paper menus on the table. Colorful pottery plates decorated the walls and streamers of cutout paper flowers hung from the lattice ceilings while Mexican music blared from a speaker somewhere.

After a curious look at the two gringos, the other patrons turned back to their food. The lone waitress, who looked young enough to be in high school, approached them with salsa, tortilla chips, and two large glasses of ice water.

She asked for their drink order and gave the new faces a dazzling smile, hoping to inspire a healthy tip.

"Two Budweiser's, *por favor.*" Buddy smiled back at her, partly because he nearly always smiled, and partly because he had a weakness for pretty girls. "What's your name?"

"Rosario. And there's no enchiladas left."

"No problem. We're burrito kind of guys anyway."

"The *machaca* is the best."

"Okay. Bring us a couple each."

Buddy's eyes followed her. She looked good from the back, too.

JT chugged his glass of water and set it back down on the table. "So, what do you think?"

"I think she's beautiful." Buddy watched Rosario disappear into the kitchen.

JT groaned. "Get a grip, man. She's young enough to be your daughter. Besides, I was talking about the property."

"Hey, you're the expert," Buddy countered. "Why do you think I brought you? Certainly not for your looks."

JT gave him a sideways glance. "I know why you brought me." He salted and dipped a tortilla chip and plopped it in his mouth. "You thought if you could get me to look at the Mesquite Mountain Inn, I'd fall in love with the place and want to be partners in the project."

"That so, huh?" Buddy tried to keep a straight face. He took off his glasses and blew the dust off them. "Did it work?"

Before JT could answer, Rosario appeared at their side with the two beers and a pitcher of ice water.

"What's there to do around here, Rosario?" Buddy asked, figuring she had to be at least twenty-one to serve drinks.

"Not much." She wagged a finger at them. "Are you the new owners of the hotel on Blood Mountain?"

Buddy and JT looked at each other. "News travels fast."

"*Si,* it's a very small town. Almost anything anyone does is news."

"I'm beginning to find that out," Buddy nodded. "Tell me. Is there any truth to the story about the gold mine on the mountain?"

Rosario smiled kindly. "Oh, the mine is still out there, somewhere, on the north side of the mountain. But it doesn't matter. All the gold is gone."

"So much for retiring early," Buddy joked, flashing his movie-star smile. "And what about—you know—that guy that committed suicide last week?"

Rosario's smile vanished and her eyes turned to ice. "I'll get your lunch," she said, turning away.

"Great job, Buddy-boy," JT whispered after Rosario left the table. "You sure have a knack with the ladies."

"What did I say?" Buddy asked, looking dumbfounded. He glanced around the room but no one seemed to take notice of him except Pablo who stared at him with a puzzled frown on his face. Somewhat relieved that Pablo remained at his station behind the bar, Buddy nervously tapped his fingers in time to the lively Mexican music and hoped to blend in.

When Rosario returned with the burrito plates, Buddy sought her eyes. "I'm terribly sorry, Rosario," he apologized. "I didn't mean to upset you."

"Juan was my boyfriend," Rosario suddenly blurted out, her eyes filled with pain. She lowered her head, embarrassed, tears dripping down her cheeks. Then she raised her head and her voice and cried out toward Pablo. "And he didn't commit suicide. He was murdered!"

"*Silencio*! *Callate, Mija!*" Pablo's voice boomed from across the bar.

Rosario turned her back to him and muttered something in Spanish, not loud enough for him to hear. Buddy crouched down, wanting to sink beneath the table. All the eyes in the room turned toward them. *So much for blending in.*

"What did they say?" Buddy whispered, after Rosario left. "Other than *por favor,* my Spanish is pretty rusty."

JT leaned closer to him. "He told her she better shut up. She told him to take a hike."

Back inside the car, JT nodded in the direction of the cafe. "Well, that was most interesting."

"Down right freaky, if you ask me."

49

JT shifted in his seat, adjusting the seat belt. "So you won't mention the thing about the murder to Heather."

"No way, *amigo*. My lips are duct-taped shut." Buddy turned the air conditioning on full blast. "And speaking of Heather, do you think she'll have a problem with you going in with me on this?"

"Heather? Oh, heck no. You know Heather. She'll think this is a great idea."

ɞɷɞ

"You did what?" Heather Carpenter's eyes flashed open and her jaw dropped. "Jackson Thomas Carpenter, have you lost your mind?"

JT sat on the sofa and stared at his wife of eighteen years. He never expected this. What in the world was he thinking? How could he be so wrong about her reaction? He looked around the cavernous living room where sunlight streamed through floor-to-ceiling windows. Photos and accoutrements of their lives stared back at him from around the room, a room filled with expensive and elegant furniture. How could he possibly imagine that Heather would be willing to give up their four-thousand-square-foot home to live in a hotel suite in Mesquite?

"JT." Heather stood over him with her hands on her hips and eyes blazing.

He could only focus on how beautiful she looked. Real-woman beautiful, with dancing eyes and hair the color of iced tea that glowed like copper when the sun hit it. Eighteen years she lived with him and loved him. He surely slipped a cog when he made a decision like that without consulting her.

"JT?" Heather asked, her voice sounding far away. She frowned, and peered down into his face. "Are you okay?"

He shook his head slowly and buried his face in his hands. "I'm so sorry," he finally said, his voice breaking. "I guess I really blew it."

Heather's eyes were wide with fear now, and the anger melted from her voice. "Please look at me," she pleaded, staring down at him. "What in the world is going on with you?"

He lifted his head and saw fear on her face. Then he saw his dream of leaving the LA rat race disappearing like sugar at an ant's picnic. "Please sit down," he said, gently reaching for her hand. "There are some things we need to talk about, things I should have been talking to you about all along."

The next morning Heather awakened early. She turned over in the king-size bed and pulled the down comforter up to her chin. The room felt cool, almost cold, when the air conditioner clicked on. JT liked it that way. It was dark with only a thin ribbon of light outlining the blackout shades, and a light scent of lavender hung in the air.

After staring at the ceiling for several minutes, she finally nudged JT. "Honey, are you awake?"

"Mmm." He didn't even twitch.

"You know, sweetie," Heather said, pushing herself up on the pillow, "I've really been thinking about this hotel thing. I know I sounded a little upset yesterday." She stared straight ahead, barely able to see the rectangular eye of the flat-screen TV in the darkened room. "A lot of that was because you never said a word to me about it before you made a decision," she continued. "You really should have consulted me, you know. After all, I am your wife and partner."

"Mmm-mm." JT scrunched his pillow around his head, still fatigued from his trek around the Mesquite Mountain Inn.

"I really didn't know you were so unhappy with the contracting business. You never told me how you were feeling."

Only the sound of regular breathing came from the other side of the bed.

"Okay, okay. I know you complained about dealing with red tape and government agencies. But I really didn't understand how badly you hated it." She glanced over at the huge lump beside her. "Well, I sort of knew, but..."

JT listened and made no response. He had learned a *few* things in eighteen years of marriage.

"Anyway, now that you shared all that with me, I can understand why you want to change your life."

His brain perked up but he didn't move.

Heather put her arm over him and massaged his neck and back. "So, I started thinking. Your idea of renovating this hotel is kind of like that dream we had about opening a bed and breakfast, remember?" She smiled, remembering their early life together and her voice warmed. "You were flipping houses then, and we talked about getting a fixer-upper big enough for all of us, even your mom and dad, plus extra rooms to rent out. I was going to be the cook, remember? Only this would be bigger. A lot bigger. We'd have to hire someone to do the cooking and the cleaning."

The rhythmic breathing from the other side of the bed stopped.

"So now that the twins are in college and are all settled in the duplex, we really don't need this huge house anymore," she continued on, snuggling up to him. "In fact, sometimes I feel kind of lost in it, it's so big." She laid her head on his side. "So, I guess what I'm saying is, this could be the right time for us to make a change, and that I agree with your decision. Let's do it."

JT's eyes snapped open. His skills at salesmanship astounded him. He had convinced his wife to move after all. "Great," he said, and rolled over on his back, hardly believing his good fortune.

"Then I started to think," Heather said, combing her fingers through the mass of hair on JT's chest. "Maybe we could hire Rachel to come to work for us."

JT's eyes widened and he stopped breathing again. "Rachel?"

"Yes, Rachel. My sister."

He wondered if he could pretend he was still asleep.

Heather didn't wait for an answer. "You know she's worked in the hotel industry for ten years, and you know for a fact that she's excellent at her job."

"Yes, yes, I remember." JT stared straight ahead, not daring to turn to his wife.

"She's all I have left, sweetie. You and I both know the boys will never really come home again." Heather's head rested on JT's chest, breathing in his scent. "Oh, they'll come home, all right, but even now, the last couple of years, they spend more time with their friends than with us. It's our fault, too. We're the ones who raised them to be strong, independent young men."

"Well, what's wrong with that?"

"Nothing's wrong with it except that I miss them. You know how I am. I want my family. That's all I've ever wanted. Now the boys are gone and Rachel is three thousand miles away." She buried her face in JT's chest.

"And you think having Rachel come to work for us will actually help our situation?" he asked, incredulous.

"It would help *my* situation." Heather propped herself up on her elbow and squinted at her husband in the dim light. "I know what you're thinking. Rachel used to be a handful and the two of you used to have your problems. But she's changed. Really. She's matured. She's in therapy again."

JT swallowed hard, his eyes glued to a spot on the ceiling, his jaw clenched. Bad memories flowed back to him, memories of when Rachel and Heather's parents died. Rachel was only thirteen at the time, so JT and Heather took her in and raised her. His mind flashed over the many nights Rachel climbed out her bedroom window and snuck out of the house, and he had to pick her up from parties because she was drunk. He recalled losing it during the awful fights they had, yelling at her at the top of his lungs. Not his best moment. The early morning calls from the police station were not a pleasant memory, either.

However, JT remained calm. He didn't want to blow it again with Heather. He had spent most of the night trying to convince her that selling the construction business was the way to go. He talked about the excitement and adventure of remodeling the old hotel, knowing Heather itched to start another decorating project. He also played on the fact Heather loved and trusted Buddy, having adopted him like the brother she never had. Then, like any deal, JT accepted the fact that you had to negotiate.

"Well, I think it's a great idea for Rachel to come for a visit," JT said, trying to muster enthusiasm in his voice and convince himself it wasn't a bold-faced lie. "She hasn't been out to see us in a long time. But you know, honey, she may not even like Arizona, being the city girl she is. Isn't she afraid of snakes or something?"

"Spiders, actually. Rachel has arachnophobia." Heather mulled that thought over in her mind. "And you may be right. We'll invite her out for a vacation. Next time I call her, I'll ask her what she thinks about it."

Heather laid her head on JT's chest, and a sly smile formed on her lips.

Eddie:

That night, on the other side of LA, three men stood in an abandoned warehouse at the end of a quiet street. Its interior, dimly lit with the light of a single lantern, stretched the men's shadows along the concrete floor and partway up the wall. Smells of metal, oil, and solvents lingered in the cavernous space; blackness filled the rest of the building.

There were no windows to offer a view either in or out, and the voices of the three men reverberated from the cold, gray surfaces.

A fourth man, who called himself Angelo Cappaletti, sat bound to a chair with rope. His head hung down to his chest, his shirt torn and soaked with blood. His eyes were swollen shut and his lips were cut and bleeding from being punched against broken teeth.

A bucket of water occupied the space next to his chair, but other than that, the warehouse was empty.

One of the men grabbed a fistful of Cappaletti's hair, yanked his head back and stuck a gun in his mouth. "One more chance, Angie-boy. What's it gonna be?"

"Hold it, Eddie," the second man cautioned, squinting at Cappaletti. "He looks dead." Reaching down, he picked up the bucket of water and threw half of it in Angelo's face. The prisoner made no response. The man reached over and felt the artery on Angelo's neck.

"He's gone, Eddie."

Eddie spewed out a string of obscenities and jammed his Glock back in his shoulder holster. Then with a kick of his boot, he sent the bucket flying across the floor. Water flew and the bucket landed with a resounding crash. After one last look at the dead man, he gritted his teeth, and the three men walked toward the door.

"Tough LA cops," Eddie hissed through his teeth, then spit on the floor. "What a joke."

He swore all the way to the car. He knew Marino was not going to be happy.

Alex Tucker:

The anonymous caller phoned 911 at midnight. "Pick up a body" a man's voice simply said. He recited the address of the abandoned warehouse and hung up.

The dead man's eyes were swollen shut and covered with blood, so he didn't look much like the picture on the driver's license that identified him as Angelo Cappaletti. Someone had knocked out four of his teeth and cracked his skull, but later tests showed that the internal injuries killed him.

When the LAPD ran Cappaletti's fingerprints through the lab, the results shattered the whole division. The dead man was one of their own, Detective Tony O'Hara, who recently had gone deep undercover.

As part of the job, Tony had been out of touch with his partner for a couple of weeks, but managed to email some information back to his computer at the station.

Alex Tucker was one of O'Hara's friends who went to the morgue. Afterward, instead of going home, Alex drove to the station, commandeered O'Hara's file, and printed out everything he needed.

His tall, muscular frame hunched over his desk as he quietly studied the file. Three hours later, he still sat there, eating corn chips from the vending machine and drinking what the department tried to pass off as coffee.

The room felt warm, and Alex looked up. The ceiling fans were turning but did little to cool the room. At least they moved the air, he considered. That was more than the block glass windows did, high up on the east side of the room. He ran his hand through his wavy, black hair, and felt the wetness at the back of his head.

"Hey!" he called out to no one in particular, not bothering to look around. "Somebody crank up the AC!"

He buried himself back in the file. His shirt, a once crisp white one, hung limp, unbuttoned at the neck, and his tie was loosened. His sleeves had been rolled up to the elbows and sweat circles appeared under his arms.

"Hey," he called out again, wiping his forehead with the back of his sleeve.

"Shut up, Tucker," a voice behind him responded. "Forget the AC. It's time you went home."

Alex recognized the voice of the commander, Marty Griswald. He spun around in his chair. "What are you doing here?"

"In case you didn't notice," Griswald replied, leaning against the desk and studying his watch, "the sun's already up and I usually get to work around this time."

Alex did a quick check of the room. They were alone, and the sun filtered in through the dusty windows.

Griswald wore one of his pink shirts. Pink flattered his dark-chocolate skin, and he was big and masculine enough to get away with it. Always a flashy dresser, he loved bright colors and trendy styles, wearing a different jacket every day of the week. He made sure he would always be dressed for a meeting with the mayor or the press. The jackets also covered his gun and the gut that threatened to fall over his belt.

"Do any good?" He glanced down at the pile of papers on Tucker's desk.

"The file indicates these guys are an offshoot of the Guerrero cartel," Alex answered, leaning back in his chair. "From what I can tell, they've killed hundreds of people in three countries and two states." *And they killed O'Hara*, Alex thought bitterly, remembering the condition of his friend's body.

"They've been at war with the Zetas for a long time now," Griswald offered.

"True, but now two other cartels are involved…and the *Federalies.* They can all kill each other off for all I care, but there's been too many innocent lives destroyed in the crossfire." He turned his head away, not wanting Griswald to read his face. "Way too many."

Griswald's eyes softened. "Listen, Tucker, I know it's killing you about O'Hara. All of us are feeling it. But you need to go home and get some sleep."

"I'm fine," Alex snapped, his voice rough from years of smoking, and turned back to the papers on his desk.

"You're anything but fine, and if you don't feed yourself something better than those corn chips, you won't be able to think your way out of the bag they're in. Now go home. "

"On one condition." Alex spun around and looked intently at Griswald.

"And that is?"

"I get the assignment." Alex's leg nervously started tapping up and down. "Four weeks, that's all I ask."

"Nope. No can do."

Alex's leg stopped tapping. "You *have* to give this to me." He stared up at Griswald with eyes so dark they looked black. "I already talked to Burnwood and she said you'd make the final decision." He lifted an eyebrow. "You know I already have a head start on the case, right?"

Griswald grunted and looked away. "A head start? Exactly how did you manage that?"

"Take a look." Alex turned back to the papers scattered on his desk. He pulled out a map and laid it on top of the pile. "This is where they start, here in Columbia. Then they go to Mexico City." He traced along a red line on the map with his finger. "Then from Mexico City to Alixta, Mexico, here," he said, stopping his finger, "right next to the border."

Griswald looked down at the enlarged section of map Alex held and tapped his fingers impatiently. "So?"

"So I happen to know somebody who lives there, in Alixta, an American ex-patriot. He owns a big cattle ranch south of the city, in the hills." A glimmer flashed across his eyes. "He has connections."

"Connections?"

"Yeah, very good connections," Alex said, the corner of his lip turning up. "And he owes me."

Griswald said nothing, stared back down at the map, thinking, his lips pursed.

Alex grabbed a red pen. "See this little area here?" He made several marks on the map near the border. "It's all farms, on both sides of the border. So my guess is a crop duster flies low, right under the radar, and slips across the border."

Griswald picked up the map and studied the red circle Alex made. In it, a line ran through the middle of a tiny dot. Miles of uninhabited land filled the rest of the area. "And they land in Mesquite?" He looked incredulous. "There's nothing there."

"Exactly. What better place to base an operation? The only problem they'd have left is getting the stuff to LA." He nervously rubbed his hands on his jeans. "Once it gets to LA, there's an eighty-per cent chance Marino gets his hand in it. So unless we follow it up the line, we have no proof. But even with Marino out of the way, a dozen guys will pop up in his place if we don't get to the source."

Griswald looked around the room. It was painted drab beige with long fluorescent lights overhead, and had the feel and smell of a dank basement that even the windows did nothing to alleviate. He couldn't think of a counterargument.

"Most of the border patrol agents are stationed near the bigger cities or they're watching the river," Alex said, continuing to press his point. "Even with parts of the border wall up, they can't cover every inch of the border. You know that, Marty. All I'd have to do is figure out where they land and follow the drugs to California."

Griswald shook his head. "You think you can just drift into a little town like that and blend in? No offense man, but what are we talking here? Three or four thousand people?"

"Not true," Alex countered. "It's more like ten, and lots more agricultural people move in during the season, along with tourists in the winter. There are RV parks, that sort of thing, along with the usual banks and stores. Even an upscale hotel."

Griswald pulled down his half-glasses and looked over them. "And you know this?"

"Yeah, I know this. I used to visit my uncle there when I was a kid, mostly on school vacations."

"No kidding? You've actually been to Mesquite?" He glanced over again at the little dot on the map.

"Yeah, dozens of times." Alex rubbed the stubble of his two-day old growth of beard, mentally tallying up his visits. "It just so happens my uncle Dewey Tucker still lives there."

"So?"

"My uncle, the *Deputy Sheriff* Dewey Tucker, still lives there." Alex raised an eyebrow and smiled. Then he reached in his drawer for uncle's card.

Chapter 4

The morning sun seeped in around the edges of the drapes, reflecting off the empty turquoise bottle, spilling its brilliance into the half-light of the room. Rachel Ryan suddenly sat bolt upright in bed, drenched with sweat. She groped around the nightstand for a cigarette before she realized she'd quit. She swung her long, slender legs over the edge of the bed, painfully stood and walked to the kitchen, trying to shake off the fragments of the bad dream that still clung to her like shards of glass.

After turning on the coffeemaker, she sat at the counter and stared out the window over the sofa. The sofa was red, which she hated. It sagged, and it took up more than half of the wall space on the other side of the room. It had but one redeeming quality: it was free, one of the many items left by the previous tenant.

Rachel's head ached. She rubbed her temples with her fingertips, listened to the coffee drip into the glass pot, and inhaled the hazelnut flavor that spilled into the air. From her stool, she could see the trees on either side of the Charles River. The sugar maples, now intensely colored, almost looked fake. *Boston was so beautiful in the fall.* She sighed and felt a pang. She wondered how much longer she'd be able to enjoy that view.

She ran her fingers through her hair, now matted from missing two days of shampoos, twisted it into a pile, and pinned it on top of her head. Opening a cabinet, she pulled out a mug and a bottle of aspirin. She downed two aspirin with a gulp of hazelnut coffee laced with ice cubes and sat back on the stool waiting for her head to stop throbbing. *I think it will be a while before I pull this stunt again,* she thought.

She jumped when the phone rang, nearly knocking over her cup.

"Hey, sis, what's wrong?" It was Heather.

"I'm okay." *Of all the times I have to pick up the phone without checking the caller ID.*

"You sound awful, honey. I called your office but the front desk said you didn't come in. I've been trying to reach you for three days. I've been worried. Are you sick? Have you been drinking?"

Rachel's voice sounded low and weary. "No—yes—and I quit my job." She figured she might as well get it all out at once. Her sister wouldn't stop until she wormed out the truth anyway.

"Oh, sweetie, what happened?"

Rachel's eyes flitted around the room while she decided how she would explain, and then settled on the truth. "I'm afraid my Irish temper got the best of me."

Silence echoed on the other end of the phone.

"I see," Heather finally mumbled. "Have you—" She paused again, hesitant. "Have you been taking your meds?"

"I stopped. Too many side effects. Let's not go there."

"Well, honey," Heather began, searching for the right thing to say, "you're so good at what you do, I'm sure if you ask, you could get your job back."

"Um, I don't think so." Rachel grimaced. She stared out the window at the river, suspecting her days of seeing that view were quickly dwindling. "Not after what I called my boss…to his face."

Heather pondered that for a moment. "I see." *Apparently the therapy wasn't helping that much.* "Well, look on the bright side, sweetie. Now you can fly out for a visit."

"I need to start looking for another job." Rachel's voice sounded dull and she propped her head in her hand, grabbed a handful of hair, pulling it loose from the knot on her head. She did not want to have this conversation.

"You could easily do that over the Internet from here," Heather insisted. "We have email, phone, fax, everything you need. Even paper and pens."

Rachel twisted the phone cord around her finger and tried to think of some excuse to turn down the offer. Nothing came to mind. "Sis, I haven't seen you in three years," Heather entreated. "I miss you. I'm so lonely with the boys gone." Then she paused, softening her tone. "If you don't come now, when will you come? Once you get a new job, you won't get a vacation for another year."

Rachel's brain was reeling. She couldn't think of a reply. Even worse, she knew Heather was right.

"I know we talk on the phone and e-mail, but it's not the same as seeing you in person." Heather pouted, willing to stoop to using a guilt trip. "I want to see you. You're my only sister. You're the only aunt the boys have. You wouldn't even recognize them if you saw them, they've grown so much. Do you even remember they've already started college?"

"Of course," Rachel affirmed, crossing her fingers. She remembered sending Justin and Joseph graduation checks in the spring, but never gave it another thought.

"Rachel, please. I really need to you to come," Heather begged. Her tone snapped Rachel out of her stupor.

She sat upright. "Heather, what's going on? Is there some kind of problem?" She was awake now, leaning forward into the phone.

The line fell silent while Heather tried to organize her thoughts. "I don't know. Well, I," she stammered, "I think JT may be having some problems," she finally admitted, "like maybe that syndrome that happens to middle-aged men."

"You mean when they run out and buy red convertibles and get twenty-year-old girl-friends with fake boobs?"

Rachel gasped and covered her mouth, suddenly realizing her diplomatic skills were at an all-time low.

"I'm sorry. I didn't mean—"

"JT is *not* having an affair." Heather's voice turned sharp. "And he didn't buy a red convertible. He bought an old broken-down hotel in Arizona. Well, he actually didn't buy it. Buddy did." She paused. "Well, actually Buddy didn't buy it, he inherited it." She paused again and sighed. "It's a long story."

"I'll bet that's right." Rachel remembered Buddy and decided anyone that happy needed to be medicated.

"JT wants to get out of the contracting business." Heather choked out the words. "He says the business has grown so big and every-thing is so political he just wants to sell out and have a simple life. Two companies have already made him an offer."

Rachel was speechless. She pictured her big brawny brother-in-law. He never made a decision based on emotion in his whole life. What could possibly be going on with Mr. Practical? Was he in some kind of trouble?

"Rachel? Are you there?"

Rachel reined in her imagination. "Yes, I'm still here. I was just thinking. This isn't the first time Buddy and JT have taken on a project together."

"That's true, but it was always in conjunction *with* his business. Now he wants to *sell* the business. He wants to sell everything, even the house."

Rachel's eyes were wide and they darted around the room. *Perhaps JT has finally flipped out.* "But you still have the condo, right?"

"Yes, but Justin and Joseph just moved into it. It's near the university, you know."

Rachel's mind whirled. The last time she saw the twins, they were thirteen and their voices were changing. She had completely missed their early teen years. She tried to get a grip but she didn't know what to think. Her head hurt. "What about," she asked, grasping about for any excuse, "you know—JT?"

"Oh, he really wants you to come," Heather lied. "He can't wait to show you the place." She raised her eyes to the ceiling and mouthed the words "Forgive me."

Rachel wondered about that. Could he have changed that much? Yet, she doubted

Heather would lie. Perhaps JT was mellowing with old age. After all, he was probably creeping up toward forty-five or forty-six. Practically a fossil.

"Rachel? Are you there?"

Heather's voice pulled her out of her thoughts. "Yes, I'm still here. I'm still thinking. I don't have the slightest idea of what to pack."

Heather smiled to herself. Her voice purred on the other end of the line. "So does that mean you'll come?"

⁋⁋⁋

JT sat high up in the seat of the loader and switched gears, grinning from ear to ear. He thought about how quickly he had sold the contracting business. The buyers didn't even quibble about his asking price. Now the piles of paperwork and miles of red tape were only a memory.

The front edge of the bucket dipped down in response to the levers in his hands, and scooped up a boulder bigger than a bathtub. With a quick jerk, JT made the loader drop the boulder precisely at the edge of the new pool

74

he was building at the Mesquite Mountain Inn. He grinned again. He hadn't lost his touch.

The fact that he was working in weather that was a hundred and two degrees didn't bother him in the least. No longer chained behind his massive oak desk, he was using his muscles again, and working in the great outdoors. He even had a tan.

JT swung the loader around to his off-key chorus of *Born Free* and scooped up another rock. He dropped it with a thud, and nudged it another foot into place, next to the big boulder.

Movement caught his eye, and he saw a gorilla of a man in a tank top and faded blue jeans walking toward him. JT shut off the tractor and jumped off, dropping his ear protectors down to his shoulders.

"Are you Mr. Carpenter?" The man called out in a voice to match his size.

When JT moved closer, he noticed the man's long, straight hair tied back in a ponytail and his dark, weathered skin.

"Sure am," JT replied. He quietly studied the man, trying not to stare at the scar that ran from the man's eye to his chin. "What can I do for you?"

The man looked down at his feet for a moment and then hesitantly at JT. "My name is Anthony Chavez, but everybody calls me Toro. I need a job and I saw you're looking for people."

"I am." JT tried to size up the man in front of him. "What kind of work can you do?"

"I can fix almost anything made of wood or steel," the huge man replied. I can paint. I can do landscaping. I can lift two fifty pound bags of cement at a time and probably roll one of those boulders in place by hand."

"I can believe that." JT nodded, squinting through his sunglasses, noting the bulging muscles on Toro's arms. He also noticed the tattoo of a spider web across his shoulder and a snake down his arm. "Done any hard time?"

A moment of surprise registered on Toro's face, and then he looked down at his feet.

"Yeah. Five years. I'm out on parole, early time for good behavior."

"What were you in for?" JT continued to scrutinize the man in front of him who looked like he could beat three or four average-size men in a fight.

Toro took a deep breath and exhaled slowly. "I killed a man in a bar fight."

JT said nothing while the sun beat down on them both. Workers with jail time were nothing new to him. But killing a man…that was a whole different ballgame.

"Listen, Mr. Carpenter," Toro continued, "I really need a job. I live in a trailer with my mother who's on social security. My father died while I was in jail." The huge man paused, looked down for a moment, then right back at JT's eyes. "I know I made a big mistake, but I don't plan on making another. I don't drink anymore and I don't do drugs. I'll understand if you don't hire me, but if you do, I can promise you, you won't ever be sorry."

The seconds ticked away and the heat seared the two men. Sweat dripped into JT's eyes and he reached for his handkerchief. He really needed to hire a new man or two since a couple laborers failed to show up after they received their first paycheck, but he didn't have the time to check the background on this man.

"See that dumpster in the back?" JT asked, making his decision. "We're pulling out all the old carpeting, drapes, and furniture, down to the bare walls, and throwing it out. Then we're going to repair, re-carpet, and repaint every one of those rooms. Think you can handle that?"

"Yes, sir." Toro broke into a huge smile revealing a gap where an upper tooth had been.

"Go find the super out back and tell him to put you to work. You're legal aren't you?"

"Sure am, Mr. Carpenter. Thank you." Toro held out his hand. "You won't regret this."

When Toro walked away, JT noticed Buddy waving to him by the cooler in the shade of the guest rooms. JT walked over and pulled a gallon jug out of the ice.

"Did you hire him?" Buddy asked.

"Yes, I did." JT chugged the cold water and let some splash down his chest.

"A guy that big and mean looking could be trouble."

"I take it you met him. You could be right."

They both watched Toro disappear into one of the suites on the hill.

JT scratched at his hairline. "But it's possible he could end up being one of the best workers and most loyal people we've hired."

"Hey, you're the boss of this chicken outfit." Buddy's signature smile was back on his face. "By the way, Heather called. She said to call her whenever it was convenient."

"Okay, thanks." JT sat down in one of the patio chairs and set the icy jug in his lap. His hair stuck to his scalp with sweat and he welcomed the slight breeze that cooled him.

"She said Rachel planned to come out for a visit," Buddy said, trying to sound nonchalant.

JT looked right through him. "Don't even think about it, kid."

"Why? She is one beautiful woman." Buddy recalled their meeting on her last trip west. "Great legs, face like an angel."

"Oh, for Pete's sake, Buddy." JT rolled his eyes. "That's your problem with women. You always go for the looks instead of what's in here." He tapped on his heart. "Trust me, Rachel is not for you." He put the gallon jug to his lips again.

"You're prejudiced," Buddy said. "Just give me one good reason."

JT wiped his mouth with the back of his hand. "Okay. She's too high maintenance. She's too neurotic. She's too skinny, and she drinks too much."

"That was four reasons."

79

"Hey, do what you want." JT shrugged. "You're a grown man. Just don't say I didn't warn you." He pulled his handkerchief out and wiped the sweat off his face. "It feels like a hundred and ten today."

"It's only a hundred and two, but it's more humid than yesterday. Maybe you should take a break."

"I am taking a break. Besides, I like to sweat. It gets rid of toxic poisons from your body."

"Then by all means, have at it."

"Thanks." JT looked around. The Mesquite Mountain Inn had come a long way in a few short weeks. The courtyard glowed with magenta bougainvillea and Mexican bird of paradise, which seemed to grow a foot a day. Passion vines and jasmine twined themselves around a portico that covered the sidewalks surrounding the perimeter of the courtyard. They hadn't lost a single plant, succulent, or cactus.

"So what have you been up to?" JT asked, changing the subject. "I noticed you talking to a woman earlier."

"The gray-haired lady? She's a science teacher who lives in Mesquite. Her name is Vicky Donovan, I think. She's been here for years and wanted permission to come on the property and hunt for scorpions. I told her she could take all she wanted. She also asked if she could set up her telescope on the mountain the night of the new moon, whenever that is. I told her she could come anytime."

JT reached for another gallon jug and handed it to Buddy. "Here, drink. You don't want to get dehydrated," he said. "You'll be puking your guts out if you don't watch it."

"Okay, boss," Buddy teased and took swig. "I need to get back to work, anyway. I arranged for the liquor license, ordered the glassware and booze, and had the guys uncrate the café furniture. The dinnerware just arrived. Now all we need is a cook and bartender and we could at least have a decent meal and brew."

JT's gaze shifted past Buddy. "Speaking of a decent meal and brew, don't look now but a former, and I do mean former, fan of yours is here."

Buddy turned and greeted the pretty waitress from Pablo's. "Rosario."

"You're Byron McCain, right?" Rosario brought her lovely smile with her and extended her hand.

Buddy held on it to a few seconds longer than necessary. "Only if you call me Buddy," he answered, flashing his grin back to her. "What can I do for you?"

"I know that when you open your bar, you will need at least four bartenders." Her look turned serious. "I want to be one of them."

"Okay," Buddy said, nodding tentatively, while guessing her age. "Can you legally mix drinks?"

Rosario's dark hair fell in deep waves past her shoulders and she tossed it back, laughing. "Yes, and I can do better than that. If you give me some ice and a blender, I can make you the best margarita you ever tasted. I have everything I need with me." She patted a small cooler she carried.

"Well, that's the best offer I've had all day," Buddy said, still grinning. "Follow me."

When JT walked into the lounge a short time later, Buddy and Rosario were huddled together over the blender. "Hey, JT, come over and taste this," Buddy called to him.

JT walked over to the red vinyl barstool and sat down. From behind the bar, Rosario poured the blender's frozen concoction into a salted glass and watched JT take a sip.

He licked his lips and raised his eyebrows, mimicking a wine connoisseur. "It's smooth, tangy...yet sweet, not bitter." He took another sip. "Mmm. I do believe this is the finest margarita I've ever tasted," he said, holding the glass up.

Buddy beamed. "I'm glad you agree with my assessment because I just hired Rosario."

JT turned to Rosario. "So you want to quit Pablo's?"

She nodded. "It's hard when you have to work for a parent. Besides, bartenders make more money than waitresses. At least waitresses that work at Pablo's. I am a single mother with a seven year old son to support." Her eyes dropped. "Before Juan was killed, he helped me out some, but now…"

The mood changed like a cold wind blowing through the room. "We're really sorry about that, Rosario," JT said. His voice was soft and kind. "We're sorry about what happened at Pablo's, too. Someone at the tax office told Buddy that Juan died by suicide."

"That's what they want you to think," Rosario snapped. Her nostrils flared. "I know better. I lived with Juan. He would *never* have killed himself. I *know* he was murdered."

"But who would do such a horrible thing?" JT felt repulsed at the thought of it.

Rosario held her hands out and then covered her face with them. "I don't know. I may never know." She dropped her hands and looked at JT. "He was kind and smart. He had no enemies. Everyone loved him." She turned her head slightly and looked off. "Sometimes I wonder if it had anything to do with the lights on the top of the mountain."

"Lights? What lights?" Buddy frowned, aware there were no electrical lines further up the mountain than the hotel.

"Juan told me he saw green lights at night sometimes. Different times. He wondered if they were from aliens." She smiled a little and her eyes twinkled. "Not the kind from Mexico. The kind from outer space." She pointed up in the air with her finger.

"So that's where the UFO rumors came from." Buddy said, remembering his conversation with the deputy sheriff.

"Perhaps." Rosario's eyes grew serious. "But Juan wrote down every time he saw the lights, in a book. He wrote in it the night he was killed. I know what he saw was true. He was not the only night irrigator to see them." Rosario began packing up her supplies. Then she stopped. "But I know Juan. He would be the only one who would go up the mountain to find out what they were."

✑✑✑

Rachel kicked off her Jimmy Choo shoes and tossed her Prada bag the minute she walked into her apartment. She took off her jacket, sank down on the sofa, and unbuttoned her blouse. The job interview she so carefully dressed for did not go well. Even worse, it was her third interview that week that did not go well. *Let that be a lesson to you, Rachel. Never quit a job before you land another one.* She threw her blouse over the back of the sofa. *And never humiliate your boss in front of his own boss, even if he totally deserves it.*

She let out a deep breath of air through pursed lips. There was no question in her mind, now, about her trip to Arizona. It was going to be a one-way. She didn't have a job. That meant no apartment to come back to. She gazed around the room and tried to shake off her anxiety. Except for the view, it was no big loss. The place was small, it smelled musty most of the time, and it was a sub-let; even the furniture didn't belong to her. Neither did the dishes nor the pots and pans. Not that she'd want any of it, anyway; it was just miss-matched junk.

In a way, it made things simpler, she told herself. She didn't have to debate what to pack. She'd simply take all her clothes, all her personal items. Well, probably not the coats and winter boots. She thought about the contents of her overflowing closet. Maybe she'd sell a few things. After all, she could use the cash. Besides, didn't they wear just blue jeans out west? Well, it was a good thing she had thought ahead and picked up a few heavy-duty boxes, regardless. She could ship some stuff out that afternoon. Then the picture of her closet popped back into her mind. She would need four of the boxes just for her shoes.

Jesse Ray:

On October 1, Jesse Ray Greever unlocked the door that said "Greever's Aviation. We fly to Hell and Back," and noticed the large envelope on the floor. It lay on top of the mail and showed no address. Having received messages through the slot on his door for the last forty years, he was in no hurry to pick it up, or his mail, which was probably overdue bills and political ads. He made a pot of coffee, scratched his four-day-old gray beard, and checked his calendar for the day's plans, which, he already knew, had nothing penciled in.

He picked up a mug that sat on top of his desk and blew the dust out of it, not bothering to rinse it from its last use. The dust settled on magazines and papers that lay in disorganized stacks around the perimeter of his desk, leaving only a small area where he could actually work.

He dug around in one of the desk drawers, pulled out half of a stinky sandwich and a small bottle of whiskey. He sniffed the sandwich and made a face. It smelled too far-gone to eat, although he considered it, and threw it in the trash. He scratched his crotch, then poured a little of the whiskey into the mug and topped it off with the freshly brewed coffee.

When he finally picked the envelope up off the floor and tore it open, Jesse Ray gawked at the stack of one-hundred-dollar bills that tumbled out. The unsigned letter looked pretty simple. Someone wanted to pay for a quick flight that night, and two nights following, flights where he had to buzz someone's home. Very closely.

The grizzled old man flopped back into his chair, legs stretched out wide, and counted the money. It was three thousand dollars. He read the letter again. He thought he knew who the sender was. After all, Mesquite was a very small town.

There weren't that many people mean enough to pay, or who could afford to pay, for a stunt like that. There were even fewer people confident enough to send him cash to do a job without a guarantee that he'd do it. He wouldn't have considered it at all except that his checkbook showed a balance of twelve dollars, and he suspected the rest of the mail consisted of overdue bills. He was nearly out of food and nobody planned to spray crops for another week. Even then, there would be three other aviation companies lining up for the jobs.

He squinted up at the stain on the ceiling, hoping the answer might appear. It didn't. Instead, a picture of a steak-and-egg breakfast flashed in front of his eyes, one with a big stack of pancakes on the side with extra syrup.

Jesse Ray scratched his crotch again, folded the money, stuffed it in his pocket, and left.

❧❧❧

By the time Rachel yanked her luggage off the turnstile, flagged down help, and slid behind the wheel of her rental car, the digital clock flashed six-ten. She looked around, hoping she could make it to Mesquite before dark.

She left the airport wondering how she ever let her sister talk her into making the trip. She hated snakes, she was petrified of spiders, and she was sure the dump of a town she was going to was full of both. Then she remembered. She didn't have a job *or* a place to live.

It wasn't the end of the world, she decided. She would use the time at JT and Heather's place to plan her next step, send out some resumes, and possibly end up working in Phoenix or San Diego.

The little hotel would be interesting to see, too. If *interesting* was what one could call such a change in someone's lifestyle. She wondered if JT and Heather had completely flipped out. They had the big home, the ocean, the culture of a big city most people dream about, and were leaving all that to get involved with an old, rattrap hotel miles from nowhere. Why, they didn't know the first thing about running a hotel and neither did Buddy.

She suspected the closest Buddy ever came to hotel work was the job of convincing some bimbo to join him in a suite somewhere. Maybe the strain of living in LA finally became too much for all of them.

Before long, the skyline of Phoenix disappeared from the rearview mirror while Rachel followed Heather's map that took her through a vast desert. The interstate rolled out like an endless ribbon of gray before her, and she yawned, sorry now she insisted on driving herself from the airport. At the time, all she could think of was being trapped in Deadsville, bored out of her mind, without her own means of escape.

It had been a long day and Rachel rubbed the tense muscles at the back of her neck. She finally reached the summit of Butterfield Pass and began to descend the winding road. Coming out of a long curve, she stared in awe at the sunset, which took her completely by surprise.

Majestic, dark purple mountains stood out in stark contrast to the coral sky. Whispers of cirrus clouds above them were shaded in myriad colors from violet to peach. Then she saw it: Blood Mountain. Heather was right. In the dimming light, it looked exactly like the color of blood. It was breathtaking.

When Rachel exited the freeway and turned south, she could see what she guessed was the town of Mesquite at the base of the mountain. One at a time, lights were blinking on behind a patchwork of brown and green fields. Mesmerized by the vista, she watched the coral sky turn to gray while twilight fell, nearly lulling her to sleep.

A tan pickup truck suddenly appeared in front of her. She jerked the wheel to the left and sped around it with a rush of adrenalin, missing the turn-off to Mesquite. It wasn't until she had raced two miles down the road that she realized her mistake and noticed the speedometer registered seventy.

Remembering the two outstanding speeding tickets back in Boston, she immediately decelerated and looked for a level place to turn around. She braked quickly and spun a U-turn across the road onto the shoulder. When the car came to a stop, she double-checked the map Heather had drawn, flipped the car back in Drive, and stepped on the accelerator. The car didn't move. The desert sand was soft and loose, like a fresh bag of sugar, and one of the tires began to spin. Unsure of what to do, Rachel tried pressing harder on the accelerator. That was a big mistake. The car rocked back and forth and the tire sank even deeper into the sand.

Rachel leaped out of the car, furious with her predicament. She slammed the door hard and stomped awkwardly onto the shoulder, her high heels sinking in the sand. After surveying the situation in what little light was left, she let out a few obscenities and kicked at the buried tire with great fury. Immediately she yelped in pain, hobbled back to the front seat cursing and yelling, and sat down to rub her foot.

Defeated, Rachel realized she had to suffer the humiliation of calling for help. She picked up her cell phone and flipped it open. No service. When she looked up in the dimming twilight, she could barely see the outline of tall mountains on either side of the road and realized she was miles from help.

A flash of light suddenly blinded her. She could hear a truck pulling up in front of her, but the brightness of its lights forced her to look away. Rachel's heart began to pound.

The door popped open. In the glare, she saw the outline of a tall, muscular man walking toward her. Fear froze her to the seat when she realized the mess she was in. She was stuck in the sand in the middle of nowhere, with no gun, no pepper spray.

Her mind quickly raced over the techniques she had learned in self-defense class and she swallowed hard, terrified she might have to use them.

The man continued walking toward her. Rachel's blood rushed through her veins and her breathing quickened. Her heart beat so fast she feared it would burst.

Then the man stopped about six feet in front of her. When he stood between Rachel and the light, his shadow fell on her, enabling her to see his face, the face of a man obviously amused by her predicament.

"Need some help, miss?" The man's voice sounded as rough as the three-day growth of beard on his face, and Rachel felt her heart stop when she watched one side of the man's mouth turn up in a sneer.

Chapter 5

Later that night, about three miles from town, two pickup trucks met on a canal road and parked, their engines still running. The two drivers stood in the road talking. The taller man lit a cigarette and leaned against the bed of one of the trucks. The other man, the little one who looked to be more than a head shorter, seemed agitated, and paced back and forth, making dramatic gestures with his arms.

With the grace of a dancer, the taller man suddenly grabbed the shoulders of the little man, spun him around, and slammed him against the truck, still holding the lit cigarette in his right hand. He held him there about a minute before he released him. Then each man climbed into his own truck and drove off.

JT lowered his binoculars, puzzled. While sitting on his balcony, scanning the desert for coyotes and his expected visitor, he witnessed the interesting encounter between the two men. It was too far to see their faces, too dark to see the color of their trucks, so it was their dance that raised questions in his mind.

"What are you doing?" Heather slid down into JT's lap. "Looking for Rachel?"

"Exactly."

She rested her hand on his arm. "You know, for all your sputtering and groaning, you really do love her."

"Of course, I love her, Heather. Every gray hair on my head is due to her, but I love her. She's your sister." He held the binoculars up to his eyes again and scanned the dirt road that led to the hotel. "I think she was stupid to drive from the airport herself, but Miss Hard-head insisted she wanted her own car."

"Yes, I know." Heather leaned back in her chair. "She is a bit stubborn."

"A bit? Not to mention she's got the sense of direction of a turnip." JT raised his eye-brows without taking his eyes off the road. "Wait. I see lights."

"Let me see." Heather grabbed the binoculars from him. "It's a car. It must be her."

By the time Rachel screeched to a stop at the hotel entrance, Heather and JT were already there to greet her. After giving Rachel a big bear hug, JT climbed into her car and drove it to the back of the property. He parked it in front of the casita next door to the one he and Heather occupied and began to tote Rachel's bags up the stairs. Judging by the number of suitcases he lugged, he figured Rachel must have brought every piece of clothing she owned and paid a hefty extra-baggage fee for the privilege of doing so…and that was after the four boxes of shoes she already had sent.

The two sisters followed on foot but slipped farther and farther behind. Heather kept pointing things out she didn't want Rachel to miss, and Rachel kept stopping every few steps for a closer look at something unfamiliar.

"This is adorable. I couldn't imagine it looking like this." Rachel's head bobbed around in all directions, taking everything in. "And it smells so good, kind of flowery, tropical, like an exotic perfume."

"Thank you, honey. I'll make sure to pass on the compliments, and I will definitely give you the full-blown tour tomorrow," Heather promised, glancing over at the courtyard. "But I have to admit it does look pretty dramatic at night with all the colored spotlights on the trees. JT and Buddy really have done an incredible job."

After climbing the flight of stairs to Rachel's suite, Heather motioned to the balcony at her right. "You'll have the most incredible view here. From our spot on the balcony, we were able to watch you drive up."

Rachel turned to the view and drew in a breath. "Oh, my."

Heather couldn't help smiling to herself. This was turning out even better than she expected. She inserted the key card and opened the door. "Here's your new home."

Rachel stepped into the room and surveyed the suite. A sofa bed and chair, flanked by sturdy mission-style end tables, beckoned her into the room. On the opposite wall, an entertainment center contained the TV; a square dining table with two chairs sat against the back wall.

Rachel carefully studied the room, drifted over, and tapped one of the shades perched over a copper lamp. "Nice. Real mica, not plastic," she commented, noticing how the light cast a warm glow on the patterned upholstery.

She turned, slipped out of her heels, and sank her toes into the carpet. A large, copper-framed, desert landscape hung over the table, completing the look. She walked over to the chair and felt the fabric. "Good choice, Heather. I bet you did the decorating."

"Of course," Heather said in a bright, bubbly voice. "I had a lot of fun doing it, too. I tried to give it a southwest look, but a sophisticated one, not like Roy Rogers. Like it?"

"It's beautiful. I absolutely love it." Rachel walked over to a small adjoining kitchenette, and ran her hands along the granite-topped bar set against the wall opposite the bathroom. The bar held a sink, with a refrigerator tucked beneath the counter, and a microwave on top. She peered into the cabinets above the counter; they held dishes and glasses. "First class. It has everything you need."

"Well, we tried; and Rachel, I want you to know we thoroughly sprayed the whole suite for insects. I personally inspected it this morning to make sure there were no spiders in residence."

"Ah, bless you, my child."

Heather smiled, but she really wanted to jump up and click her heels. She held out her hand toward the bedroom and Rachel followed it. A king-size bed with a circular headboard and a half-sun carved on it dominated the room. Heather opened the armoire opposite the bed with a flourish, revealing a computer and printer. "Ta da," she said. "It's all hooked up to the Internet."

"Great." Rachel looked around, still amazed by the difference of what she saw and what she had expected to see. The extra-large room included a leather chair, a double dresser with a flat-screen TV above it, and a closet. "Wow. This is even bigger than my apartment in Boston." She whirled around. "A person could live here."

Heather smiled impishly. "That's the whole idea."

❧❦❧

Later that night, Heather appeared at Rachel's door with a plate of little sandwiches and two bottles of root beer. Stars sparkled against a velvet sky as she followed Rachel out to her balcony.

"JT didn't want to come?" Rachel asked casually, dropping into one of the lounge chairs.

Heather avoided her sister's eyes. "I'm afraid he was beat. He was headed for bed when I left."

"Hmm," Rachel mumbled, wondering if that was the truth.

Heather set the tray between them. "Here, eat," she insisted. "Did you get a chance to unpack?"

Rachel grabbed a root beer, disappointed it wasn't a margarita. "Well, I made a dent. But I can't believe the walk-in closet that size in a hotel room. Not to mention all the clothes hangers." She took a sip of root beer and pressed the cold glass to her cheek. "What's the temperature here? Eighty?"

"It's probably ninety, but don't forget, it's a dry heat." Heather laughed at the old joke. She leaned back in the lounge chair and put her feet up. "So tell me, how was the trip over? I was afraid you wouldn't be able to read my map."

"It was fine, no problems," Rachel fibbed, completely avoiding her stuck-in-the-sand experience. She figured if she owned up to her stupidity, she'd have to listen to a lecture from her big sister about speeding, not paying attention, and driving on the median when the sign said not to. "But I have to confess I really didn't want to come. I'm afraid I expected the Mesquite Mountain Inn would be some spider-infested, creepy, falling-down dump."

"You mean, like the Bates Motel?" Heather teased, taking a quick sip of her drink and appraising the guilty look on Rachel's face. "It could have been like that when the guys took it over. JT didn't let me come here until he finished our suite. I even had to pick out the furniture without seeing the actual room."

Rachel picked up one of the little sandwiches Heather had made and examined it. It was egg salad, her favorite. Heather had even cut the crusts off the edges and made little triangles like she used to.

"So where is Buddy? Did he ever remarry?" Rachel put one of the little triangles in her mouth and chewed. "No, you certainly would have told me that."

"He'll be back from LA tomorrow. He bought a new plane, you know. A Beech Bonanza." Heather gave Rachel a penetrating look.

Rachel squinted back with a mouthful of egg salad. "Don't start with that," she mumbled.

"Hey, did I say anything?" A look of wide-eyed innocence formed on Heather's face. "I was simply telling you—"

"Fine. But for the record, I don't want to get married. I may never want to get married, and I don't even want to *talk* about getting married. I have a career, or rather *had* a career, and that's what I really want in life."

"Okay, okay. I get it," Heather said, waving her hand in front of her face. "Absolutely no fix-ups."

"Thank you. I appreciate that." Rachel relaxed against the chair and gazed out at the sky, amazed at how many more stars were visible compared to Boston. She inhaled deeply of the jasmine and natal plum that perfumed the air, delighted to enjoy plants blooming in the fall. She thought about those things, the suite she would be staying in, the little egg sandwiches that her devoted sister made, and let out a deep sigh. "This is the life, huh, sis?"

"And being here with you makes it so much more special, sweetie."

"Thank you, Heather. You always say the nicest things. No wonder everyone loves you." Rachel looked over at her sister and wanted to kick herself for not coming sooner. Then she noticed a particularly bright light in the southern sky. "Say, what's that?" She pointed to it, directly in front of them.

"Hmm. A star?" Heather cocked her head quizzically.

"It's getting bigger. That's odd."

"It must be a plane. Listen, I hear something."

"It's getting louder."

"It's definitely a plane, but why isn't it moving?"

They both stared transfixed at the light. It grew larger by the moment, the engine now a roar.

Heather screamed. "Because it's coming right at us!" She grabbed her sister, and pulled her to the floor.

Instinctively, they covered their heads when the plane flew directly at them. Suddenly, the plane shot straight up. It banked sharply to the right, and then flew out of sight.

Within a minute JT bounded up the stairs, out of breath, his face red. "Are you okay?"

"Other than having a cardiac arrest, you mean?" Rachel was helping her sister to stand.

"I thought he was going to crash into us," Heather said breathlessly, her hand over her heart. "Who *was* that?"

JT gazed at the southern sky, now clear and quiet, trying to get his anger under control. "I don't know. By the time I got outside, the plane was too far away to see." He turned back to the sisters, his eyes hard, with purpose. "But tomorrow I plan on finding out."

❧❧❧

Venkman Farms covered nearly five thousand acres of the fertile valley below Blood Mountain, and JT sped right through the middle of it. Billowing up clouds of dust with the big tires on his pickup, he hardly noticed the brown fields on either side, still wet from irrigation. Tips of pale green lettuce leaves were barely pushing up through the soil.

JT gripped the steering wheel tighter, and turned onto the road that led to the farm office. He expected Franz Venkman would already be at work. The old man's workaholic reputation had already reached JT's ears. So did a few other pieces of gossip.

Venkman put the word out early that he didn't want the Mesquite Mountain Inn resurrected. JT also heard that he tried to intimidate most of the town's workforce into ignoring the hotel's want ads for manual laborers. It pretty much worked, too, at least at first, and JT had to import some of his old crew from LA.

A very tough and determined competitor, JT learned early on to pick his fights, and a petty fight with Venkman was one, he decided, was a waste of time. But the possibility of Venkman's hiring a pilot to buzz his home changed the whole dynamic. He bristled at the thought of it and realized that leaving the LA rat race didn't guarantee a future free of rats.

Arriving in front of the farm office, JT was surprised to see the building appeared quite ordinary. He expected something special after Deputy Tucker's lengthy description of the Venkman's marble mansion that sat on the edge of the golf course. Perhaps Franz didn't feel the need to impress the field hands like he did the townspeople. Then again, Tucker mentioned that it was Franz's wife, Kat, who came from money. Maybe she was the one who paid for all those fine Italian marble floors and columns that so impressed Tucker.

JT was surprised a second time when he was ushered into Venkman's office. When Franz stood up to shake his hand, he proved to be more than a head shorter than JT, even in his cowboy boots.

Venkman's body was evenly proportioned, but he was small, almost delicate looking, except for the beak nose. His hair was thin and straight, an off-white color, probably blond at one time, and was combed over the dome of his head with a low part. His eyelids drooped, and his eyes peered out underneath the folds like little blue balls of steel. His ears were too large, too, but overall, JT felt disappointed. He expected Franz to look menacing, more like a giant Viking with steroid muscles.

Instead, Venkman appeared to be friendly and not at all surprised to see his visitor. He offered JT coffee and a cigar from the box of Cuban Cohibas on his desk.

JT accepted the coffee but turned down the illegal cigar and sat in the low leather chair in front of the desk, trying to size up the little man in front of him. Napoleon complex was the first thought that came to JT's mind, but before he had time to explore that idea, Venkman set his cigar down in the ashtray and skipped the usual pleasantries.

"So, what can I do for you, Mr. Carpenter?" Venkman's eyes were neutral and the smoke from the fragrant cigar rose and curled, releasing more of its aroma.

"You can call me JT, for starters." JT leaned forward in his chair, trying to sound friendly. "I've come here today because I like to be a good neighbor and I have a problem I'm hoping you can fix."

Venkman lifted one eyebrow and looked out from beneath hooded lids. "What problem is that?"

JT's voice was quiet, but firm: "Last night a plane coming from the direction of your farm barely missed hitting our home."

Franz stiffened. His eyes grew even smaller and bored into JT like steel screws. "A plane may have come from the direction of my farm, but it did not come *from* my farm, if that's what you're implying. We had no planes out at all yesterday and we won't even be spraying lettuce for at least a week."

"I see." JT stared back at him, trying to discern the truth. Neither man spoke and tension filled the void.

Venkman picked up his cigar and looked sideways at JT.

"Why would I want to buzz your home, in the first place?"

JT shifted in his chair, wondering if he should go there. "I've heard a few things," he said, his voice drifting off.

"That I wanted your property?" Franz broke in, asking in a manner as if it were the most ludicrous thing he'd heard.

"Actually," JT said, and paused to consider his response. "Yes."

"Well, let's get right to the bottom line here, shall we? We're both busy men and I'm sure we've already found out a lot about each other." Venkman rolled the cigar in his thin fingers. "People say a lot of things about me and some of them may be true," he said, pausing, "but I don't think you'll find anyone who'd tell you I'm stupid."

He tapped the ash off his cigar and stared at JT with those little balls of steel. "First of all, I'm a farmer, not a rock collector, or a hotel operator. Second, if I *was* interested in your property, and I'm not saying I am, I'd offer to buy it. But not now." He smiled with a lift of his chin. "I'd make you an offer later, after you put a bunch of time and money into it, and needed to get rid of it."

"But we're not selling," JT countered.

"You will eventually." Venkman's voice was patronizing. "A city man like you will get bored with that hotel. When you find that it won't make the kind of profit you're used to making, a man like you will get bored real quick." He took a drag from what was left of his cigar and exhaled the smoke up toward the ceiling. "I am a patient man. I can wait."

He suddenly turned and jabbed his finger at JT. "But I am not a stupid man. It would be stupid of me to take risks to try to intimidate you into selling."

JT stood up, deciding to end the meeting. "Very well. I'm sorry I bothered you, Franz." His voice had an edge to it. What he really wanted to do was yank the little twerp out of his chair by the few hairs left on his head. "Like I said, I want to be a good neighbor so I thought I'd bring this to your attention first. I meant no offense." JT started to walk away, but turned and added, "But if you do happen to know of anyone who likes to buzz people's houses, I'd appreciate it if you'd tell him that I will be taking appropriate measures to protect my family and my home."

JT jumped into his Ford, slammed the door, and drove away. He fumed all the way into town rehashing his conversation with Venkman. Maybe the old man was telling the truth. He wasn't stupid, either. Maybe he didn't hire anyone to buzz the hotel. Well, if not, then who else would pull a stunt like that? And why? If that plane had come a few feet closer, they'd all be dead now.

When JT arrived in town, he turned south off Main to Tamarack. The sky in front of him had turned white with clouds and blowing dust filled the air. The little park across from the town hall was empty, guarded only by giant ficus trees, the wind weaving through their branches.

In the parking lot of the sheriff's office, bright flags straining against the wind greeted JT. Once inside, he informed Deputy Tucker about the incident with the plane. Tucker quickly picked up the phone and made a couple calls while JT paced the floor and surveyed the office.

A layer of tan dust covered everything. Papers and files were stacked haphazardly on all horizontal surfaces. Even a black widow brazenly lazed in a web-filled corner, giving visual testimony to Tucker's lack of housekeeping activities. While JT continued to pace on the cheap vinyl floor, the deputy finished his last conversation.

"Sorry, I can't be of much help," Tucker said when he hung up. "Nobody admits to taking a plane out last night. None of the crop dusters anyway."

"What about Venkman?" JT asked, still assigning the blame in his mind. "He must own a plane. Didn't you tell me he had a son?"

Tucker held up his hand and walked around to the front of his desk. "Look, JT, most of the farmers around here have their own planes, but I reckon nobody's gonna own up to doin' the deed even if it was an accident."

"Which it wasn't."

"Okay." Tucker nodded. "You may be right. But right now I can't do nothin' more than have you fill out a complaint." He handed JT a form. "Here, sit down and take a load off. I'll nose around later and see what I can find out."

"I'll bring it back tomorrow," JT said, folding the form and putting it in his shirt pocket. "Right now I've got a ton of stuff to do." He turned to leave and nearly bumped into a man who walked through the door.

"Meet my nephew, Alex Tucker," the deputy called out. "He's visitin' here from California. Alex, this is JT Carpenter, one of the new owners of the Mesquite Mountain Inn."

JT quickly took stock of the chisel-jawed man with curly black hair. "Nice to meet you," he said, shaking the younger man's hand and noting his firm grip. The short-sleeved knit shirt and jeans Alex wore accentuated his muscular shoulders and slim waist. He looked like a cop or a physical trainer. "Are you in law enforcement, too?"

"Heck no, he's a writer," Tucker quickly answered for him. "Came here to do a story on small town crime."

JT turned to Alex. "Is that so? I didn't expect to find much crime here. Except for someone trying to kill people with airplanes, that is." He shot a quick glance at Tucker.

"You'd be surprised," Alex said.

"I bet I would. I'd like to hear about it sometime. Come by and see us while you're here. We're remodeling the inn and you might be interested." He looked Alex over again. "You look like you work out. We're putting in a small exercise room near the pool. You're welcome to come over and use it."

"Thanks, I noticed there's no gym in town, and I'd really like to see the hotel again. Uncle Dewey took me up there when I was a kid, and he said you made a lot of improvements."

"That we have. Come by any time." JT nodded pleasantly. He looked back at Dewey with a squint. "Not much of a family resemblance is there."

Dewey tried to keep from smiling, but his cheeks balled up and his mustache twitched. "Nope," he drawled, "It's a cryin' shame I got all the looks."

JT laughed and walked out, shutting the door behind him. The two inside watched him through the dusty window until he was out of sight.

"What was that writer business all about?" Alex demanded. "We agreed—"

"No, we ain't never agreed. I got my reasons, too." Dewey's voice remained calm as he wagged a finger in Alex's face. "I know you college boys from the big city think you got it all figured out, but you gotta remember I been around here longer than you been alive. Right now, I got some problems here, too, and nobody in these parts needs to even *suspect* you're LAPD."

Alex opened his mouth to speak but Dewey held up a hand. "Sorry, son. You're in my jurisdiction now. You want my help? We do it my way."

⁓⁓⁓

By noon, JT finished his other errands and swung by the post office to pick up the mail. The post office was crowded with people, all of whom greeted JT with small-town friendliness, or plain old curiosity. When he checked out the community bulletin board, he was happy to see that his help wanted poster hadn't been torn down again. He read some of the other ads, and then a man with a neat copper-colored mustache and beard greeted him.

"You must be one of the new owners of the hotel," he said, holding out his hand, a wide smile on his face. "I'm Weezer Chaffee. We're happy to have you here."

The tall, slim man was dressed in Wranglers and a western shirt. JT guessed him to be thirty-something and in the farming business. "Thank you. JT Carpenter," he said, shaking the younger man's hand. "So tell me what you do. Are you a farmer?"

"No, I'm the manager of the local Southwest Chemical. We sell pesticides and herbicides to farmers."

"Ah, you're just the man I need," JT said. "Something is starting to eat up the new flowers I've just put in."

"Well, actually I only volume sell in fifty-pound bags or more," Weezer said, smiling, "which I don't think you'll be needing." With his forefinger, he pushed up his cowboy hat and scratched his head, revealing a full crop of wavy auburn hair. "But I tell you what. I'll come by later. I've wanted to come out anyway to see what you're doing with the old place. Maybe I can help, after all."

JT watched the tall man in blue jeans walk away. Something about him looked familiar, maybe because he was gifted with beautiful teeth and smiled a lot like Buddy.

Turning to leave, JT brushed by an older, gray-haired man who stank like dirty laundry. His hair was wild and he needed a shave, badly. JT said, "Excuse me," but the old man barely opened his mouth to grumble and even that was enough to send a plume of whiskey breath in the air.

Well, I guess not all small-town folks are friendly. JT watched the old man get in line at the window.

JT left the post office through the double glass doors, and the old man turned and followed him with his eyes until he couldn't see him any longer.

"Jesse Ray, what do you need?" the postal worker asked him. She looked to be a tired sixty, probably close to retiring, with a few wrinkles and a double chin.

Jesse Ray jerked his head back. "Pack of stamps, Edna," he grumbled, laying a hundred-dollar bill on the counter.

"Doing any spraying lately?" the woman asked, handing him the stamps.

Jesse Ray blinked and drew back, a scowl on his face. Mumbling something unintelligible, he picked up the stamps and change, turned, and left.

❧❧❧

When JT arrived back at the Mesquite Mountain Inn, Heather ran down the stairs to greet him with a hug and kiss. *She sure seems happy now that Rachel is here,* JT thought.

Not that she wasn't happy before. She just seems more excited, more animated, more...something. It might be his imagination, but lately he seemed like the only one around not on happy pills.

"So, did you find out about the plane?" Heather jarred him back to the present.

"There was no record of anyone flying in the area at that time," JT replied, "but I'll be ready next time, if there is one." He took a couple of large packages out of the truck and handed Heather a small sack.

While they climbed the stairs to their suite, JT glanced back at the pool and saw Rachel drifting lazily on a rubber raft. His mind jogged back to meeting Alex Tucker and re-membered the man wore no wedding ring. "Is Rachel enjoying herself?" he asked.

She's finally relaxing, and amazingly, she's quite impressed with our new acquisi-tion."

"Yeah, you're right. That is amazing." JT stopped on a stair to wait for Heather. "Any-thing else going on?"

"We had a few visitors," Heather said. "Claudia Camarina, the flower shop owner, some applicants for jobs, and Stanley Belin-ski, from Mesquite Realty."

"Stanley Belinski? He's been by twice before," JT said. "What'd he want?"

"He said he had a buyer for our property if we were interested." Heather moved to the landing while JT unlocked the door.

"Again? Did you till him to get lost?" JT pushed the door open with his foot. The scent of fresh linen sheets greeted him. Heather was burning her fancy candles again.

"What? And be rude? Anyway, he gave me his card. He wants you to call."

JT took the card and dropped it in the wastebasket. "I pass by his office all the time. I should stop in and tell him to stop bothering us. That's two offers already and we haven't even been here a month. It's worse than LA."

"Anyway," Heather continued, "I made sure he and Claudia, the flower shop owner, were on the Chamber of Commerce list for the open house party."

"Open house party?" JT gave her a blank look. "We're having an open house party?"

"Of course. Rachel says we need to have one. She offered to plan it."

JT opened his mouth to protest then closed it. "Okay, whatever." He pulled a card out of his pocket. "Here, give this to Rachel, then, and make sure this guy's on the list."

"Weezer Chafee?" Heather asked, reading the name on the card. "That's an odd name."

"Yeah. I didn't ask," he said, and gave her a wink.

Heather smiled at him, one of those smiles that lit up her whole face. He quietly studied his wife. *Yeah, she is more than just happy. She's actually joyous, more alive. Huh. I suppose I could put up with Rachel for a while.* His mind flashed to the two men he met. *And it might help if I found someone to help keep her occupied.*

"Claudia said what we're doing here is already a help to the local economy. She brought us a bouquet of flowers." Heather dropped her package on the table. "She's really glad we're here. Everybody I talk to seems to feel that way."

"I've run into the same thing." JT sat down on the sofa and patted his thigh, his invitation to Heather to sit on his lap. "But don't forget, honey, opening this business isn't personal. They like us because it means money to them. Belinski's interest isn't personal. It's just a big, fat commission for him."

Heather sat in his lap, her body dwarfed by his. "I know. It's always about the money," she said, repeating one of JT's favorite quips.

"But they still like us." She looked up at JT. "Don't they?"

JT hugged his wife. "Honey, anybody who doesn't like you is plain crazy."

Heather put her finger inside the neck of JT's shirt and began to rub the hair on his chest. "So I was thinking about that realtor, Belinski." She pulled back with a puzzled look. "He seemed more than just interested in a sale. He actually seemed anxious. You know, worried-like, sweating a lot." She ran her fingers across JT's chest and looked up from under her eyelashes. "So, is it possible that this property is worth a lot more than what we've been led to think?"

JT kissed his wife gently on the lips. "What I think is that you are also very smart for a young chick."

❧❧❧

The aroma of juicy T-bones sizzling on the grill wafted over the pool area as the sun dropped behind Blood Mountain. JT flipped the steaks over when Buddy drove up in his BMW and pulled into a parking space in front of him. He stepped out of the car with a flourish and greeted everyone, giving Heather and Rachel each a hug.

"It's good to see you again," Buddy said to Rachel, flashing her an appealing smile. "Are you enjoying the place?"

His warmth was disarming and Rachel couldn't help but smile back. "Very much so. My suite is beautiful. It's just perfect, really. In fact, the whole place is absolutely charming."

"That so?" Buddy blinked in surprise. "Coming from you, that's quite a compliment." He held out a chair for her to sit down at a poolside table. It was attractively set with brightly colored place mats, white hotel china, and a colorful mixed bouquet in the center.

"You know, Buddy," Rachel said. "Because I've only worked for large hotels doesn't mean I can't appreciate a small desert hide-away."

"Humm. Desert hide-away," Buddy repeated, pulling a chair out for Heather. "I like the sound of that, don't you, Heather? It sounds romantic, adventurous."

He lifted up a colorful gift bag, pulled out a bottle of wine, and set it in front of Heather. "Like a bottle of fine Bordeaux, perhaps?"

Heather thanked him then shot JT a worried look. JT raised his eyebrows and made a face to indicate he didn't care. If Rachel got blasted, it might show Buddy some of his sister-in-law's less attractive qualities.

But Buddy was busy with the gift bag, pulling out a corkscrew, and then with a dramatic flourish, four wineglasses heavily wrapped in tissue paper. He unwrapped the stemware and set them in front of Rachel saying, "A welcome gift for a lovely lady."

Rachel stared at the glasses. She had seen similar Polish crystal in a jewelry store in Boston. The designs cut into the jeweled-colored stemware sparkled under the tiny lights that hung above them. "They're beautiful," she murmured, picking up one of them. "I don't know what to say." She turned to Buddy with a sincere smile. "Thank you."

"You're welcome." Buddy nodded and poured the wine into the glasses, setting one at each plate. "I thought this dinner might warrant something more than our standard hotel barware. So, my dear Rachel, when you drink out of them back in Boston, you can remember this night by the pool of a romantic, adventurous, hideaway hotel."

Rachel laughed, tossing her white-blonde hair. "I'll drink to that," she toasted, deciding not to mention she never bought a return ticket.

JT rolled his eyes at Buddy's corny blather. He speared the steaks and placed them on a platter. *I ought to slap that kid silly,* he thought. *He has no more sense than a box of rocks.* JT sat down and passed the platter. *Oh, well, I warned him. It's his neck, not mine.*

After much laughter and conversation, Buddy finally pushed his plate away. "No more for me." He turned to JT and asked, "So, do you think the mad bombardier will return?"

JT scooped the last of Heather's homemade potato salad onto his plate. "I thought we'd sit out on the balcony later, and see if he does."

Buddy poured the last of the wine into Rachel's glass. "Oh, that should be fun," he said facetiously. "Did you happen to notify the authorities?"

"First thing this morning I went to see Dewey Tucker, but he wasn't much help."

Buddy nodded sympathetically. "I met him when I arrived at the airport tonight, but he never mentioned that." He turned to Rachel, suddenly remembering something.

"Dewey did tell me you had quite an experience on the drive over, though. I'm really sorry."

Everything turned dead quiet and the blood rushed to Rachel's face. "I-I'm not sure what you mean," she stammered, and reached for her wineglass.

JT and Heather exchanged puzzled glances.

Buddy plowed on, "You know, when you drove up here and got stuck in the sand."

Heather stared at her sister. "You got stuck in the sand on the way over? And you didn't call us?"

"You got stuck in the sand?" JT repeated, nodding. "Oh, so that's why you were late."

Rachel downed the rest of her wine, wadded up the napkin in her lap, and angrily slapped it on the table. "For Pete's sake. It's no big deal. So what if I got stuck in a little sand making a U-turn. A guy in a truck pulled me out."

"A guy? What guy?" Heather looked worried.

"How should I know? Just some guy. If this little burg was capable of even the most minimal level of telecommunications technology I could have called you."

"But you told me—"

JT suddenly stood up hoping to avert the possibility of Rachel's temper going into overdrive. "Okay everyone. This was a great dinner, but I happen to know my darling wife baked a delicious chocolate cake earlier and it's calling our names." He motioned for everyone to get up. "So let's all walk over to our place, shall we?"

⌘⌘⌘

JT had chosen the top floor of the first casita on the slope of the hill because it had the best view of the valley. Like all second-floor suites, it had a large window in the back bedroom with a view of the mesquite grove. In the evenings, he and Heather enjoyed the bonus of a large family of crickets that lived among the trees and serenaded them with their chirping.

Heather pulled JT inside with her when she went in after the iced tea and chocolate cake, leaving the other couple alone. Buddy and Rachel sprawled out in the lounge chairs that lined the long balcony off the living room, watching the lights of the city below. A thin sliver of moon sat low in the sky. The temperature had dropped, a gentle breeze stirred, and the dozens of natal plum plants below them released their perfume into the air.

"It smells absolutely wonderful here," Rachel exclaimed, breathing in the fragrance that floated up to them. "I've never seen so many stars." She leaned back in the lounge chair in awe. "This is the most incredible night."

"Yes, it's so romantic," Buddy cooed in a falsetto voice, teasing her.

"Buddy," Heather protested, overhearing him when she walked out. "It's no wonder no one will marry you. You don't have a serious bone in your body," she scolded in a pretense of disgust.

"Oh, I've had lots of offers for me hand, me love," Buddy replied with an exaggerated Irish brogue and a wave of his hand. "But me heart belongs to a blonde Irish lass by the name of Rachel Ryan."

"Oh, give me break." Rachel laughed, making a face.

"Yes, cut the blarney," Heather chimed in, setting the cake on a table.

JT, who stepped outside with a baseball cap on his head, walked over the wrought iron railing on the edge of the balcony. No one noticed the Winchester rifle until he pulled it up to his side.

Heather's mouth dropped open when she spotted the weapon. "JT? What in the world are you doing? "

"Just sit tight." JT replied in a calm, even voice, his eyes riveted to the sky.

Suddenly everyone else shifted their attention to the blinding light that appeared in front of them.

"Oh, no, not again," Heather cried, mesmerized by the light while she watched it grow larger.

The sound of the airplane engine increased to an ear-shattering roar as the plane flew directly toward the group. The four of them were totally frozen in their places.

When the plane was about a hundred yards out, JT looked out beneath his hat, lifted the long-barrel rifle to his shoulder, and fired. His shot hit the windshield to the right of the pilot and the plane lifted immediately, banked to the right, and sped out of sight.

JT took off his hat, leaned his rifle against the wall, and sat down. He reached for his iced tea while everyone stared at him in shock.

"Now what were you saying?" he asked, acting as if nothing unusual happened.

Chapter 6

Vittorio Marino gazed out of his office window at the Pacific Ocean far below him and lit a cigarette. He propped his feet up on the mahogany desk and inhaled while the phone rang. He waited for a couple more rings, glanced around the office at his collection of Italian antiques, picked up the receiver. "What?"

"It's me."

"I know it's you, stupid. I got caller ID. I told you never to call me on this line."

"I couldn't get you on the cell. There's a tower down out here."

"So make it quick."

"There's this little problem with my partner." The caller paused. "Since we had to deal with that Mexican, he's just freaked out."

"Well, un-freak him." Marino snapped. "What do you think we pay you for? Don't be wasting my time with this." He leaned back in his chair and took a drag of his cigarette.

"You can't change the date?"

"No. Everything is all set. Same deal as usual. So you better be ready. Only this time, butt-head, no mistakes." He ran his hand over his slicked-back hair. "*Comprende, amigo?*"

"I understand perfectly," the caller answered and disconnected.

❧❧❧

Rachel opened her eyes and saw the digital clock flash to 5:08. Still on eastern daylight time, she groaned. She flipped the switch on the coffeepot on the way to the shower and came out shortly, dressed in a pink T-shirt and shorts. Slipping on a pair of Birkenstocks, she felt happy to be able to skip the usual routine of panty hose, slip, skirt, and heels. After drying her hair, she decided to wear it pulled back. She opened the top drawer and reached for a barrette. Then she froze, her eyes glued to a hairy, brown tarantula larger than her whole hand.

Momentarily paralyzed, she couldn't move her hand, and her mouth froze open in panic. Not able to breathe, she uttered weak little cries from the top of her throat. Then suddenly, she sprang back with one huge leap and ran out, flying down the stairs until she hit the bottom, finally crying "Spider!"

Toro dropped the can of paint he carried and ran up the walk. Rachel pointed to her suite. "In the bathroom."

A couple minutes later Toro came out with the spider cupped in his huge hands and stood in front of her.

"They don't bite much, Miss Rachel." He looked sympathetic. "They just look ugly and scary."

Rachel met his eyes. "Actually, I know that, Toro," she said, sinking down on the bottom step, calmly reviewing the previous scene in her mind and hoping there were no other witnesses. She brought her knees up to her chest, hugging them. "I just happen to have a phobia about spiders."

Toro nodded at her sympathetically, as if he understood.

"I know it's stupid," she continued, her voice calm and detached. "And I've really been working on trying to overcome my fear.

My therapist suggested I read up on them. So I did. I know the only types of spiders I need to be careful of, *here,* are the black widows and brown recluses. In my *mind,* I know that perfectly. In fact, I can even look at pictures of them now without shivering."

Still hugging her knees, she sighed deeply and looked up at the big, gentle man. "But when I stuck my hand in the drawer and *touched* the thing, I was so shocked, I just panicked."

"I know." Toro nodded. "It wasn't the spider so much. It was the surprise, too." He brought his cupped hands near his face and peeked in. "He's alive and looks good." Toro looked at Rachel, puzzled. "Miss Rachel, I sprayed your suite right before you came. Inside and outside. Mrs. Carpenter told me to make sure nothing could get in. This little fellow should be dead, but he doesn't even look *sick.*"

He caught a movement at the corner of his eye and looked over at the bougainvillea bushes. Lupe, the cook, was hiding there, watching them. He scowled at her and she quickly scurried off. "Miss Rachel," he began very gently. "I swear to you I sprayed your apartment. I know I'm gonna be in a heap of trouble because of this little guy but I know I did my job right." He opened his cupped hands. The spider sat there looking at him.

Rachel drew back, holding her hands up in front of her face. "No, don't."

"See, if you don't hurt them or startle them," he said while softly stroking the spider, "they actually make nice pets."

"Not for me," she said, her face contorted.

"Okay, I'm gonna take my little friend here and tell Mr. Carpenter what happened before I lose my job."

"Oh, please don't." *The last thing I need is JT hearing about my running from a stupid spider.* "You won't lose your job, Toro, you can count on it," she assured him. "I know you sprayed thoroughly. I could even smell it when I first came in."

Toro lumbered away and Rachel pressed her head to her knees. She remembered filling the empty drawers in the bathroom with her personal effects. Heather checked the room, too. So if Toro sprayed, how could a spider work its way in and still be alive? A sickening feeling washed over Rachel. *Did someone deliberately put that spider in my room? And, if they did, why? Was it JT's idea of a sick joke? But who else knew?*

Franz Venkman heard the pop of the front door when it opened, freeing itself from sticky layers of varnish. His large ears picked up the sounds of soft footfalls and the movement of fabric when his son, Otto, quietly crept down the hall. He heard the buzz of fluorescent lights when Otto turned them on in the office behind his and the soft click of the door closing.

Franz glanced at his watch and pressed the button on the intercom. "You're an hour late."

Otto jumped and his face turned ashen.

"Get in here." His father's tone sounded demeaning, metallic.

Otto opened the door, straightened himself, and took a deep breath. He ran his fingers through his dark blond hair, smoothing it, dreading the confrontation with his father. This time, he decided, he would hold his ground.

Otto stood in front of his father, taking the advantage of being taller. "What's your problem? So I'm an hour late. Big deal. I happened to be sick all night and barely slept. Even irrigators get sick days," he heard himself say. He squeezed his eyes shut. He sounded defensive, whiny.

"You were sick all night? Again?" Venkman's disbelieving tone washed over his son. He snorted. "Otto, Otto, don't you think I know your so-called sickness requires a six-week stint in rehab?"

Otto felt himself flush and he clenched his fists at his side. "So now you're a doctor?" he spat back, a wave of sarcasm rising up. "Oh, that's right," he said, "I forgot you give physicals to the pretty little Mexican who drops by."

Franz jerked his head as though he had been slapped. He glared at his son, but he softened his voice. "You knew I needed you here this morning."

"And I'm here," Otto shot back assertively. "Your appointment with Sherman isn't until nine-thirty. I left you the file with everything you need in it, if you'd have bothered to look around." He picked up the accordion file lying on the edge of the massive desk and dropped it down in front of his father. "Anything else?"

Franz looked down at the file and then dismissed it with a toss of his hand. "Clem over at the John Deere dealer is bringing by a new cultivator tractor he wants us to try." He spoke calmly, acting as if nothing happened between them, and glanced at his watch. "He'll be here any minute. You make the decision."

Franz picked up the file and stood. In his last action, he took two Cohibas from the box on the desk before he walked off.

Otto stood for several moments in silence before he realized he was shaking. It was so typical of his father to berate him, humiliate him, and then turn around and act as if nothing happened. "You make the decision," Otto said aloud, mimicking his father in a falsetto, sing-song voice. His emotions roiled in him like a cold fist twisting his heart, and he spotted the family photo on his father's desk, the one with him and Anna at the seashore with their parents. He picked it up, and with all his strength, flung it against the wall. It hit with a resounding crack, and the glass and frame exploded into a hundred pieces.

Without bothering to clean up the mess, Otto walked back to his office and opened a tall, metal file cabinet. At the back sat a bottle of Maker's Mark. He still shook when he poured himself a double and downed it, feeling the burn down his throat. He sat down, elbows on his desk, and ran thin, slender fingers through his hair. *It's not you, it's him. One day he'll die and you'll have the farm.* He repeated his little mantra over and over until the trembling ceased. He didn't know if it was the self-talk or the bourbon that did it, and he didn't care.

The stack of mail addressed to Venkman Farms caught his eye and he started going through it when the outer office door popped open. Otto heard the familiar sound and put the mail inside the desk drawer. He didn't bother getting up, knowing Clem always found his way to the offices in the back.

He jumped back, surprised, when it wasn't Clem, but rather Jesse Ray Greever, who burst into his office and leaned over his desk.

"I'm done," the grizzled, old man bellowed. "Get yourself another pilot."

"What are you talking about?" Otto pulled away, trying to distance himself from the wild, belligerent man who leaned into him only inches from his face. Jesse Ray's breath was sour with booze and he smelled as if he didn't bathe for weeks.

"Cut the crap, Otto. You know what I'm talking about," Jesse Ray slurred, and then laid a stack of one-hundred dollar bills on the desk.

Otto stared at him for several seconds, debating what to do. He reached out to take the money.

Jesse Ray's large hand clamped down on his. "Not so fast, my little friend," he said. "You owe me for expenses."

"What expenses?" Otto asked, barely hiding a smirk.

"Your friend shot my windshield, busted it all up. I was lucky he didn't kill me." Jesse Ray let it all sink in. "It's gonna take more than a thousand to fix the plane but we'll call it even."

"You didn't finish the job." Otto was firm, not moving his hand.

"It ain't gonna get finished. Not by me." Jesse Ray applied more pressure to Otto's hand, squeezing it until Otto loosened his grip on the money. Jesse took back the stack of bills and slipped it in his pocket.

"It's too bad you feel that way." Otto tried to keep his voice from cracking. "We're spraying lettuce next week."

"Listen, you little weasel." Jesse Ray leaned across the desk and huffed his curdled breath right in Otto's face. "I've done kissed your ass for too many years, grateful for those crumbs you've tossed my way. You'll give me my usual share of those spray contracts or Daddy's gonna find out exactly what you been up to…and he ain't gonna be none too happy when he finds out the deputy's been called."

When Jesse Ray left, Otto broke out in a cold sweat. He rubbed his throbbing hand, glad no bones were broken. What a mess, he thought, shaking his head in disbelief. *Of all the things that could have happened. JT actually shot at the plane? And now that stupid excuse of a pilot thinks he can blackmail me?* Otto stood to his full five feet-six, took a deep breath, and exhaled slowly. *Calm down,* he thought. *Calm down. You can fix this.* He twisted his hands together nervously and glanced back at the file cabinet.

જ૭જ૭

When Rachel looked at her watch, it read ten-after-ten. Her early-bird sister still hadn't arrived. She didn't answer the phone in her suite, either. A little irritated, Rachel left the main building and walked toward the rear of the property.

A hummingbird with an iridescent green head and a red throat swooped down at her and hovered over the hibiscus blossoms printed on her blouse. She stopped and held her breath, watching it hover so close to her face, not wanting it to leave. Finally, after perusing the cloth flowers and finding nothing to eat, the tiny bird zipped off to a nearby ash tree. *Wow, that's never happened before,* Rachel thought, and pondered other things that were new to her. Rachel reached Heather's suite, climbed the steps, and pounded on the door.

Inside, Heather turned her head and moaned. Her neck crunched as it moved. "Who is it?" she called out.

"It's me, Rachel."

"Just a minute." Heather swung her pale legs over the side of the bed. The pain in her neck radiated over her shoulders and down her arms. Even her fingertips ached. She pushed herself up; from her waist down, her whole body felt as if it were on fire.

When Heather finally opened the door, Rachel looked at her and gasped. "What's wrong?"

"Come in." Heather motioned to the carafe of coffee sitting on the counter, untouched and still hot.

Rachel's hand shook as she filled two mugs and added flavored creamer from the refrigerator. She glanced down at the jar candle next to the carafe and sniffed at the lavender fragrance that rose from it, but it did nothing to calm her. She sat down at the table across from her sister and searched Heather's face, frightened by the pain in her half-closed eyes. "Heather, tell me what's wrong."

Heather slowly brought the mug to her lips then eyed the prescription bottle on the table. The travel alarm next to it indicated she still had two more hours to wait for her next dose. She took a deep breath. "Rachel, please don't overreact to this. I have fibromyalgia, and I'm having a pretty bad attack this morning."

Rachel frowned. "Fibromyalgia? What's that?"

"It's a whole lot of pain and fatigue that comes and goes. There's no cure, but there's meds that help."

Rachel snapped up the medication and read the label. "This is synthetic morphine," she said, looking up. "You're taking morphine?" She felt her chest constrict. "They give this to people who are dying of cancer."

"They give it to people in other kinds of pain, too." Heather's voice sounded soft and flat. "Trust me; it's not that big of a deal."

"It's a big deal to me." Rachel's face darkened. "How long have you had this?"

"Years."

"Years? You've been ill for years and you never told me?"

Heather's voice was barely audible. "Well, I'm telling you now."

"I'm just sick over this. How could you not tell me?" Rachel demanded, slamming the container of pills on the table.

Heather shook her head slowly and took Rachel's hand. "Sweetie, I need you to calm down. It will only make it worse if you're upset."

"But—"

"It's okay," Heather interrupted, holding up her other hand. "I really am okay. I'm in pain, that's true, but nobody dies from this. Ever."

Rachel searched Heather's face, wondering if she was telling the truth.

"I know it's a bit of a shock for you to see me like this," Heather continued, "but after a day of bed rest, I'll be fine. You'll see."

Rachel's eyes continued to stare, fearful, accusing.

The frustration crept into Heather's voice. "Listen, Rachel. I hardly ever saw you once you went out on your own. Even though we talked on the phone, it wasn't the same. You always seemed so involved in the drama of your career and overwhelmed with your own problems, I didn't want to add mine to the batch." Heather's eyes left her sister's face to follow the slow-turning blades of the fan above them. "Besides, you never asked me how *I* felt."

Rachel's jaw dropped. "I see," she finally said, seared with the truth. Embarrassed to see herself through her sister's eyes, she hung her head. She remembered that during her last visit, JT told her quite bluntly to grow up. "It's not all about you," he had harshly informed her.

Rachel jumped up and walked to the open patio door. She clenched her jaw and blinked back tears. Cirrus clouds formed a high layer of gauze between her and the sun, and two jets spewed long, lazy contrails across the southern sky. She stepped onto the patio and watched Toro haul a roll of old carpeting out of one of the guest rooms and she returned his wave when he spotted her.

Rachel felt calmer when she walked back into the room. Heather sat quietly, staring at her coffee. "You're right," she said softly when Heather lifted her eyes. "I've been pretty self-centered."

Heather pictured her baby sister as she had been years ago and warmth crept into her voice. "Sweetie, you've had good reason. You were at a very critical point in your life when Mom and Dad were killed, barely a teenager. That's a pretty big trauma, even for an adult."

"That was over fifteen years ago." Rachel turned her face to the open door. "I can't keep using that as an excuse for immature, neurotic behavior."

"Then Matt was killed."

"Stop." Rachel jerked around as if someone yanked her with a rope. "I don't want to talk about that. It's in the past. He's gone, period. I should be over it by now."

"Rachel, don't you see?" Heather implored. "The reason you're having anxiety right now is because I'm sick, and deep down you're afraid I'll die, too, like everyone else you've loved."

"Stop it, stop it!" Rachel covered her ears with her hands, powerless to keep the scab from being ripped off her heart. "Stop trying to psychoanalyze me." She softened and dropped her hands as tears leaked from her eyes. "Don't you think I know all that? I've paid for enough therapy. I know the "why."

"But?"

Rachel shrugged. "No one could really tell me how to fix the problem."

"Maybe you gave up therapy too soon."

Rachel looked away. Sheer curtains by the open door twirled in the breeze, scattering a fistful of leaves on the floor. She stood up and shut the door, noticing the sky was turning milky with cloud cover. "Do you think it will rain?" she asked, wanting to change the subject.

"Don't count on it." Heather smiled, having heard it rained in Mesquite about once a year.

Rachel sat down again and Heather watched her for a few moments. "I don't want to upset you any more than you are," she finally said, "and I don't know if this will work, but I have an idea, if you're willing to give it a try."

Rachel looked at Heather warily. "This isn't going to be another you-need-God lecture is it?"

"No, I've given up on that."

"Okay, so what is it? I'm willing to try almost anything at this point."

Heather leaned forward, feeling as if she stepped out on a paper-thin layer of glass. "Here's the plan," she said, taking a deep breath. "Stop analyzing yourself and your behavior for the time you're here." She stood, grunting as she did so, and walked to the sink.

"That's it?" Rachel was dumbfounded.

"Not exactly." Heather rinsed her cup under the faucet and turned to her sister. "I'd like you to work for me, Rachel. I really need your help."

Rachel was speechless. Wonder Woman asked *her* for help?

"It pains me to admit it, but this project is a lot bigger than I imagined it," Heather confessed. "When JT kept telling me about the hotel, I kept thinking Bed-and-Breakfast. I just couldn't comprehend the size. So now I'm in over my head, and I don't want to tell JT since I'm the one that asked for the job to begin with." She walked over to the table and sat down. "The truth is I'm suffocating under everything I need to do. That's why I've been sick."

Rachel continued to stare at her sister. This was the first time in the history of their relationship that Heather opened up to her about her own difficulties.

"I have all kinds of jobs you can easily handle," Heather continued, "and you'd be getting me out of a big mess."

Stunned, Rachel slowly nodded. "Okay," she said, happy her sister actually needed her. Her hotel experience would be a real asset, too. "I'm ready. Let's write out a list of what you need me to do."

"Since you asked," Heather said, reaching over for the notebook on the table, "here's my to-do list."

Rachel took it from her and quickly read the two pages of notes. "No problem," she quipped. "What do you want me to do this afternoon?"

"There you go, getting all cocky again," Heather teased. "Pride goeth before a fall, you know."

"I know. I said I'd help, but I never promised to be humble." She hugged her sister tightly and walked out the door. She stuck her head back in and grinned wickedly. "Hey, remind me later to tell you about the tarantula I found in my room."

"What? Rachel Ryan, you come back here," Heather shouted at the closed door.

❧❧❧

Some days Alex Tucker felt as if he lived in his truck, and this day was no exception. Heading back to Mesquite, he navigated the narrow, rutted road carefully. Mexican roads, even highways, were often poorly maintained. Feeling a little on edge, Alex stayed five kilometers under the speed limit and checked his rearview mirror frequently for *Federales*.

Being a cop didn't necessarily work to his advantage out of the country. In fact, with all the recent tension at the border, he knew a few folks on the south side of the wall who would happily shoot him on sight if they found out his declared business wasn't "tourist." Hoping he'd look less like a cop, Alex kept the bottle of tequila and the few trinkets he had purchased on the seat next to him. He also grew his beard for three days, skipped a haircut, and tossed on a large gold chain and bracelet under a black silk shirt before he left. He flipped down the visor and checked himself. The sunglasses did it. He definitely could pass as a gangster, or a major drug dealer. The important thing was, he *did* pass, and thanks to his rancher friend, he had been able to meet the right people.

Expanses of low desert slipped by his window with an occasional creosote bush and prickly pear cactus adding touches of dusty green. The elevation was too low for saguaros now. That meant he wasn't far from the border.

Desert soon turned to farmland and Alex spotted an occasional outhouse on a canal bank. Then a small village appeared, devoid of grass or landscaping. Barefoot children ran happily among the plain adobe homes.

When Alex finally arrived within the border city of Alixta, shops and tables lined the streets. Vendors hovered over them, hawking pottery and purses and everything else a tourist could possibly want. He felt safe. Tourists rarely encountered problems here because their money was too important to the local power structure, and the police were in evidence everywhere. So were the Federales, armed with their assault rifles.

Siesta time, for those that still partook, was over, and locals lined up in front of taco stands where the aroma of barbequed pork and carne asada drifted down the block. Alex's mouth watered as he pulled into the long line of vehicles that snaked through the streets, waiting to cross the border. By the time he entered the Mesquite town limits, he felt exhausted and hungry, but he was satisfied; he had gathered all the information he needed. Now, if he could only get the rest of the plan to work.

Chapter 7

It was nearly quitting time for the employees when Rachel wound her way out of the kitchen. She stopped in her tracks. Loud voices boomed through the door of the employees' lounge. Although she didn't understand a word of Spanish, it was obvious an argument was escalating. She flung open the door. Toro and Lupe jumped, stopping in mid-sentence.

"What's going on?"

Toro and Lupe looked at each other.

Rachel gasped. "Lupe. What happened to your face?" She stared, alarmed at the large bruise near Lupe's left eye. "—and your arm?"

Lupe's eyes dropped. "It's nothing, *señorita.* I fell."

Suspecting Lupe had just lied to her, Rachel turned to Toro and glared at him. "You better tell me what's going on," she demanded.

"Lupe needs to tell you that," he said and suddenly shouted at Lupe in Spanish.

Lupe burst into tears and turned to Rachel, her hands flung out in a pleading gesture, talking rapidly in Spanish.

"Stop it!" Rachel shouted. She shot Toro a warning look and then lowered her voice to a near whisper. "I want someone to explain to me in English exactly what is going on here."

"I think Lupe has something to tell you about the spider," Toro said, staring at Lupe.

"The spider?" Rachel turned to Lupe with a quizzical look on her face. Then it occurred to her. *Other than Toro, Lupe is the only other person who's been in my suite. Heather would have told her to check for spiders.* "Lupe? What about the spider?"

"I so sorry, I so sorry, *señorita*," she said, bursting into tears again.

Rachel pulled up a chair in front of the crying woman and held her hands. "Okay, Lupe," she said, ratcheting her voice down a few notches in volume. "Nobody died. Now what exactly are you sorry for?"

Lupe kept her eyes on her hands. "*Mi esposo*, my husband. He make me put spider in room." She began to cry again.

Rachel's mouth dropped open and she turned toward Toro. "What? What is she talking about?"

"Some guy paid her husband five hundred dollars to get Lupe to put that tarantula in your room."

Lupe continued to cry. "He bad man, *señorita,* bad man."

Rachel was stunned. "Who is a bad man?"

"Lupe told me she didn't know who the man was," Toro replied. "She went home and told her husband how she had to clean your suite extra good because you were afraid of spiders. Her husband bragged about her job to somebody, some guy. He told him you were afraid of spiders. That man, he's the one who gave Lupe's husband the money and the spider."

"Hold on a second, Toro." Rachel shook her head in bewilderment. "Are you saying some guy I don't even know paid Lupe's husband to make sure she put a spider in my room? That's sick. It doesn't even make sense."

Toro hunched up his shoulders. "That's what Lupe told me and Lupe doesn't lie. She said she told her husband no, that she would lose her job. But her husband hit her and told her if she didn't do it, he'd kick her and her daughter out in the street."

Rachel's eyes flashed with anger at the thought of a man hitting Lupe and threatening her. "Lupe, look at me," she said in a quiet, controlled voice.

Lupe finally looked up, tears streaking her ample cheeks, and wiped her face with her hands.

"You are not going to get fired, Lupe. Understand?"

"*Si, señorita,*" Lupe sniffed. "*Gracias, gracias.*"

"If your husband asks you to do something bad again, you tell me first. Understand?"

"*Si, señorita.*" Lupe nodded vigorously.

"Now go ahead and punch out, and come back to work tomorrow, just like normal. Just don't tell your husband that you told us what happened."

"Oh, *señorita, gracias, gracias.*" Lupe grabbed Rachel's hands and squeezed them.

Rachel finally walked out into the sunlight, still bewildered, and turned to Toro.

"This is the craziest thing I've ever heard. What in the world do you make of it?"

Toro stepped up beside her, his massive body shading her from the setting sun. "I don't know, Miss Rachel. It don't make sense to me, either. Why would someone try to scare you?"

"Yes, why indeed?" Rachel pondered the reasons and scanned the employees' parking lot wondering if that someone might be hiding nearby. The cracked and gravelly blacktop held one vehicle, the pieced-together old Chevy that Toro drove.

"But who? I hardly know anyone here." Rachel looked up, anger starting to surge through her. She narrowed her eyes at Toro and her mind raced over all the people she'd met since she came to Mesquite. "I've only met a handful of people, Toro, and they hardly know me." A look of resolve settled on her face. "If they did, they'd know something like this makes me all the more determined to stay."

‹››

Rachel went back to the café, poured herself a big glass of ice water, and sat in the corner booth where everyone met to eat. She dropped her head into her hands and massaged her temples.

Afternoon light subdued the normally bright room, giving the coral walls a golden glow. It was too early for anyone to show up for dinner, and she felt grateful for the solitude. It had been a long day.

"What are you doing?" JT's voice startled her and she jumped, nearly falling out the booth. "A tad nervous, are we?"

He smelled like Irish Spring soap and his hair was still damp from a shower. She gave him a dour look. "If you had the day I did, you'd be nervous, too."

"Why, what happened?"

Rachel considered telling JT about the spider but thought about Lupe. *The poor woman doesn't need to be interrogated by JT. She's terrified enough. Besides, JT is the last person that needs to know I ran away from a stupid spider.* Rachel let out a deep breath. "It's a long story you don't really need to hear. Right now I need you to tell me about Heather."

"What about her?"

"Why didn't you tell me she was sick?"

"You were never around to tell."

Rachel winced at the sting. "You've never been subtle, JT, but I guess I deserved that."

JT slid in the booth across from her. "Oh, don't get all stressed out about it. Heather's had these attacks for a few years. The best thing she can do is rest in bed like she's doing and take her pills. She'll be better tomorrow."

Rachel studied his body language, then considered JT probably never told a lie in his life. She lowered her head and drummed her fingers, trying to figure out how she was going to say what she wanted to say.

"So what happened?" JT asked, giving her an opening.

"Heather asked me if I'd take over some of her responsibilities here," Rachel blurted out. "I did a few things that needed to be taken care of today as far as food service and designed a few forms, but there's a lot more that needs to be done."

"I'm sure that's right. I was wondering when she'd finally admit she bit off more than she could really chew." JT's eyes drifted away. "She's been working far too hard, and she never knows when to quit."

"Exactly. That's why I want to stay around for a while and work here. Maybe six months.

I could book in a few groups and associations, advertise, set up the catering department. Just until you guys get the hotel on its feet." She finally caught his eyes. "You know hotel sales have been my forte, JT. Eventually you're going to have to hire *somebody*."

JT looked down, rubbed his chin.

"Please, JT, I know your first reaction is to say forget it. But let me finish."

"Rachel, I know you're very capable—"

"Wait, please. You and Heather spent five years of your lives taking care of me. Then you even paid for my hospitality degree." She put her face directly in front of his so he had to look at her. "Please give me a chance to pay you back."

"That's not the issue."

"I know. I know. The real issue is that I've been a thorn in your side in the past." She paused and sipped her ice water. "If there was any way I could change history, believe me, I'd do it in a heartbeat." JT didn't respond. "Look, you know very well I can do anything related to hotel work. You don't even have to pay me. I'll work for room and board."

JT rubbed his hairline, starting to analyze all the pros and cons of Rachel's proposal while she had enough sense to keep quiet. He left the booth, went into the kitchen, and put a pan of enchiladas in the oven. He switched on the coffee machine when he walked back into the cafe. Rachel remained silent.

"Okay," he finally said. "You can stay for six months. You can be the sales and catering director. It will be your job to bring in group sales, develop advertising, hire a chef, develop a menu, and plan catered events for all the meeting rooms. Plus anything else that comes up."

Rachel's face lit up. "Thank you, thank you, JT. You won't regret this."

Embarrassed, he brushed her away, and then gave her a penetrating look. "However, if you screw up, you're history. You know that."

"I know that."

"Okay," he said, mollified. "Now come with me."

Rachel followed JT over to the pool and sat near the steps at the shallow end. While he headed over to the control panel behind her, Rachel started to think. *What the heck just happened? I allow my sister to suck me into a guilt trip, and then I beg my brother-in-law for a job? Where I'll be working directly for him? Have I totally lost my mind?*

A hum and a gurgle distracted Rachel, and she turned her eyes toward the cave made of boulders that JT had built at the far end of the pool. A river of water slid down over the top to a large semicircular rock shelf, and then cascaded over the shelf like a silver curtain, partially obscuring the entrance to the cave. Inside the grotto, a swirling pool of water began to bubble and steam.

"Oh, it's beautiful." Rachel jumped up and clapped her hands in childlike amazement. "It looks totally natural."

"That's because we used our own natural rocks, right off the mountain." JT beamed, coming around the front. "Plus a little cement and chicken wire here and there."

Rachel walked closer to the waterfall, inspecting it. "You obviously spent weeks working on it."

"Well, that too."

The bits of silica and mica embedded in some of the boulders sparkled in the sun. Rachel reached out her hand to touch them. "These even feel real." She looked from one boulder to the next. "You can't tell the real rocks from the ones you made."

"Only if you knock," JT said. "I'm afraid the hollow sound is a dead giveaway."

"So who goes around knocking on rocks? I say they're absolutely perfect. Just look how everything fits together. It looks like a tropical grotto." Her voice trailed off and her eyes drifted to the landscaping that bordered the pool. "Now, if we can only find out what's eating all our flowers—"

"I think I can help with that," a voice behind them said.

Rachel and JT whirled around to see Weezer Chaffee with a big smile on his face.

"You did a great job with that pool, JT," he commended. "I can't believe what a difference it makes. In fact, the whole courtyard is amazing. It's way better than the original."

"Thanks. It's good to see you, Weezer." JT shook his hand, noticed he wore no ring on his other hand, and quickly introduced him to Rachel.

Rachel stared at the lanky man in front of her, taking in his Wranglers, boots, and Stetson. "Are you a real cowboy?" she blurted out without saying hello.

"No." Weezer smiled, a slow, sexy smile, and then looked into her eyes. "But if you like cowboys, I can be one."

Rachel's ivory skin flushed pink and she found her eyes riveted to his, unable to speak.

161

"Actually, I'm just a humble entomologist." He smiled again. "I kill bugs for a living."

Rachel recovered, pulled away from his eyes. "Well, you're definitely my kind of guy," she said brightly, happy to hear the words "kill" and "bugs" in the same sentence. "Your name sounds familiar," she added, thoughtfully. "I think I just mailed you an invitation to our open house party."

"I hope so. I love a party." Weezer took a step closer to her, drinking her in.

I'll bet you do, Rachel thought, taking a step back, dropping her eyes. "Well, right now, someone is having a real party with these flowers," she said, pointing to a spot where something had eaten several blossoms down to stubs.

Weezer knelt down to inspect the flowers at close range. JT looked over at Rachel and asked, "Do you remember when we talked about your position? The "and anything else" that was included in the job description?"

"Yes?"

"Well, the flower problem is one of the 'and else's.' So see what you can do about it. I need to run."

Rachel felt awkward alone with Weezer, and her skin flushed again. "So what's the verdict?" she asked, trying to sound business-like.

Weezer stood up. "Darlin', you got rabbits."

The setting sun haloed around Rachel, turning her hair to spun gold. She could feel Weezer's eyes on her.

"Rabbits?"

"Yeah, jackrabbits, or even little brown rabbits." Weezer stood up and squinted into the sun. "You seen any around at dusk or early in the morning?"

"I've seen little grey-brown bunnies, and I think a couple tan ones." Her face turned soft. "They were so cute."

Weezer laughed. "Well, those cute little critters are definitely enjoying your landscaping."

"Oh, dear." Rachel looked down at the denuded plantings. "That's a bad deal for us. So what are our options?"

Weezer moved closer to her, his eyes still on her, and Rachel caught a musky, gamey scent surrounding him. "You can either get up early in the morning and shoot their butts with a pellet gun when they show up for breakfast, or…"

Rachel's eyes immediately reflected distress. "Or?"

"Peace offering," Weezer responded with wink. "Carrots, lettuce, and other food they'll like better than your flowers."

"Okay, I think I can handle that," Rachel nodded with relief. "Now let me show you something else." While she led Weezer over to a garden behind the main building, the sun slipped behind the mountain. She pointed out a miniature bougainvillea that sported only thorns on several of its branches. "Another rabbit party?"

Weezer picked off a couple leaves, or rather what was left of them. "No, these pests are quite a bit smaller," he said, turning the leaves over in his hand. "I actually have something to take care of this, but it only comes in industrial size quantities, something you hardly need."

Rachel's face expressed her disappointment.

"But since I hate to see a beautiful woman in distress," Weezer said, looking deeply into her eyes, "I'll make up a little baggie for you that your gardener can mix with water. It should last you a year."

"That sounds great." Rachel dropped her gaze to his lips and the mustache softly feathered over them. A flash of heat rushed over her and her knees felt weak. She continued to sense the electricity between them as they walked toward the main building, chatting, laughing. When Rachel turned the corner, she was startled to see the golden coat and flaxen mane of a horse standing in the shade.

"Is that your ride?" she asked, staring at the animal.

"Sure is."

"You lied," she teased. "You *are* a cowboy."

"When I need to be." He smiled that sexy smile again Rachel felt down to her toes.

She watched him mount up and cantor off into the sunset. A real lady-killer, she decided. The kind she needed to stay far, far away from.

✧✦✧

After dinner, Rachel walked to the far end of the lobby where her new office was located. She opened the french doors and entered the small room, seating herself at the desk Heather normally occupied. She leaned back in the chair. It was a comfortable room, enough for two or three clients to sit in front of her. The phone sat perfectly situated at her left. She smiled. She and Heather were both left-handed, but other than that and the ivory skin they shared, they had inherited very different genes from their parents, so much so, they hardly looked like sisters.

When Rachel glanced at the top of the desk, she noticed a large brown envelope with Buddy's name on it. In the top right-hand corner, someone had neatly printed the name Rosario Garcia and a phone number. The envelope smelled heavily of a woman's perfume, as if someone scented it on purpose. She brushed away the little ping of jealousy she felt and turned the envelope over. It wasn't even sealed. She set it aside, but before five minutes passed, she picked it up again.

Buddy won't be back from LA for another day or two, she rationalized. *What if this is something really important that I need to call him about? Perhaps I should inspect it. After all, it is on my desk. No one would ever know, anyway.*

After a brief struggle between her conscience and her curiosity, she carefully undid the clasp and slid out the contents of the envelope. It was a stack of photocopies, some sort of diary written in Spanish by someone with the name of Juan Rodriguez. *Oh, great,* she thought, but when she flipped through the papers, an English translation followed, written in a feminine hand.

The diary detailed sightings by the writer, along with sightings by others, of mysterious green lights appearing on Blood Mountain. Rachel put the papers down, puzzled. *What the heck is this all about?* She read the diary through twice more. The third time, she made a tiny mark on a calendar on the nights the lights were seen, wondering if there was some kind of pattern. Then she carefully put the diary back in the envelope and closed the clasp.

✧✧✧

The sunset was unusual for autumn. Stratus clouds formed bands of gold against the horizon, and then turned flaming orange, as if the sky caught on fire. The edges of the clouds gradually softened and dulled to the color of red wine. Finally, the grays of night descended, and they ushered in the thick, black night of the new moon.

Two men in trucks, without headlights on, crept up the winding north side of Blood Mountain. In the darkness, they reached a mesa not far from the top, and the trucks slowly moved along the half-mile span. One man jumped out at intervals to drag plaster boulders off to the side, and remove piles of brush they placed there the month before. The second man snapped reflectors onto metal pipes nearly buried in the sand. Within a half-hour, the two men transformed the mesa into its original purpose of thirty years prior: a rough but serviceable airstrip.

At the end of the landing area, the men pulled some brush and debris away from a jagged wall of rock that ascended over sixty feet above them. Behind the brush sat a massive boulder, made of concrete and chicken wire, ten feet high and so wide it required the two of them to move it.

When the two men finally pushed the artificial boulder to the side, they exposed the opening to a cave. One man entered and lit a lantern, casting an eerie glow in the roughly hollowed-out dome. A large stainless steel hopper sat in the center, dominating the room, flanked by tables on either side. The other man backed his truck up to the entrance and together they unloaded a sealed container and thirty bags of Parathion, a commercial insecticide.

They worked silently, moving with a smooth, easy rhythm, like two dancers having practiced their moves many times.

"I need a break," Little announced, wiping his arm across his forehead.

They walked outside, pulled out cigarettes and lit up, thinking their own thoughts while the nicotine calmed their nerves and the night breezes washed over them, drying their sweat.

"Dewey Tucker's been asking questions again," Little said without preamble.

"So?" his partner asked.

"You know he doesn't think Juan's death was a suicide."

"So what?" The taller man filled his lungs with smoke and exhaled. "We've plowed that ground before. It really doesn't matter what the old man thinks. He's no FBI. He can say it's murder till the cows come home. Everyone else believes it's a suicide and that's the perception that counts."

Little stared at him. "Are you nuts? That's the stupidest thing I've ever heard. All he needs is one little piece of evidence."

"And what might that be, Einstein?"

Little stayed silent.

"You see?" The man crushed his smoke under his heel. "Even if that dimwit suspected the both of us, he couldn't prove a thing. Absolutely nothing. No clues, no DNA, nothing."

"We could have buried him."

"Right," the tall man answered sarcastically. "Then we could sit and chew our nails while people conducted search parties for him all over these mountains." He stood up. "Just put the whole thing out of your mind. Everyone else has. We need to get back to work."

Opening a box near the entrance, each man pulled out a white jumpsuit. They stepped into them, quickly zipping the suits up to their necks. Large white masks came next with round filters over the mouth, and then goggles that fit snugly over their eyes. The white gloves and tight white caps were last. They nodded to each other. Everything looked good.

After reentering the cave, the men opened the bags of Parathion and poured half of each bag of poison into the hopper until it was full.

Little checked his watch, pointing to it, and the other man nodded. Everything was set.

Little took two green lanterns, climbed over the rocks to the top of the peak above the cave, and waited.

❦❧❦❧

Vicky Donovan worked her way up the east face of Blood Mountain, the camera bouncing against her chest with every step. Although she was fit for a woman of fifty-seven, she began to tire of having to carry the large telescope on her back, the cooler full of snacks and the lantern that illuminated the path in front of her. It also didn't help that she tipped the scales with an extra thirty-five pounds.

Stopping by some flat-faced rocks to rest, Vicky set the cooler down and pulled the telescope off her back. Maybe this wasn't such a hot idea after all. She really wanted to study Orion's belt, but was the science class that interested in photographs of a constellation? Now, maybe if they all hiked up here at night, they might be. On the other hand, kids today…ah, they'd probably spend their time necking and not looking at the stars.

Vicky decided to leave the cooler and come back for it later, and she slipped the camera off her neck and put that in the cooler, too. She bristled at the thought of Laura standing her up at the last minute, forcing her to carry everything by herself. She'd thought about putting the hike off another month, but she had already waited a long time. Laura might come up with an excuse then, too.

No, this trip was too important to postpone. New moons came only once a lunar month. It was the darkest night and she would have the best view of the heavens. Besides, she was anxious to get to the top of Blood Mountain.

After a quick rest and half of a chocolate bar, Vicky hoisted the telescope onto her back and slung the binoculars around her neck. Picking up the lantern, she continued up the hill. When she found a level area near the top, she stopped, out of breath. It was close enough, she decided. At three thousand feet, the view was magical. Mesquite appeared as a dim dusting of lights, and the stars above looked close enough that someone could pick them like cherries.

Placing the lantern on a nearby rock, Vicky carefully set up the telescope. She had almost finished fine-tuning it when suddenly a bright light appeared out of nowhere. Oddly, it seemed to grow larger. Hearing the drone of an engine, she stepped out from behind the telescope and squinted at the oncoming plane. It steadily dropped in altitude and Vicky gazed at it curiously, watching the light get closer. The noise of the plane quieted, and it came directly at her. Spooked, she quickly ducked behind a rock and flattened herself on the ground.

The plane banked and dropped behind the peak behind her. She watched it disappear from sight and heard the engine die down and stop. *How odd,* she thought.

Curious, Vicky climbed over the rocks in the direction the plane had gone. When she could go no farther, she sprawled out on the rock ledge, face down, and caught her breath. Light reflected from below, and she inched herself up, just enough to see over the edge. She adjusted the binoculars against her eyes then gasped in shock.

Two men, totally covered in white Tyvek suits and looking like something out of a science fiction movie, were removing packages from the small plane. Vicky gaped at the bizarre scene below her, her mind spinning out scenarios of what could be going on. Whatever was taking place, she suddenly realized, was probably illegal.

In a panic, she pushed herself up awkwardly. At the same awful moment, a chunk of rock cracked and teetered on the ledge, then tumbled and bounced its way down to the airstrip, until it reached the feet of one of the men. He looked up and encircled Vicky in a white, powerful beam of light.

Terrified, Vicky turned and ran down the trail, scraping her legs and arms along the way. She jumped over cactus, slipped on the gravel-covered path, and watched her lantern bounce down the hill and land against a boulder. She jumped up in the dark and ran to her lantern, but its light was dimming. She ran on and on, and when she finally emerged from around a bend in the trail and saw the faint glow in the sky from the Mesquite Mountain Inn, she sobbed with relief. Her lantern had just died completely.

The trail widened and she ran again, tears running down her face, and she slipped once more on loose gravel before she reached the edge of the parking lot. It was then she saw the truck racing toward her. Exhausted and out of breath, she dug for her keys and ran to her car and reached the door just as the truck pulled up to her. In horror, she watched the two men in white jump out of the truck. She shook so hard she had barely inserted the key in the lock before she felt strong hands gripping her and she struggled, scratching and kicking, trying to push the man away. Then the second man, the tall one, threw a cord around her neck and pulled. Vicky continued to struggle, her feet kicking the air, her hands grabbing at the tightening cord, gasping for air with a wheeze that sounded inhuman.

Gradually her movements slowed and blackness descended on her. The wheeze from her throat subsided and her body shook one last time. She slowly sank to the ground and lay totally still.

Chapter 8

The two men in white, soaked with sweat, climbed back into their truck and left the parking lot. They wordlessly wove their way through the darkness of the moonless night and slowly climbed the north face of Blood Mountain, driving the twisted road back to the airstrip.

After entering the cave, it took a few seconds for Little's eyes to adjust to the light. He surveyed the stainless steel table near the back of the cave that held the thirty packages they unloaded from the plane and risked their lives for. Each bundle, smaller than a bag of sugar and weighing less than three pounds, was sealed with wide white tape in the shape of a cross. Each package contained seventy-six thousand dollars' worth of cocaine. Over two million dollars lay within a few feet of him.

His partner gestured for Little to get back to work, and began his own task of hauling the partially empty bags of Parathion under the hopper one at a time.

Little picked up a hypodermic needle and inserted the tip gently beneath the tape where it formed the cross on one of the packages. Slowly he withdrew a minute amount of white power and carefully expelled it into a jar that had a tiny hole in the lid.

He was satisfied, and no one ever missed the trace amount. Finally, with the tip of a heat tool, he delicately touched the tape, sealing it, and set the bundle on the opposite table. He reached for the next package.

In turn, the taller man took each package and carefully placed it in the center of the bag of insecticide. With a deft touch, he pulled open the slide gate under the hopper and watched the insecticide flow in and around the cocaine, totally obscuring it. After resealing the bag, he marked it in the corner with a small, discreet dot.

When they finally completed their task, the men went outside to take a break. "Give me a couple cigarettes," Little said, "I'm out." His lighter shook when he lit one, but he calmed himself while he sucked the smoke greedily into his lungs.

"This is my last time," he said, expelling the smoke into the dark. "I just can't do it anymore. That's two people we've killed in a month."

"You knew what this was when we took on the deal," his partner responded calmly. He drank deeply from the jug of water between them. "Look, things were bound to happen eventually. The Mexican got in the way and so did the old broad. We had no choice." He turned to the red glow of the cigarette beside him. "Unless, of course, you'd prefer to spend twenty years in prison."

"Yeah? Well, now we could both fry." Little's voice became very small. "You didn't have to kill her."

"Right. We could have let her tell the whole town what's going on at Blood Mountain. Maybe even put it in the paper."

Little filled his lungs with smoke and didn't answer. A slight breeze swept over them and he zipped down the top of his suit, welcoming the cooler air on his chest. "Let's finish up," he said.

It was close to four in the morning by the time the two men returned the site to its abandoned façade, and swept the area of any signs of human occupancy.

They walked to their trucks and Little said gently, "She was my high school biology teacher, you know."

"Mine, too, and it's regrettable." The tall one threw a large bag of trash into his truck. "But we can't change what happened. We have to go on. Just be cool, act normal. Nobody can prove anything. Trust me. I've covered all the bases."

Little looked at him, puzzled. "You just don't get it, do you? I really don't care what you got covered." His voice was weary. He threw down his cigarette and crushed it to the ground. "I'm out. Period. End of story."

He climbed into his truck and brushed the hair and sweat back from his face. It wasn't until he arrived home and turned on the light in the bathroom that he saw the blood.

ღღღ

The following morning, the sun hid below the horizon when Rachel walked to the main building and entered the hotel kitchen. She stood alone in the dim light, smelling the lingering sent of bleach and disinfectant. Determined to do battle with her long-eared visitors, she assembled a plate of vegetables from the walk-in, artfully arranging carrots, celery, and lettuce, humming as she worked. Her sneakers squeaked on the vinyl floor when she crossed the kitchen, hoping she could come up with a more permanent solution to their bunny problem soon, without hurting Peter Rabbit's family.

She stepped outside the back door of the kitchen and the sky greeted her with a wide band of pink on the eastern horizon. The air felt cool and delicious. A roadrunner scooted out from a cluster of olive trees with a little critter in his mouth, and darted past, surprising Rachel.

She gazed out toward the desert, scanning the area for signs of furry visitors. A pair of taupe-colored rabbits hopped out from behind some rocks near the employees' parking lot. They lifted their heads, sniffed the air, and looked in her direction.

Rachel stood statue-like for several moments before they turned and bounded toward the courtyard. Stealthily pursuing them in the dim light, she stepped through the cracked and buckled parking lot until she spotted something out of the corner of her eye.

Someone had parked a car at the edge of the lot. Rachel looked at it quizzically. She was sure the old Subaru belonged to no one who worked at the hotel. So why was it there?

Rachel approached the car, noticed something lying on the blacktop by the front tire, and smelled something bad. The dawning sun suddenly splayed over the object and Rachel froze in place like a pillar of salt. The object was a woman, her head bent at an awkward angle as if her neck were broken, her eyes and mouth open in terror. Rachel knew she was dead.

ひひひ

The ambulance whined and rumbled up the twisted road, followed by Deputy Tucker in the county SUV. Out of the way, and far enough to be out of the view of the body, Buddy and JT sat by the entrance to the kitchen, waiting.

Deputy Tucker approached them in yesterday's clothes, thrown on in a hurry, lugging along as if he missed his morning jolt of Joe. "Where's Rachel?" he asked.

Buddy stood and handed him a paper cup filled with freshly poured coffee from the coffee station they thoughtfully had set up. "She's inside, in the lobby."

"Ah, thanks," Tucker said, raising his cup. "I needed this." He drank the whole cup down and handed it back for a refill. "Rachel okay?"

"Right now, yes."

Before the deputy could ask another question, the medical examiner pulled up in a black Lexus and squealed to a stop. "Hold up on that refill, will ya," he said, walking away.

Tucker met the ME at the car, taking the camera she handed him. She looked striking, with clear skin the color of hazelnuts and black hair pulled back in a stylish bun. After exchanging a few words with Tucker, they both put on gloves and knelt down by the body.

While the ME checked the dead woman and took her temperature, Tucker took pictures of the crime scene from every angle.

The EMTs milled around, and the sun was up five fingers before Tucker approached JT and Buddy again.

"Know anythin' about this?" Tucker held out a plastic bag filled with broken china and vegetables.

"Rachel brought that out to feed the rabbits," JT said.

Tucker looked puzzled. "Don't they breed enough around here without extra food?"

"I guess Weezer Chaffee told her she—"

"Weezer come by here?" Tucker blurted.

"Yeah, yesterday. He stopped by and gave us advice on landscaping problems."

The deputy looked down and rubbed his chin, which hadn't yet received its morning shave. The ambulance doors slammed shut and everyone turned to watch it rumble off, but this time the siren remained quiet

Tucker and JT talked a while, and then Tucker excused himself, saying he needed to speak to Rachel.

"Just be careful," JT warned. "She can be a bit unstable."

When Tucker walked into the lobby, Rachel and Heather were reading catalogs on a sofa that had recently been uncrated. A couple of large, attractively framed prints were propped up against the sofa, their wrappings still lying on the floor.

Tucker was glad to come inside and sniffed. The air smelled good, he thought, kind of spicy, which beat the heck out of the smell of the dead. It didn't matter how many years he'd done the job; the smell never got better.

"Sorry, Rachel, but I need to ask you a couple of questions."

Rachel looked up. "Sure, no problem," she said, a little too brightly.

Tucker noticed Rachel's hair and makeup. For someone who had just gone through a trauma, they appeared undisturbed.

"Can you tell me what happened? Start right at the beginning."

Rachel closed up her catalog and set it aside. She related her story of how she arose early, went to the kitchen and made up the plate of vegetables, and found the woman.

"When I saw the woman, I must have dropped the plate," Rachel said, calmly." Anyway, I called 911. That's it."

Tucker stopped writing and stared at Rachel. *She could be reciting a grocery list for all the emotion she shows. And JT said to be careful?* "So what were your first thoughts when you saw her?"

"Well, I knew she had been strangled, and she was all twisted up with flies going in and out of her mouth."

The deputy frowned at her reply. "How do you figure she was strangled?

Rachel gave him an odd look. "Didn't you see the ligature mark around her neck?"

Tucker drew back. Rachel insinuated he had overlooked the obvious. It took some effort to keep the irritation out of his voice. "It might *look* like she was strangled," he said, a little sarcasm dripping out, "but we won't know the actual cause of death until the body has been autopsied by the ME. In the meantime, don't say nothin' to nobody. Understood?"

Tucker caught a look from Rachel that came close to an eye-roll. He felt himself bristling at her lack of respect for him and developed an instant dislike for the uppity young woman.

"So Deputy, you're saying someone attacked her when she was getting back to the car, right?"

Rachel was definitely beginning to irritate him. "I ain't saying nothin' yet," he answered, deliberately refusing to give her any information.

"Well, her keys were on the ground in front of the car door, and Buddy said something about her bringing a telescope up the mountain. Since there wasn't one in the car, I have to assume it's still up there, somewhere."

It wasn't what Rachel said, but rather her tone that wore on Tucker's nerves. He looked over at Heather who pretended to be engrossed in her catalog, ignoring Rachel's comments.

"One last question, Rachel," he said, wanting to conclude the interview. "Did you touch the body?"

"Did I touch the body?" Rachel repeated, looking bewildered. She fixed her eyes on Tucker as if he were a total idiot. "Do you think I'm flippin' *stupid*? I told you I could tell she was dead."

Tucker went back outside, muttering to himself, and then noticed JT and Buddy approaching him with the coffee refill.

"I'm getting a little concerned, Deputy," JT said as he handed him the cup. "Do you think the four of us are in any danger here?"

Tucker avoided JT's eyes. "I honestly don't know." He glanced at the trail heading up the mountain, dreading the hike he'd eventually have to take. He pulled out a bandana and wiped his glasses. Folds of skin nearly covered his eyes.

"So what about this so-called suicide that happened before we moved in?" Buddy asked.

"Don't look at me. I never called it a suicide." Tucker squinted at him. "Some folks around these parts might want people to think Juan killed himself, but as far as I'm concerned, it's still under investigation."

"Do you think it would be a good idea to bring in some night security?" JT asked.

"Can't hurt none," Tucker admitted. "I might even know someone who could help."

"That sounds great," JT said. "Are you thinking about your nephew?"

"Yeah. He's sleepin' on the sofa now, so if you gave him a decent bed and a meal now and then, I'd be willin' to bet he'd do it for free while he's here. I'll ask him, and let you know. Meantime, I need your personnel records and statements from all of you. We can take care of it this afternoon, if you want."

He walked away, and then had a thought and turned back. "Uh, JT? Your sister-in-law? She's a little different, huh?"

JT stared at the deputy. "Man, you don't know the half of it."

187

The rest of the day went by in a blur. JT asked the day labor to clean up the parking lot first thing, then decided to go ahead and crack-seal it, and followed that with a good seal-coating. It was something he planned to do, eventually. But the fact that someone murdered a woman there and her bodily remains leaked into the cracks that proliferated over the parking lot, JT decided to make quick work of blotting out the spot—and hopefully the memory—with a thick, black coat of sealant.

After he lined out the workers on the parking lot job, JT dug out the personnel papers Tucker needed, and drove himself and Rachel over to the sheriff's station so she could give the deputy her official statement. By the time they returned to the hotel, ate a late lunch, and JT checked his phone calls, the reporters from three area newspapers were waiting in the lobby. He decided his best course of action was for him to be considerate and polite, even though he felt like a tender morsel with a flock of vultures circling overhead.

Rachel managed to escape. She hid out at Heather's where she and her sister made microwave popcorn and watched a couple of movies.

"Are you doing okay?" Heather asked when *The Pink Panther* finished.

"For the tenth time, I'm fine. You've been asking me that every fifteen minutes."

Heather gave her sister a penetrating look. *That's because I know you're not fine. Nobody is fine after they find a body, not for a while, anyway.* "I haven't been that bad, have I?"

"Yeah, you have, but I forgive you. I know you can't resist mothering me."

"I could come over and spend the night at your place," Heather offered.

"Heather, no." The pleasantness left Rachel's face. "I don't need you to and I don't want you to."

"Okay," Heather agreed, backing off. "In that case, why don't we go over to the cafe and see what Lupe's cooking up for dinner?" She looked at her watch. "I'll bet JT and Buddy are already there."

The café stretched along the south side of the main building, with booths lining the outside wall. A line of windows hung above them, still undressed, awaiting the custom drapes Heather had ordered. Two rows of tables filled the inside of the room, surrounded by rattan chairs, which had just arrived. Buddy and JT were already sitting on two of the new acquisitions, drinking coffee, and talking over the day's happenings.

As soon as Lupe spotted the two women enter the café, she served them drinks, and then brought out a meal of pot roast with seasoned vegetables. The food was delicious, but the dinner was uneventful, and that worried Heather. She kept stealing glances at her sister, concerned she showed so little emotion after discovering Ms. Donovan's body. It just didn't seem like normal behavior to her. *Then again*, she thought, *not a whole lot of what Rachel does is normal.*

Heather walked beside Rachel on the way back to their casitas, with Buddy and JT following. "You're in for the night, right, sis?" Heather asked, suspecting Rachel might go out later to snoop around.

"Yeah, I'm pretty tired. Not to mention stuffed full." Her voice sounded weary. "I may read a while."

Rachel said her good nights and walked the few feet ahead to her own place. Heather watched her from her own steps, watched until Rachel entered her own suite and pulled the door shut behind her.

இ૭இ૭

Rachel hadn't meant to deceive, but she wore a path pacing back and forth across the living room, and knew she'd have to leave the confines of her suite and get outdoors.

She picked up an Alaskan mystery by Don G. Porter to bring out by the pool then took a steak knife from the drawer and slid it under the cover. It was probably too dark to read, even with the lights out there. However, the book and the knife were a comfort, if nothing else, and if someone came by to disturb her solitude, her exciting novel provided a good excuse to leave.

Instead of walking to the pool, however, Rachel went over to the parking lot.

A thin layer of sand now covered the seal coat, and a big sign said "Keep Off." Not about to ruin her three-hundred-dollar sandals, Rachel stood at the edge and stared at the trail at the other side, trying to visualize what happened earlier that morning. She could see, in her mind's eye, Vicky running down the path to her car, frightened enough to leave her belongings up the hill. But why? She must have stumbled upon something or someone on the mountain scary enough to run from, and run fast. The scrapes and cactus spines on her legs proved that, but what, or whom, did she see?

"Miss Rachel."

Rachel gasped and nearly jumped out of her clothes. She turned and saw the booming voice belonged to Toro. He walked toward her.

"I'm sorry I scared you," he said, noticing her ashen face and her hand over her heart. "But you shouldn't be out here by yourself."

"I'm just fine, Toro," she lied, waiting for the adrenaline to stop racing through her veins. "I was just looking at the view, enjoying the quiet."

"Yeah, it's that all right, but Mr. Carpenter said I need to make you to go inside if you were still out here."

"Is that *so*," Rachel sniffed, feeling like a child caught past curfew.

"Yes, miss." Toro just stood there waiting, hands by his side.

"Well, it's too dark to read, anyway," she said, trying to mollify herself. *There's no sense getting Toro in trouble.*

Rachel said good night, but Toro insisted on walking with her to her casita and he waited until she was safely inside before he continued his rounds.

Once inside, Rachel dropped her book on the table. She was reluctant to go to bed. She was afraid to go to sleep, and even worse, she was afraid to dream.

After setting the alarm clock twelve hours ahead, Rachel finally fell into bed, armed with her book and a glass of gin. She sipped the gin, and read until her eyelids drooped.

She kept on reading. In three minutes, her eyes closed and the book fell from her fingers. She lay in bed, the light on low, and expelled soft breaths as she slept.

Two hours later, her mother and father came to her in a dream. They floated through the air in wispy garments, eyes wide open, a single bullet hole in each of their foreheads.

Rachel was thirteen again. She watched, in panic, while the faces of her parents wobbled and stretched like those in a fun-house mirror, and finally morphed into the face of the woman she found dead on the blacktop.

Rachel screamed in terror, recognizing her own voice when she jerked herself awake. Her nightgown stuck to her body, soaked with sweat, and her hair hung in damp strands.

Her hands shook, yet she held the comforter up in front of her, as if somehow it could protect her from the visitors in her dream. But the dream stuck with her, thick as tar, and she stared into the dimly lit room, waiting.

Chapter 9

Heather woke up with a bad feeling and turned over in bed. She glanced at the digital clock: 7:16. She thought about Rachel, who had said she was going right to bed when they dropped her off at her steps the night before. Heather remembered watching her climb the stairs and waiting for the two clicks when her sister locked the door. She'd be up by now, Heather assumed, and picked up the phone and called. No one answered.

After a shower and a full cup of coffee, Heather called again, this time on the cell. No answer there, either. Heather wondered where her sister could be, and went down a short list of possibilities. Rachel never jogged. With their mother's metabolism, Rachel never needed to. She always carried her phone. So, why didn't she answer? When Heather finished dressing, she tried to call again with the same results.

Heather pounded on the door a little after nine. "Rachel. Rachel, open up."

Rachel opened the door a crack and peeked through. "What?"

"What do you mean, 'what'? Open the door." Heather pushed her way in. "Why didn't you answer your phone? I was worried sick." Heather's eyes flashed around the room.

"Sorry. I shut off the ringer so I could sleep," Rachel replied, moving quickly to block her sister's line of sight.

Heather studied Rachel's face. It was red, puffy, and her eyes were nearly swollen shut. She still had on her nightgown.

"What happened?" As soon as Heather asked the question, she realized she knew the answer. "You had nightmares again."

Rachel turned away, but Heather followed her. "I was afraid of that."

"You know, Heather, you're doing the mother thing again. You're hovering."

"Yeah, and you're hiding something." Heather took a step toward the coffee table and Rachel shifted her position in front of it.

"Why don't you just show me, Rachel? You know I'm going to find out anyway."

"Oh, for Pete's sake," Rachel huffed, but she moved.

A wide-brimmed hat, water jug, and camera sat on the table.

"What the heck is that?" Heather demanded to know. She knew the answer to that question, too.

Rachel surrendered. "Look, sis, why don't you sit down and we'll have some coffee."

They sat at the small dining table with their two glass mugs imprinted with the hotel logo. Over coffee, Rachel told Heather about her nightmare, and described how it had changed from her previous ones.

"Oh, honey, I'm so sorry." Heather leaned across the table and squeezed Rachel's hand. "That's why I was so worried about you yesterday. You were far too calm for someone who went through what you did."

"We all have to deal with things any way we can, Heather. That just happens to be my way."

Heather held the mug in both her hands and took a small sip. "Did you ever fall back asleep?"

Rachel nodded. "I think I stayed awake in bed afterwards for a good three hours, the cover pulled over my head, just thinking about Mom and Dad…about the murder here." She stood up, went to the sliding glass door, and pulled the drapes open. Bright sunlight flooded into the room. She cracked the door open to let in some fresh air.

"I've made a decision, Heather," she said, turning to her sister.

"A decision? About what?"

"A decision about the woman. I have to find out who killed her."

"What?" Heather's eyes widened. "What do you mean?"

Rachel's eyes darted all over the room. "I'm not sure I can explain this." She paced back and forth in front of the glass door. "I've spent years with shrinks, trying to get rid of those nightmares. Nothing has helped. Now, this thing with the faces changing..." she said, her voice trailing off.

Rachel stopped and stared down at the carpet while Heather sat quietly and waited.

Rachel lifted up her face. "I believe that if I find the person or persons who killed Vicky Donovan, the nightmares will go away."

That didn't make any sense to Heather, but then she wasn't the one with the nightmares, either. "So what are you planning to do?" Once more, she knew the answer, and turned to look at the coffee table with the sun hat on it. "You're going up the mountain."

"I have to. I have to do something. At least if I find the telescope, it will help."

"Rachel, no, please. You're only going to get yourself in a pile of trouble."

"Don't be silly." Rachel's eyes shifted away, avoiding her sister's gaze. "What kind of trouble could I possibly get into?"

"You'll be going up that mountain against the direct order of Sheriff Tucker."

"Sheriff Tucker, Sheriff Schmucker. A lot of good he's done us. Besides, he's only a deputy, and a stupid one at that." Rachel folded her arms resolutely against her chest. "He should be up on that mountain himself, looking for that telescope, but I bet he's not or even planning to. Why, he's so fat, I bet he couldn't even climb these stairs."

"That may be true, Rachel, but he told us that everyone had to stay out of there until he finished his investigation. Regardless of his position, he is the authority figure here."

"Like I care about that?"

"Exactly."

Rachel looked around impatiently. "Well, my darling sister, I'm not going to argue about it. If you'll excuse me, I need to change my clothes and head out," she said, turning away.

Heather clamped her hand down on Rachel's hand. "Oh no you don't. You're not going up there now. It will be at least a hundred and two today. That means you'll have to carry three gallons of water with you just to stay alive. I swear, Rachel, you do this and I *will* call JT."

Rachel wailed at her sister. "Don't you understand why I need to do this?"

"Of course I understand, sweetie. Don't you remember how I'd come into your room when you had your nightmares, and hold you, and put cold towels on your head?"

Rachel looked down, feeling like thirteen again, and tears splotched her feet. She couldn't speak.

Heather went to her and hugged her for a long time. "Okay, sis, this is what we're going to do. You meet me in the kitchen at four o'clock. The sun will be dropping and it will give me time to round up a weapon."

"That sounds good."

"I'll pack two backpacks with everything we need."

"We?"

"Yes, we. That's the way it has to be, Rachel."

"But what about your, your—"

"Fibromyalgia," Heather finished for her. "I feel good today. I told you I'd be better, and I need to exercise. So either I'm going with you, or I'm calling JT."

"Aw, geez, Heather."

"Stop griping. Remember, we leave at four o' clock. If you go off without me, I'm telling JT."

After packing the two backpacks, Heather set them by the back door of the kitchen. Rachel walked in and looked down at them, puzzled. "What did you pack? We're going for a hike, not a vacation."

"Look Rachel, it's still a hundred degrees out. We've never walked up there before, and we need to prepare ourselves for anything. Here, take the binoculars."

Rachel looped them over her neck. "What about the weapon?"

"Here." Heather shoved a can of pepper spray into her hand.

Rachel stared at the can. "This is a weapon?"

"What? You were expecting an AK-47?"

Rachel smiled. "Well, one could always hope." She hoisted one of the backpacks and slung it over her shoulders.

After opening the back door a crack, Heather peered out at the parking lot, which was now dry and still covered with a thin coat of sand. Relieved no one was in sight, she gave a quick nod to her sister, and then they both raced across the blacktop and started up the wide trail that led to the east peak of Blood Mountain.

The sun was a white-hot ball in the western sky and the temperature was still ninety-eight degrees. Having already walked the rugged terrain for nearly an hour, the sisters' pace began to slow.

"Now, remind me whose bright idea this was," Heather grumbled.

"I didn't see me twisting your arm," Rachel replied from her position in the lead, "but I'm glad you thought of the sunscreen," she added, sitting down on a large chunk of flat rock. "Otherwise we'd be french fries by now."

"I think you must mean Irish fries," Heather giggled, putting down her pack.

"Okay, if you want to get picky about it," Rachel said, pulling out one of the large jugs of water, "then it's half-Irish, half-Swedish fries." She took a big swig and handed the water to her sister.

Heather took several large gulps and handed back the water. "Well, even if we don't find the telescope, I have to admit the view itself is worth it." She gazed down at the valley floor and the neat patchwork of crops. "It's amazing."

Rachel pulled out the binoculars and zoomed in on the surrounding area. Rocks, rocks, and more rocks filled her view, with an occasional saguaro or palo verde tree to soften the scene. "Wait," she said. "I think I see something." She lowered the binoculars then brought them back up to her eyes. She handed them off to Heather, walked up a little farther, and turned right.

"Over here," Rachel called out. "It's a cooler."

Heather sprinted up the hill after her with a fresh burst of energy. "I wonder if it was Vicky's."

"Let's find out," Rachel said, lifting the lid. "Phew. What a smell."

"Yuk. Look at the ants."

"There's the camera. I think we better not touch it."

The sisters looked at the mess in the cooler then Rachel closed the lid. "Look, the little thingy on the bottom is open so all the ice melted and the water drained out.

"Yeah, and all the ants came in for a feast," Heather said. "This must be hers."

"Well, at least we know we're on the right track." Rachel looked around. "She probably took as long to get here as we did. She may have been tired and left the cooler, planning to come back for it."

"So now what?"

"We go that way," Rachel said, pointing.

Heather groaned softly and continued up the hill. The climb became steeper. Dried skeletons of brittlebush poked up between the rocks, their yellow blossoms gone for months. The women kept their distance from the prickly pear and cholla cacti, but stopped to inspect the first saguaro that stood in their path.

"Look," Heather said, pointing to a hole in the saguaro the size of a biscuit cutter, partially filled with twigs. "It's some kind of little animal house, most likely a bird."

Rachel studied the huge cactus a moment. "Hmm. They're pretty ugly when you get close up."

Heather giggled. "We'd be pretty ugly too, if we sat around in the sun for a hundred years." A small, sand-colored lizard scooted past her feet. The lizard's friend, meanwhile, practiced his push-ups on a flat rock a few yards ahead. "You got the right idea, little guy," she said, heading his way. The lizard zipped away when she climbed within a few feet of him and Heather plunked herself down in his spot. "This is it. I'm not moving anymore," she announced, finally giving in to her fatigue.

Rachel could see the exhaustion on her sister's face. "Heather, I am so sorry. I never should have let you come."

"You didn't *let* me come, remember? I invited myself. I just didn't expect it to be this hot up here, or the climb so difficult." She pulled up a foot and started rubbing the muscles on her calf." Did I tell you JT put Toro on night security?"

"No. I think it's a good idea though." Rachel decided not to mention she saw him the night before. "Until this situation is all over with, anyway."

"Deputy Tucker's nephew is going to stay with us and do security, too."

Rachel sat down beside her sister. "Oh, that's all we need. Another stupid, fat-tub hanging around."

Heather shook her head. "You know Rachel, have you ever thought about discussing your hatred of the police with your therapist?"

"Why? I already know why I hate them."

"They did the best they could, you know."

"No, they *didn't,* Heather." Rachel pointed a finger at her sister. "You and I both know Dad would never, *ever* have killed Mom, nor would he have killed himself. I don't like anyone saying he did, period. End of discussion."

Heather couldn't think of a thing to say.

"I do have an idea, though," Rachel said, changing the subject. "You sit and rest. Drink some water and eat some trail mix. I'll go up a little farther, around the next bend, and see what I can find. By the time I get back, maybe you'll be rested up enough for us to start back down."

"Sounds good to me," Heather said, glad to leave behind the conversation about their parents. She lay back on the boulder with a towel folded under her head. "The sun's gone down behind the mountain, so we need to head back anyway, before it gets dark."

Rachel navigated the hill and noticed a large boulder ahead. It was pitted and darkened from long years of exposure to the elements. She climbed up on it and scanned the area through her binoculars. Jubilant, she turned around and called to her sister. "I found the telescope," she hollered.

Rachel raced back down the hill to Heather, but when she arrived, her face fell. "Uh, oh."

Heather turned and gazed down the path. A well-built man with dark curly hair climbed the hill with ease, followed by a huffing and puffing Dewey Tucker. Buddy and JT were trailing behind them.

Heather grimaced when she turned back to face Rachel. "I left a note, just in case we got lost." Then she added weakly, "Sorry."

For a moment, Rachel had a bizarre thought that she should hide in the rocks somewhere. She quickly scratched that idea. Besides, at least the first two hikers already spotted them. She caught JT's eye next. He looked madder than a baptized cat. Her eyes zeroed back on the lead man who looked more and more familiar. "Oh, no," she muttered, realizing the dark haired man was the very one who rescued her when she was stuck in the sand. The very one who made it clear he was totally amused by her stupidity.

"Well hello, ladies," Dewey Tucker said, after gulping large quantities of breath. He steadied his gaze at Rachel and he did not look happy. "I believe you and my nephew, Alex, have already met."

Rachel felt his glare and she looked down, embarrassed. From underneath her lashes she could see the irritating smirk on the face of Alex Tucker and wanted to slap him. "The telescope is up ahead, on the right," was all she could say, her voice cracking.

Dewey turned to look at JT. "You guys take them back. We'll check out the area and meet you later."

With downcast eyes, Rachel and Heather headed down the mountain, followed by JT and Buddy. Neither man said a word, but Rachel could feel JT's anger boring a hole in her back. She never looked back.

Twilight faded by the time the group reached the parking lot. After a quick good-bye, Rachel hurried away, trying to separate herself from the group. She practically ran toward her suite, scattering faded blossoms that littered the sidewalk. When she put her hand on the stair rail, a voice boomed out at her.

"Just a minute, young lady."

Rachel winced at the familiar voice. She turned to JT. "I don't want to fight," she said quietly, not wanting to look up at the bear of a man in front of her.

"Oh, there's not going to be a fight, Rachel," JT said with great control. "This is strictly a one-liner." He paused for effect, anger blazing from his eyes. "You will not, under any conditions, involve my wife in any of your schemes, ever." JT's voice was low and controlled to the point that Rachel would have preferred a loud scolding.

She finally looked up at him, contrite. "For what it's worth, I'm sorry."

JT simply stared at her, his eyes boring into hers. Then he turned on his heel and walked back to Heather and Buddy.

ⱻⱾⱻⱾ

JT threw the backpack on the floor when he and Heather walked into their suite.

"I'm going to take a quick lay-down," Heather said, fatigue in her voice. "Care to join me?"

They lunged for the bed, cuddled, and Heather looked up at JT from beneath her lashes. "You're not mad at me, are you, sweetie?"

"Heather, I was worried sick."

"That's why I left you a note, honey." Heather snuggled her face up against JT's neck. "I didn't want you to worry, but Rachel had it all planned out to go up there alone. With one little bottle of water, yet. I just couldn't let that happen."

"I know, sweetie," JT reluctantly agreed. "Sometimes I could just throttle that girl."

"JT, you know she can't help it. I don't care what kind of therapy she's had, she still walked into that room and found our parents dead."

"Yeah," JT remembered. "That's one day I'll never forget."

Heather lifted her head. "Even worse, the police insisted it was a murder-suicide. You know it wasn't. Just because our father had some brain problems, they didn't even investigate."

"I know, honey, I know. Don't get yourself upset." JT stroked his wife's cheek, her hair, and pressed her face to his neck. "You know there's nothing we can do about that now. Just let it go, baby, let it go."

"You won't send Rachel away?" she asked. "I need her."

JT felt tears on his neck. "No, I won't send her away. I think with the boys gone, you may need to mother somebody, and Rachel could use some maternal guidance as well as anyone."

"I'm not sure she'd go for that, but it's obvious she's hurting. I want to be there for her. I want to help her."

"That may not be possible."

"I can try."

"Yeah," JT agreed, realizing he wasn't going to change Heather. It didn't look like Rachel would be lining up a new therapist, either. The best he could hope for is that Rachel would fall in love with some guy and run off...but pray it wouldn't be Buddy. He focused off into the distance. "Well, I guess I'd rather put up with Rachel than that slobbery St. Bernard you were thinking about getting."

The Hibiscus Café—as it was finally named—smelled deliciously of fried onions and peppers when Rachel reluctantly made her way to the corner booth. JT greeted her pleasantly, and she was grateful, remembering he never stayed angry long and never held a grudge. Heather and Buddy were their usual cheerful selves and acted as if nothing out of the ordinary had happened.

Rachel spied the large bowl of tortilla chips on the table and began munching on them as the group began talking about current hotel business. Rachel felt relieved. It appeared JT had forgiven her, and the tension gradually eased out of her shoulders.

The delicious aroma coming from the kitchen made Rachel's mouth water. When she was about to ask what they were having for dinner, the door opened and Dewey and Alex Tucker walked in.

Rachel pictured herself jumping up and running out of the room. Too awkward. Besides, she was starved.

"You're just in time for dinner," JT said, greeting them.

"Please be our guests," Heather added, signaling to Lupe to bring more iced tea and glasses. She moved over so Dewey and Alex could slide into the booth.

"Any interesting developments?" Buddy asked, while the two men settled in.

"Looks like the girls did find the place where Vicky Donovan set up for the night," Dewey answered with a quick look toward Rachel. "I reckon she picked the spot because it was flat and had a good view. She was probably tired of walkin,' too. I know *I* was." He took a glass of tea from Lupe who arrived at the table. "I reckon she didn't get much time to look around, though, judgin' from the time of her death."

"So you think she saw something and tried to run to her car?" Rachel asked. She looked at Dewey, completely ignoring Alex who sat opposite him.

"I'd reckon that's about what happened."

"That means we need to find out who and what she saw." Rachel said.

Dewey raised his eyebrows and pointed a finger at her. "Miss Ryan, I'm gonna say this one time to you. *We* don't need to find out anything. *You* need to stay close to home and stay inside at night, period. I'll take care of

213

trackin' down Ms. Donovan's killer." He dug around in his pocket for a card. "If you see or hear anything that you think could help in this investigation, call me right away on one of these numbers."

Dewey took a quick look at Alex when he handed Rachel the card. "I don't know if you know this, but Alex has moved into the hotel to provide some additional security. You could call him first if you need someone right away. I put his cell phone number on the back."

Rachel glanced at Alex with distain and spoke to Dewey, "Is he a police officer?"

"No," Dewey lied. "He's a freelance writer but he carries a gun and knows how to use it."

"I didn't realize writing was such a dangerous occupation," Rachel said dryly, still refusing to acknowledge Alex.

"He lives in LA."

"Well, that explains it."

Lupe appeared at the table with a large tray of sizzling steak strips smothered with onions and peppers. She set it on the table next to dishes of sour cream and guacamole and added a fresh bowl of salsa and chips.

"Oh, man, fajitas." Dewey beamed, rubbing his hands together in anticipation. "I reckon we got here just in time."

Lupe passed around the plates and tortillas while Buddy asked Dewey about his progress on the employee search.

"It looks like every one checks out okay except Toro."

JT reddened a bit and looked down at his plate.

"You know he went to jail for killin' a guy," Dewey said, just as Lupe left the table.

Heather almost choked on her food and quickly exchanged looks with Rachel. "He murdered a man?"

"No," JT interjected. "He killed a man in a bar fight. That's different. I knew all about it."

"Uh-huh, and you were planning on telling me *when*?" Heather asked.

"Well, actually, I didn't think it mattered. It happened years ago, when he drank. He's been sober six years. He's loyal, and he's a great worker. That's all that really concerns us. In fact, I put him on night security last night and fully trust him in that capacity."

"Well, I don't know, JT," Dewey drawled. "I still say we have to consider him a person of interest in the matter."

Before JT could respond further, Rachel jumped in. "I can't believe you'd even consider Toro as a suspect. He's dependable, and he's one of the gentlest men I've ever met. He even, sort of, well, rescued me one day."

Dewey looked at her straight-faced and said dryly, "You're not plannin' on makin' a career out of it, are ya? Gettin' rescued, I mean?"

Rachel stole a glance at Alex who was carefully piling a tortilla with steak strips and peppers while trying to suppress a smile.

"Someone deliberately put a huge tarantula in my room...and that happened after Toro sprayed and Heather thoroughly checked everything out." Rachel's voice raised a notch.

Alex pressed his lips together tightly, still staring at his fajitas.

"You needed to be rescued from a spider?" Dewey looked incredulous.

Rachel's face burned with humiliation. She looked around. Some of the men appeared to be quite amused. She gripped her hands into hard white balls and half stood in the booth. "Would you excuse me, please?" she asked, picking up her plate. "I think I'll do take-out."

In awkward silence, Rachel stepped out of the booth. "Enjoy your stay," she snapped, looking back at Alex.

Chapter 10

The next morning, under the dim light of the lone desk lamp, Rachel slumped back in her executive chair, using great effort to bring a mug of coffee to her lips. The specter of sleep had eluded her most of the night while she kicked her sheets into a tangle and struggled to keep visions of Vicky Donovan out of her mind. At two in the morning, she finally slept. At six she awakened, the ghosts of her dreams held at bay.

Lingering under a hot shower, Rachel willed her demons down the drain with the rush of softened water. She affirmed she was glad she had a job to go to, a right-brain, creative job that might keep flashbacks of Vicky Donovan away.

Her hair still damp, she threw on jeans and a turquoise tee, unlocked her office and stationed herself behind the desk. That was as far as she got. Anxiety stuck to her like a tar baby, the amber glow of the lamp turning her skin pale gold, and she simply sat and stared through the locked french doors.

Intruding into her line of sight, a vision of Vicky Donovan boldly appeared before her, eyes staring sightlessly, body sprawled gracelessly, surrounded by the smell of death. Rachel blinked hard and shook her head. She shifted her gaze to the far end of the lobby where workers were bringing in equipment to refinish the dance floor in the ballroom.

She ignored the tinny ring and blinking light on her phone. Heather had offered to take any messages until she felt ready to deal with the public again. Wondering when that would happen, Rachel doodled spirals on her desk pad, thinking of escaping back to Boston.

No way, she argued with herself. She would keep her commitment to help her sister at Blood Mountain. Heather needed her, perhaps for the first time in her life. Besides, she eventually admitted to herself, she didn't have a job or a place to stay.

The scene beyond the french doors drew her attention again. This time the men were delivering new banquet chairs. Rachel watched as the workers eventually left and southern light filtered in through the front entrance, bathing the lobby in a golden hue.

Heather's voice cracked the silence when the intercom light came on. "Rachel, I think you may want to take this call on line one. It's Weezer Chaffee."

Rachel reluctantly pressed the first button on the top row and greeted her caller.

"I heard what happened." Weezer's voice was soft and imbued with concern. "Are you okay?"

Rachel debated whether to be honest. "No, not really," she said, not having the energy to fake it. "I suppose the whole town has heard about it by now."

"They probably have. You know how small towns are."

"Well, I didn't before, but I'm a fast learner." Rachel picked up the phone cord and nervously twirled it around her finger. "I was bringing food out for the rabbits when I found her." Her voice dropped and the phone cord untangled and snapped back in place.

"Oh, darlin', I'm really sorry," Weezer said in a voice silky and soothing. "If I can help in any way, let me know. Call me any-time. You have my card."

"Thanks, but I'll be okay," she said, un-convinced, twisting the cord around her finger again.

"I don't want you to think I forgot about your miniature bougainvillea," Weezer con-tinued in his melodic voice. "I have a small bag of pesticide for your gardener."

"Thank you, I do appreciate that," Rachel said.

"I'll come by and drop it off later. In fact," he said pausing, as if the thought just occurred to him, "why don't you plan to come back to town with me? I'd like to take you to lunch at the country club."

Rachel's gaze shifted through the glass doors again and didn't notice anyone wander-ing around. She hesitated before answering, remembering the spark between them. She didn't want to start something with Weezer she didn't intend to finish. She thought about the horse, too.

"Thank you, but I don't think so."

"I have a truck," he added, tentatively, as if reading her mind.

She laughed. "I guess you can tell I don't go for animals bigger than a dog or smaller than a kitten unless they're in a zoo.

"Well, that blows my idea about a riding date," he joked, "but please reconsider lunch. You need to get away. You need a change of scenery, something to take your mind off what happened. Besides, you can check out the competition."

Curiosity about the country club restaurant did peak Rachel's interest, and she realized the longer she stayed at her desk, the worse she felt. It couldn't hurt to get away from the hotel and the instant replays of the day before.

"I do have a couple errands to do in town," she said, scrutinizing her casual attire and thinking she should change it. "Why don't I just meet you at the country club at noon?"

❦

When she drove through Venkman's farm, Rachel noticed long, perfect rows of lettuce passing by the window, each plant sprouting several new leaves. Hispanic workers, bent at the waist and covered in protective clothing, thinned the crop that Venkman Farms would soon be shipping all over the country.

Driving in the mid-day sunshine, Rachel's depression lifted. She glanced over the fields that loomed ahead as water in the canals rippled by, looking like liquid turquoise. A once-white bus with muddied tires had parked on a canal road with two portable toilets perched behind it. She shuddered at the thought of ever having to use one.

Driving on, Rachel wondered if Franz Venkman spent much time in the fields. *Do farmers work the farms anymore? Or do they sit in offices filling out government forms like most businesses do these days?* She reflected on the happy thought that Buddy and Heather were naturally gifted with the paperwork gene. She certainly wasn't, and sometimes found herself led to write bizarre answers on some of those annoying government forms, just for spite.

Arriving at the country club, Rachel pulled through the wide circular drive that fronted the clubhouse. The driveway contained a sea of grass, edged by rainbow-colored zinnias, and she could see the golf course through the tall eucalyptus trees on each side of the building.

She had changed into a simple emerald green dress for the occasion. The dress hugged her body and brought out the green in her eyes. Her hair, like of strands silk, flowed softly around her shoulders, and when she stepped into the lobby, Weezer's eyes lit up.

"You look fantastic," Weezer said, not the least bit subtle about eyeing her up and down.

"Thanks," Rachel deadpanned. "I told Heather all that expensive makeup would be worth it."

Weezer laughed. "I like a woman with a sense of humor." He offered his arm and led her into the dining room. Stepping up close, Rachel noticed that even in four-inch heels, he still towered over her.

Every single head turned when the hostess led the lean, beautiful couple to their booth. Rachel felt that much-hated flush reach her face when she noticed other patrons staring at her, and then speaking in whispers.

When they sat down, the hostess handed them menus. A waiter quickly placed stemmed glasses of ice water with lemon in front of them, greeting them with a friendly smile and a promise to return for their orders. When the waiter left, Rachel, still conscious of the stares and whispers of the other patrons, leaned over close to Weezer.

"People are staring at us. This was not a good idea after all."

"Don't worry, darlin'," Weezer said, "I'm sure all the men are thinking I'm having lunch with a super-model, and they're wishing they were me." He gave her a wink and glanced down at the menu. "Like oriental salad? They have a great one here."

Rachel was surprised at his choice, having guessed him to be a steak-and-potatoes man. In addition to the salads, Weezer ordered the crab dip and a bottle of pinot noir. Rachel asked to keep her menu and tried to memorize the contents, along with the prices, while she and Weezer made small talk.

The wine arrived quickly, and with the first sip, Rachel let the liquid roll back along her tongue and felt herself starting to relax. She looked around, deliberately meeting the gazes of other patrons and smiling. They all smiled back. "Nice place," she said, noticing for the first time the wall of windows on the opposite side of the room and the golf course sprawled out beyond it.

Weezer poured more wine into her glass. "It's always a surprise when visitors see a clubhouse like this in a little town like Mesquite."

"I can believe that," Rachel said, taking another slow sip. "Tell me about your name, Weezer. It's quite distinctive."

He laughed. "My name is William Ronald Chaffee but I picked up the nickname Weezer when I had asthma as a kid. I never did like William, or Ronald, so I kept the nickname. I have to admit, though, people do remember it."

"That's true," Rachel said. "I did."

The waiter brought the crab dip and Weezer encouraged Rachel to try it. She plopped a tortilla chip with a mass of cheesy dip into her mouth, just as a man dressed in a starched Ralph Lauren shirt and creased khakis approached their table.

Weezer shook the man's hand and introduced Rachel.

When Rachel heard the man's name, she choked on the chip, and then took a swallow of wine while she composed herself. Although surprised to hear Otto Venkman's name, she decided to act charming in spite of what she had heard about Otto's father and his unsuccessful try to obtain Blood Mountain. Somehow, she never expected Franz's son to look like the short, delicate-appearing man standing in front of her. His hair, the color and texture of corn silk, gave him a feminine look; but his nose, too large for his face, negated that. She tried not to stare at it.

"It's nice to meet you, Otto." She politely extended her hand. His grip was gentle, his fingers perfectly formed and professionally manicured. A small bandage stuck to the back of his hand marred the perfect look of a hand model. Still, Rachel couldn't imagine those elegant hands driving a tractor or even touching soil.

"I'm sorry to hear about what happened at the Inn yesterday," Otto said.

"Thank you," Rachel replied graciously, yet silently questioned his sincerity and wondered if there was anyone left in town who hadn't heard about the murder.

"We received your invitation to the open house party and appreciate your inviting us," Otto continued on, clipping his words like an actor from an old English movie.

Rachel forced a smile. "Good. I hope you'll be able to come." She wanted to sound warm and genuine but it required a lot of effort. What was it about him, she wondered, that caused instant dislike?

"Then you are still having the party, in spite of the circumstances?" Otto asked, raising his eyebrows in a condescending look.

A thought popped in Rachel's mind to slap his phony mouth, but she managed to resist and replied charmingly, "Yes, we are. The way things are going around here, I suspect that all of this will be old news by the day of the party."

"Well, then," Otto said, almost too brightly. "We're looking forward to coming."

Rachel's eyes followed him when he walked away and sat down with a much older man and woman. A heavy dose of Armani still clung to the air.

"Is he gay?" Rachel asked, and immediately clapped her hand over her mouth. "I'm sorry," she said, embarrassed. "I have the tendency to put my mouth in gear before my brain."

Weezer laughed. "No, he's definitely not gay as you'll see soon enough. He does like to put on a bit for strangers, though. I blame it on his years at Harvard business school."

"He went to Harvard?" Rachel stole another look at him. Otto looked like the clone of the man sitting opposite him, minus twenty-five years. "Are those his parents?"

"Sure are. Franz and Katerina Venkman, richest folks in town."

The waiter arrived with their salads and Rachel used the opportunity to sneak another look at the Venkmans. Katerina was pale with long gold hair puffed up on top of her head like a Gibson-girl of the early 1900s. Her long dress mimicked one from that era, too. Rachel thought she looked odd, but at least this time her thoughts didn't make it to her mouth.

Weezer poured more wine into their glasses, interrupting her silent critique of the Venkman family. They started eating their salads. The hostess passed by their booth, followed by two men, both of whom stopped at their table. The first man appeared larger than his height because of his massive, square body and thick neck. He was dressed in a suit and tie, and an apparently recent weight gain caused his chest to strain against the buttons on his white shirt.

"Hey, Weezer, how's it going?" Stanley Belinski broke into a big smile, well suited for a real estate salesperson.

Weezer made the introductions and Stanley Belinski quickly reached for Rachel's hand, his thick eyebrows knitting together. "Of course," he remembered, "You're the new sales director at the Mesquite Mountain Inn. I knew the name sounded familiar. I just received your invitation to the open house party." He turned to the man behind him. "This is my brother, George."

After a brief greeting from George, Stanley offered his condolences about the murder. "That must have been something. Unbelievable," he added with enthusiasm.

"Yes, it was. I'm still in shock," Rachel said quietly. "But we aren't canceling the party," she continued, changing the subject, "so I hope you all can come." She forced a smile.

"Oh, we'll be there with bells on," Stanley said as George nudged his brother forward to their own table.

"How's the salad, darlin'?" Weezer asked in the awkward silence.

"The one bite I ate tasted delicious." Rachel looked up at him. "I hope I get a chance to eat more of it before someone else comes by to ask about yesterday."

Weezer laid his fork on the table. "You know, Rachel, it's understandable. It's the biggest news we've had around here for a long time. I can't ever remember the time we had a murder in Mesquite."

Rachel blinked. "Really? What about the one last month, the guy that had his head blown off?"

Weezer stiffened. "I heard that was a suicide." He watched her face intently. "Why? Did Deputy Tucker say the guy was murdered?"

"No." Rachel paused, a little puzzled at the expression on his face. "I just wondered how someone could blow his own head off with a shotgun."

"It's easy," Weezer said without a hint of a smile. "You use a short barrel, 12-gauge, pistol grip and hold it real close to your neck."

"Oh," said Rachel, looking up from her salad. "How do you figure that?"

"I have friends everywhere," Weezer said with a wink.

After the waiter checked back to see if there was anything else they needed, Rachel leaned back against the booth and took another sip of wine. She studied the man in front of her. "Tell me about yourself, Weezer. Have you ever been married?"

"I was married for a short time in my early twenties. George Belinski is my ex-brother-in-law. So is Stanley." He blushed and fidgeted in his seat. "Sara and I were young. It just didn't work out." He grinned. "Now I'm married to my boat."

"That's interesting," Rachel said, and took another sip of wine. "Tell me about your boat. I can't imagine anyone out here in the desert owning one."

"There's a few of us that do. I keep mine in LA and spend the weekend there whenever I can. It's a long drive."

"I can see that." Rachel nodded. "What kind of boat it is it?"

"A seventy-five foot Hatteras."

Rachel reared up. "Wow. That's not a boat. That's a yacht. I know someone in Boston who owns one." She leaned forward and looked at him with a sly smile, partly influenced by her third glass of wine. "And here I thought you were just a poor bug killer."

Weezer laughed. "I really am a poor bug killer but I do have good taste and so does the bank. Besides, it's an old retrofit. I'm working on it in my spare time, when I get spare time."

"I can understand that," Rachel said, then allowed a lull in the conversation, letting Weezer take the lead.

He put his fork down again and looked uncomfortable. "I understand Dewey Tucker's nephew is visiting him. Have you met him yet?"

"Yes, as a matter of fact, he checked into the hotel."

"That so." Weezer took a sip of wine. "What does he do?"

Rachel began to get an uncomfortable feeling. "He's a freelance writer. Why the interest?" She cocked her head coyly. "You want to get fixed up?"

Weezer laughed. "You really are funny, you know that darlin'?" He pushed his plate aside and pulled out a pack of Nat Sherman's. He stopped. "I forget. Everything is no smoking now."

"Luckily, I don't have to worry about that anymore. I gave it up a month ago."

"Smart girl." He put the pack back in his pocket. "You know, I thought it was kind of odd that Vicky Donovan was out at your place so late at night. What was she doing there, anyway?"

Rachel pushed aside her plate and did not answer right away. When she lifted her head, she appeared troubled. "You know, Weezer, I'd really like to forget about the whole murder thing, if you don't mind. This is the worst thing that's happened to me in a long time, and I had hoped to come here to get away from it."

Weezer looked stricken. "I'm so sorry," he said. "I've been so thoughtless, darlin'. Please forgive me."

"Of course," Rachel said, glancing down at her watch. "But I really have to get back to work."

လ၁လ၁

Later that same afternoon, a man wended his way through a home store in Yuma, hoping to avoid anyone he knew. He gathered the few things he needed: a cotton rope, a gas can, and a long-handled lighter. The articles he purchased were available in Mesquite, of course, but every checkout clerk in town knew him and might remember what he purchased.

He pulled out his checkbook, then thought better of it and put it back. He dug around in his wallet for the few dollars he needed, paid the woman, and took the receipt.

When he arrived at his car, he put the items in the trunk next to his earlier purchase from a party supply: a bag of large latex balloons.

He turned the air conditioner on full blast, as he settled into the compact. He hated the little Japanese vehicle. It felt like driving a lawn mower, but he had to admit it made great gas mileage, and right now, that was important. He navigated the trip to Yuma and back home with the needle on the gas gauge barely moving.

ဢၣဢ

Rachel drifted into the lobby of the Inn and spotted Heather lounging on one of the sofas.

"Well, how did lunch go?" Heather asked.

Rachel dropped down on the sofa next to her sister, slipped off her Jimmy Choo's, and put her feet up on the table. "It was okay." She glanced around the lobby, now littered with cartons of various sizes, some opened, some waiting to be opened. "What are you doing sitting here?"

"Oh, just sitting. You know how I like to just sit around and just think."

"Hmm. So what great idea did you just think up? Besides moving the furniture around, I mean."

"You like it?"

Rachel studied the two brightly patterned chairs adjacent to them. "Yes. It's much better for conversation. I like the grouping opposite the front desk, too. People can rest while the partner checks in."

"Exactly. So, tell me about lunch."

"It was very good," Rachel nodded. "Good food, good wine, good atmosphere. I memorized the prices."

"That's interesting, but it's not what I meant. I meant with the hunk, the cowboy."

"You met him?"

"No, but I saw him from the patio the other day."

"You saw him from the patio? When I gave him the tour of the garden? Wasn't that a bit far?"

"Not with binoculars."

"Why, Heather, you little snoop," Rachel laughed. "Well, he *is* kind of sexy. You know I'm a sucker for those tall, lanky types." Then she paused, leaning back in the chair, hands clasped behind her head. "There is something about him that bothers me, though."

"Which is?"

"I don't know." Rachel leaned her head back against the sofa and looked up. "I just don't know."

☙☙☙

Rachel floated lazily around the pool on a plastic raft, still mulling over her conversation with Weezer. Something ticked in the back of her brain and she couldn't silence it. She recalled Weezer annoying her with his questions about the murder and his interest in Sheriff Tucker's nephew, Alex. But it was not that unusual for someone to be curious or even downright nosey in Mesquite. Why, even Dewey Tucker had the reputation of being a gossip.

She dropped her hand into the water and steered toward the middle of the pool. She thought about how Weezer kept calling her darlin'. Normally she would have felt patronized, but Weezer had a way of rolling the word off his tongue with that accent of his that made it sound enchanting. On the other hand, he wanted to know about everything else except *her*. That was annoying, and hard on the ego, but it wasn't whatever was making her feel uneasy.

Rachel glanced at her watch. It read five o' clock. The shadows of Mexican fan palms were stretching across the pool while the sun dipped low in the sky. She was actually glad to have some time alone with her thoughts.

"Hello, Rachel," a rough, masculine voice called out. Startled, Rachel jerked up, tumbled off the float, and splashed into neck-deep water. When she stood up, she glared at Alex Tucker.

"Don't sneak up on me like that."

"I'm sorry. I thought you heard me walking up." Alex set down two tall margaritas on a small table between the lounges. "I didn't mean to surprise you." He picked up the bath towel on Rachel's chair and held it out for her.

She waded out toward the steps. "What do you want?" she asked, annoyed by his intrusion. At least he didn't have that insulting smirk on his face.

"I hoped we could talk for a few minutes." He watched the water slowly run down her body while she walked through the shallow water toward him.

"Uncle Dewey sent you out to make nice, huh?"

"No, it was actually my idea." He sounded almost humble. "I was hoping we could start over."

A puff of dry air blew over Rachel's skin when she walked up the steps out of the pool. Goose bumps formed on her arms and she began to shiver. Alex draped the towel over her and motioned for her to sit down.

"I see you brought a peace offering." Rachel sat next to the drinks.

"I thought it might be appropriate." Alex handed her a glass, lifted his, and smiled awkwardly. "Here's to new beginnings."

Rachel glanced at him, then down at the glass. With Alex staying at the hotel, it would be impossible to avoid him, she reasoned. Besides, she was thirsty and the frosty margarita looked extremely appealing. "Okay," she said. "To new beginnings."

She took a long sip of her drink, and for the first time, did more than just glance at his face. His eyes were dark and sad and showed a deep sensitivity. A thick five o'clock shadow covered the lower part of his face, giving him a rugged, masculine appeal. One side of his mouth drooped. "You have an odd smile," she said bluntly.

"I know. It looks like I'm sneering. I can't help it."

"Nerve damage," she said, understanding the problem.

"Right. Can we change the subject?"

Rachel wished she could learn to keep her mouth zipped until her brain started working. "Okay," she started again. "How is your story coming along?" She patted her legs dry with the edge of the towel.

"It's coming along."

"May I read it?"

"I never let anyone read my work until it's finished and ready for publication."

"Uh, okay," she said, thinking that was rather odd. She settled in and leaned back in the lounge chair. "What's it about?"

"It's about crime in small towns."

Rachel took a long sip from her drink and stared off at the waterfall at the end of the pool. "Who's your favorite author?" She asked casually, wondering how long the question-and-answer quiz would go on.

"Don't really have one."

Rachel studied him. His comment was unrealistic for a writer, and his eyes drifted from sad to slightly embarrassed. "You're not much of a talker, are you?"

"No. That's probably why both of my wives left me."

Rachel bit her lip to keep from laughing. "You're funny."

"I'm just truthful."

Rachel sat up, swung her legs over the side of the chair, and leaned right into the man's face. "The hell you are. You've been lying all along."

The muscles in Alex's face tightened. "What do you mean?"

"What I mean is you're no more a writer than I'm a cop." Rachel set her drink down. "And your face was injured from getting hit too many times. But don't worry. I won't blow your cover." She started to get up but Alex reached for her wrist.

"Don't. Please stay."

"For more lies? No, thanks." She tried to pull away.

"Wait. You're right." Alex held on to her. "I haven't been honest with you for reasons I can't explain right now."

Rachel stared at him. "Then be honest now. *Are* you a cop?"

Alex met her eyes for several seconds then released her wrist. "Yes. How did you know?"

Rachel leaned back against the chair, not speaking. A cool breeze came up deliciously smelling of Mexican food from the kitchen. She pulled the towel tight. "I almost married a detective. I can tell one a mile away." Her eyes clouded.

"What happened?"

"He died three weeks before the wedding." She turned her head away, picked up her drink, and took a long sip.

"I'm sorry," Alex said. He put his hand on top of hers. "I'm really sorry. Was he killed in the line of duty?"

Rachel's mouth opened and closed, but nothing emerged. "He was shot. He shot himself." She turned her face away. "I can't talk about it."

Alex gripped her hand tighter, and then brought it to his cheek, rough with a day's growth of beard. "I'm so sorry, Rachel, but I do understand. My friend, Tony, a former partner…he was tortured, murdered, less than two weeks ago."

"Oh, no. I'm so sorry, Alex. I had no idea."

"Of course you didn't."

She grimaced. "I've been so rude to you." She flushed when she thought of how angry she had been when her car became stuck in the sand. "I never even thanked you properly for coming to my rescue. All I could think of was myself and my own embarrassment." She shook her head in disgust, pulled her knees up, and buried her face in them. "I've been such a jerk."

"Hey, don't be so hard on yourself." Alex's voice was soft and kind. "How could you know?"

After a few moments, Rachel lifted her head and turned toward the sun, a large, gold orb touching the horizon. "Someone I ate lunch with today wanted to know about you."

Alex's eyes widened. "What do you mean?"

Rachel tossed her hand as if swatting away a fly. "Oh, you know, the typical 'what does he do?' question."

"So you told him—"

"What I was told." She turned around and gave him a penetrating stare. "I may be a little crazy, but I'm not stupid. I lived with Matt for two years and I know how it works. I also have good intuition."

Alex studied her awhile. "So tell me, who is this person who's so interested in what I do?"

"Weezer Chaffee."

Alex's face showed no reaction.

"Do you know him?"

"I don't know him, but I know *of* him."

"I see. A person of interest," Rachel said, mocking Dewey Tucker.

Alex casually turned his head away. "Quite the ladies' man, from what I hear."

Rachel suppressed a smile. "Well, he is quite handsome."

"Handsome is as handsome does."

Rachel looked at him, the smile now working its way across her lips. "Yes, I suppose that's true," she agreed. "So what does our person of interest do? Besides kill bugs, that is?"

Alex pulled out his cigarettes and lit one. He inhaled deeply and stared off at the mesquite grove and the mountain behind it, letting the breeze carry the smoke eastward. "Matt was wrong to involve you in his work," he said, changing the subject.

"He didn't think so. I helped him on more than one occasion. I told you, I have good intuition. It's a gift."

"That so?" Alex said, nonchalantly. "So what does your intuition have to say about Weezer?"

Rachel drank the last of her margarita and stood up, ignoring his question. "You know, Alex, you sound just like the FBI. You want everyone to give you information, but you never share what *you* have." She slipped her feet into the sandals that sat next to her chair. "Thanks for the drink. I'll see you around."

❧❧

The phone rang after eleven that night. Rachel put her book down on the bedspread and picked up the receiver after the second ring.

"It's Alex. You weren't asleep yet, were you?"

"No. I'm reading John Sandford. In case you're interested, he writes an excellent mystery."

"Good. I'll have to remember his name next time someone asks me who my favorite author is."

Rachel could picture his rueful smile. "I'm glad you're teachable," she said, teasing. "In your present state, no one with half a brain would believe you're a crime writer."

A soft laugh came through the line. "Uncle Dewey popped that one out. You probably guessed the last thing I'd want to do in my spare time is read crime stories. He really is my uncle, by the way."

"That part I could believe. I noticed you deferred to him and have been very respectful." She found herself softening toward him. "So what did you need? You called, remember?"

"I need to talk with you and show you something. Can you go for a ride with me early in the morning?"

"I can't." Rachel was surprised at her disappointment. "Buddy and I are taking my rental car back to Phoenix and have some business to take care of. But what's it about?"

"It's about green lights near the top of Blood Mountain."

"Green lights? You mean the ones that show up on the night of the new moon?" Rachel waited, listening to the silence on the other end of the line. "Hello?"

A deflated Alex answered: "Now, how did you know that? I haven't even told Dewey yet."

"Elementary, my dear Watson. I read the diary, too."

He laughed softly and Rachel could almost see him shaking his head. "Well, that's what I want to talk about. In the meantime, I need you to watch what you say to anyone before I meet with you." He paused a moment. "Right now, that means everyone, even your sister and Buddy. No one can know what I'm doing here. I promise I'll explain when I see you."

"Okay. I can accept that."

"Call me when you get back…and Rachel?"

"Yes, Alex?"

"Be careful."

Chapter 11

The morning arrived clear and windless. The sun, still low on the horizon, sprayed gold on everything it touched. Visibility seemed endless.

"Another day in paradise," Rachel chirped, slipping in behind the wheel and sniffing the new-car smell of the rental car.

Buddy tossed a briefcase to the front passenger well before he climbed in and buckled up. "And just think," he said, flashing her his movie-star smile, "you get to spend this fabulous day in paradise with me."

"Uh-oh," Rachel teased back. "I knew there had to be a downside."

She started up the car and drove down the mountain and through the fields of lettuce that were waiting to be cut. By the time she crossed Main Street, rumbled over the railroad tracks, and navigated the dried and cracked feeder road that led to the highway, Buddy pulled the briefcase onto his lap. His to-do list sat on top and he held a pen in his hand.

"I'm beginning to worry that we won't have everything ready for the official opening after the party," Rachel fretted. She eased on-to the highway and set the cruise control at seventy-five.

"Don't worry about it," Buddy reassured her. "We don't have to be totally finished. We only need one suite and one guest room to show, and we have that. Even the meeting rooms are finished, except for the ballroom."

He looked up from his notes and pushed back a lock of sun-streaked hair from his face. The desert went speeding by. Summer had sucked the moisture from the creosote bushes, leaving them brittle and nearly colorless. The ocotillos, having long dropped their leaves, stood like tall, rickety, gray sticks.

"But I've put us on the Internet," Rachel wailed. "I've paid for advertising. I've been calling state associations."

"Even so, I don't think we'll be overrun with guests at first." Buddy pushed the brief-case between the bucket seats and into the back. "I think JT completed enough rooms to hold us for a while."

Rachel glanced over at Buddy. He flipped through papers on his clipboard. "Let me guess," she said. "It's our to-do list of what we need to accomplish today."

"Right." Buddy began reading the list aloud. "Interview chefs, go to the restaurant supply, buy a Hummer, return rental—"

"What?" Rachel's ears perked up.

"Return rental car."

"No, the one before that. You said buy a Hummer."

"Hmm," Buddy said, pretending indifference. "I guess I did." He turned to her with one of his big smiles.

"Oh, Buddy, thank you." Rachel bounced up and down in her seat. "Then you liked my idea about doing the 4-wheel drive trips in the mountains with the gourmet meals."

"Actually, Rachel, I've liked all of your ideas." He patted her shoulder. "That's why we pay you the big bucks."

Rachel turned to him. "Now *that's* funny."

ভিত্তি

Stella Belinski stood in front of the sink washing the breakfast dishes when the phone rang. She left the pan she was scrubbing and wiped her hands on a towel. Her face was round, sweet, and reflective of her Polish heritage. Pushing strands of graying hair away from her face with the habitual brush of her wrist, she picked up the phone. She did not like the man behind the icy voice on the other end of the line, but dutifully pressed the receiver to her breast and called to her husband who was sprawled on the sofa.

"Stanley. It's for you."

Belinski threw his newspaper on the floor. "I'll take it in the office," he said, walking toward the back of the house. He picked up the phone and waited for Stella to click off.

"Good morning, Stanley." The voice was sharp, cold, like a piece of tin. "How is our little project coming along?"

"Not as quickly as I had planned," Belinski answered, his voice catching. "But I'm working on a few things."

"What does that mean, you're working on a few things?" Templeton's voice was low and deceptively calm.

"It means just that. I'm working on a few angles that will convince our clients they need to sell."

"Now Stanley, if you will recall, I gave you an extension of thirty days. Your time is nearly up."

Belinski's collar suddenly felt inordinately tight, choking him. He pulled against it, trying to loosen it before finally fumbling open the top button. He didn't feel a whole lot braver even when hundreds of miles stood between him and Templeton. "Don't worry. I'll have that contract for you by the deadline," Belinski insisted, sounding a lot more confident than he felt.

"Good. I'm glad I don't have to start working with another real estate agent after all the time I've invested in you."

Belinski pulled out a linen handkerchief and mopped the sweat that pooled on his forehead and neck. "You know that won't be necessary. I told you I'll get you the property. I told you I would do whatever it takes, and I will."

"That's good. But time is running out." Templeton paused. "You have two weeks left."

Belinski heard the click, but still held the phone to his ear. Sweat dripped down his back. He slowly hung up the receiver and sat rooted in front of the desk for a few minutes before he arose and left the office.

Walking back through the family room wearing a fresh white shirt, Stanley stepped over his teenaged son who lay on the floor watching cartoons. "Don't you have anything better to do?" he snapped. The boy ignored him and continued watching TV.

On the way out the backdoor he passed by Stella with barely a glance. "I'll be back for lunch," he said.

❡❡❡

A blanket of darkness covered the desert when Buddy and Rachel drove back to the hotel with the new Hummer. Buddy pulled up to the rear entrance where JT and Heather were already waiting to inspect the new acquisition, and Rachel jumped out.

"She's a beauty," JT said, admiring the black finish shimmering under the hotel lights. "Got time for a drive?"

"Hop in," Buddy said. "You want the wheel?"

"Nah," JT said, stepping up into the Hummer. He watched Heather steer Rachel through the backdoor of the lobby. "I want a Dairy Queen. Just don't tell Heather."

"Okay. Let's cruise Main Street and see if it's open. We might even find one of the locals to drag." Buddy caught JT's look. "Just kidding, JT, just kidding."

Heather maneuvered Rachel through the lobby and brought her to the front of the round table near the main entrance.

"Beautiful," Rachel exclaimed, admiring the two-dozen yellow roses adorning the table.

"They're yours," Heather said, handing her the card nestled in the arrangement.

Rachel opened the envelope and read the card aloud, "Darlin', I'm sorry I upset you. Please forgive me. W." She read the card again, this time to herself and leaned over to smell the roses. "Well, how about that."

"What was that about?" Heather asked.

"An apology from my lunch date."

"Weezer? What happened?"

"I'll tell you about it later."

Heather frowned. "Um, Deputy Tucker came by this morning, after you were gone."

"And?"

"Well, you know what a gossip he is."

"So?"

"So he just sort of mentioned that Weezer used to be married."

"Yeah, I know that, to Belinski's sister."

"True. But did you know why they divorced?"

"What do you mean?"

"Exactly. Nobody knows why. She just up and left, suddenly, never said a word to anybody. Never came back, not even to visit."

"That *is* a bit odd, if it's true. I'm too tired to think about it now, though." Rachel turned away. "I need to go to bed."

"Wait. I almost forgot. This fax came in for you today." While her expression changed to one of excitement, she pulled a paper out of her pocket, handed it to Rachel, and then blurted out the news. "It's from Richard Markman, the Hollywood producer."

Rachel read the fax and muttered, "This is incredible." She looked at her sister who was doing a little victory dance. "He said he came here the first of August to check out Blood Mountain for a possible site for the location of his next movie and wants to know when the hotel will be ready for occupancy."

"I know," Heather tittered, giddy with excitement.

"Heather, think a minute," Rachel cautioned, holding up a hand. "This doesn't compute. The first of August the property was still deserted. Buddy said he didn't pay off the taxes until the fifth of August. Remember? He told us it was his birthday and he talked about it being the best birthday present anyone ever gave him?"

Heather stood silent and thought back. "Yes, you're right. But so what?"

"So, it's odd, that's what. How did Markman get on the property? Who showed him around?"

"Hmm." Heather blinked a couple times. "Does it really matter?"

"It should." She frowned. "The property *never* was for sale. Buddy told me it even had miles of chain link fence around it when he and JT went to check it out. So whoever showed Markman around trespassed and pretended he owned something he really didn't." She looked at her sister. "Don't you think that's a little weird?"

The excitement had fizzled out of Heather like a leaking balloon. "Only you would think of something like that," she said glumly. "But you could make a phone call and find out."

"Yes, that's true." Rachel gazed off in the direction of her office, still thinking about it. "Well, you can bet your cowboy boots I'll be taking care of that first thing in the morning."

❧❧

The night air smelled heady and shadows flickered in the breeze when Rachel walked back to her casita. She noticed lights were on in Alex's suite and called him after she bolted her door behind her.

"Are we still on for the morning?"

He answered yes, and told her to be prepared to do some hiking.

After Rachel hung up the phone, she sat for a moment and pictured his face and the cleft in his chin. He always looked like he needed a shave even early in the day, yet on him it looked good, she thought. Funny, she didn't notice he was that good-looking the night he rescued her. But then she'd prefer to erase the memory of that whole episode from her mind.

Rachel cast off her clothing on the way to the bathroom, remembering Alex had accepted her apology for that night. With that thought, Rachel turned on the shower and pulled the curtain closed. Twenty minutes later, she was dozing off in bed.

⌒⌒⌒

A man crouched in the darkness; only the whites of his eyes were visible. He dressed completely in black hoping to be less visible, guessing the hotel employed some kind of night security. He guessed right. The huge Indian walked by right in front of him, waving his flashlight behind the east block of guest rooms just twenty feet away, and never spotted him.

The man in black remained motionless behind the oleander hedge, watching, waiting for the light to move west. The Indian finally waved the light in a circle, a last check of the area, before he headed toward the courtyard.

The man in black was patient. He waited silently, like a statue, until the security guard disappeared into the courtyard gardens. He carefully toted the black bag filled with his purchases, staying in the shadow of the oleander hedge all the way up the hill. When he arrived at an old wooden shed, he quickly ducked behind it and calmed himself. He pulled the balloons out from his pocket, opened the black bag, and quickly, quietly, went to work.

❧❧❧

The sliver of moon of had already dropped toward the west. It was three o' clock and the air was completely still. Suddenly: Wuumph! BANG! The sound of the explosion jolted Rachel awake. She leaped up from her bed and stared out the bedroom window, her heart beating wildly, a scream in her throat. Blood Mountain was burning!

❧❧❧

The man in black jumped down the hill, tumbling by the hedge when the tip of the rope caught fire. It was only seconds before the flames ran the length of rope and leaped to the shed. The man didn't turn to watch the explosion, but fled through the parking lot and down the west side of the road to the junk car hidden in the rocks.

He raced the old car down the dirt road just as the few residents of the Mesquite Mountain Inn were jumping up from their dreams, frightened and disoriented.

The flames shot past the far end of the building. Snapping and cracking, they leaped skyward as sparks burst through the air like fireworks.

Rachel grabbed the phone and punched in 911. The operator said she had just received a call about the fire, so Rachel hung up and grabbed her robe, throwing it on while she ran out of the room.

Within seconds, everyone occupying the suites ran down the stairs and up the hill to the back. Toro raced up from the parking lot, beat them all there, and cautioned them to stay back while smoke and the smells of burning wood and gasoline filled the air.

A Nikon digital firmly gripped in his hand, Alex snapped pictures of the fire and the small group that gathered. The Carpenters, Rachel, Buddy, and Toro stood mesmerized, watching the flames engulf the old shed on the hill.

Long arms of orange-yellow fire flicked the trees on the hill, and teased the sagging barn close by. Suddenly the barn exploded into a giant fireball, forcing everyone even farther back.

Toro held his cell phone to his ear, still connected to 911. "Another barn just caught fire," he yelled into the phone. "Tell them to hurry!"

As if answering to his demand, a siren wailed its cry. Within seconds, the firefighters arrived and jumped into action.

Rachel gently shook her head in silence. *I can't believe this is happening.*

Buddy walked up beside her and wordlessly put his arm around her shoulders. Slowly, she leaned into its comfort.

ornament

At the bottom of the mountain, in the desert near the edge of a canal road, the man in black stood by his car, his eyes glued to a pair of binoculars while the fire burned on the mountain.

He arrived in time to see the second fireball. It billowed hundreds of feet in the air like the mushroom cloud of a bomb. He watched with interest when the fire truck and sheriff raced to the scene, his eyes following the spinning lights up the twisting hill. Shedding his clothes, he washed his face and as much of his body as he could reach with the soapy rags he'd thought to bring. The rags and smelly clothes went in the bag when he finished; he tied it, planning to burn it later. Finally, he put on a clean pair of jeans and shirt and looked himself over in the car's side mirror. Satisfied, he drove home.

∽∾∽

The air still stank of charred wood when the dazed residents of the hotel started their morning trek to the cafe. Detouring to the scene of the fire, each one gazed at the black-ened remains of the old shed and barn.

A lone beam, blistered with black alligator skin, leaned precariously against a heap of rubble. Streams of wet soot had gouged the hill with deep, dark wrinkles.

The group assembled silently in their cor-ner booth, each numb with shock and fatigue. Rachel dragged in last, not having bothered with makeup to try to conceal the lack of sleep showing beneath her eyes.

She lunged at the coffeepot in the center of the table. From behind the counter, Lupe assessed the condition of the group and immediately brewed another pot.

"Did anyone sleep afterwards?" Rachel asked.

No one replied affirmatively. They all sipped coffee, waiting for caffeine to work its magic.

Rachel turned to Heather. "I never paid much attention to that old barn and shed out there. Did you?"

Heather shook her head, but Buddy said that he and JT checked it out briefly when they first inspected the place.

"What were they?" Rachel asked.

"I don't really know what they were used for," JT answered. "Just old storage sheds with some junk and boards inside. Kind of musty smelling. I thought about tearing them down anyway." He took a sip of his coffee. "I guess I don't have to worry about that now."

Rachel looked at him sharply. "That isn't the problem."

"I know."

"I'd really like to know what's going on around here." Rachel tried to keep the frustration she felt from seeping into her voice. "The kamikaze plane was bad enough. Then we have a murder right on our doorstep and after that a fire? What's coming next?" She turned to glare at Alex. "Why isn't your uncle doing something about this?"

As if on cue, Dewey Tucker came through the front door. He trudged over to the corner in his slow, bowl-legged way and sat down next to Rachel. She crinkled up her nose at the smell of Tucker's shirt. Soot smeared his sleeves and pants. Obviously, he had been up a while, poking around in the ashes.

"Dewey, what's going on with the fire?" JT asked.

The deputy filled his cup and slowly drawled, "I was fixin' to ask you the same thing, JT."

"What do you mean?" JT appeared confused.

"I mean it looks like arson." Tucker was so laid-back he looked like he could dissolve into a big, fat puddle.

Alex laid out prints of some of the photos he had taken the night before. "I printed these off the computer so the resolution isn't that great, but you can see enough of the evidence to tell."

JT clenched his jaw and shot a look at Tucker. "You're not saying one of us started that fire, are you?"

"Aw, no, JT." Dewey barely shook his head. "If somebody's gonna burn down their own place, they're gonna make it worth the insurance. I seen the shed and barn. They weren't worth a flip."

Lupe suddenly appeared at his side with platters of scrambled eggs, bacon, and home-made biscuits. Dewey stopped talking and passed the plates around the table. After scooping copious amounts of food onto his plate, he checked to make sure Lupe was out of hearing range before he spoke again.

"As I said, I know your loss ain't that much, but given the situation here, I think it warrants a thorough investigation." He shov-eled a large forkful of eggs into his mouth and hardly chewed before opening his mouth again to speak. "I'm having a friend of mine fly out from Yuma today. She's one of the state's arson experts." He shot a quick glance at Alex. "A real looker, too."

"Thank you, it's about time something is being done." Rachel said, picking up a crisp slice of bacon.

JT shot her a warning look.

"In the meantime," the deputy continued, ignoring Rachel's remark, "Ya might want to start makin' a list of anybody that might want ya out of here." He looked around the table at everyone, in turn. "Alex said you all met up about the same time, at the start of the fire."

"That's right," Buddy said. "I heard a loud bang that woke me up. After I saw the flames, I ran out the door."

"We did, too," Heather added.

Tucker nodded. "What you heard was gasoline exploding." He pointed to one of the photos. "This is the remains of a wick that we think was used to start the original fire, just a common cotton rope."

The group exchanged questioning looks.

Tucker gathered up the prints of the fire and handed them back to Alex. "Where was Toro at the time of the fire?"

"He was already up the hill." Buddy answered. "He's the one who called 911."

"Yeah, I know. I'll be checking him out."

"What do you mean, you'll be checking him out?" Rachel asked. "You can't possibly think he had anything to do with the fire. The only reason he was up there first is because he was on security duty last night. He was *supposed* to be watching for stuff. That was his *job*." She turned her face away and looked at the others. "I don't believe it. This is turning into a witch hunt."

Tucker tried to keep his cool. "Right now, we're not huntin' anybody. We're just gatherin' information."

"That's what you said about the murder, too." Rachel's voice raised a whole octave. "When are you going to stop gathering information and start giving us some answers?"

"Rachel, stop it," JT scolded in a booming voice.

She fell back as if he'd slapped her.

"Okay guys, let's calm down," Tucker said, holding up a hand. "We're gonna get to the bottom of this, I promise you." He turned to look at Buddy. "You might be interested in knowin' Toro had a gas can in the trunk of his car last night, and it was empty."

Uneasy silence blanketed the table before Rachel finally spoke, anger smoldering in her eyes.

She refused to look at Dewey and directed her explanation to the others. "Toro always carries a gas can in his trunk. It's a regulation can and it's legal. His gas gauge has been broken for months."

Another awkward silence filled the room. No one dared speak. Heather caught Rachel's eye and dramatically pointed to her watch.

Rachel stood up, understanding the signal. "Please excuse me." Her voice took on a gracious, professional tone. "I'm sorry, but I have an important phone call I need to make."

Chapter 12

Stanley Belinski drove his Lincoln slowly over the dirt road, trying not to raise dust. He cursed the particles of sand that peppered his windshield then caught himself. What was he thinking? He could easily find his legs broken for an unpaid debt, and he was worried about dust on his fancy car? He shook his head, trying to banish the thoughts of the bad decisions he'd made during the last three years.

He noticed the autumn sun had been rising lower in the sky lately, stretching out the shadows. He looked forward to this time each year. Mornings were crisp, nights were cooler, and it didn't get hot until two in the afternoon. The weather felt as perfect as it could get, if one overlooked the occasional dust storm, and Stanley determined he would.

The Lincoln idled in front of the hotel coffee shop, air conditioning set on high, while Stanley put his mind on track. He took a deep breath and visualized himself talking with McCain, convincing him to sell Blood Mountain. He practiced his smile and greeting in the mirror.

When he stepped outside the climate-controlled comfort of his car, the smell of fire assaulted his nostrils. Was he doing the right thing? News of the fire spread quickly through the town, yet when Stanley looked around, he saw nothing out of the ordinary. The news may have spread, but apparently, the fire didn't.

"Good morning," he said brightly, entering the cafe. It was then, when the mood of the room caved in on him and he saw only somber faces, Stanley realized his contrived cheerfulness and timing were off.

Heather rose from the corner booth. "May I help you?" she asked. "Oh, I remember you," she said, recognizing the man who was discreetly combing wind-blown hair.

"Stanley Belinski from Mesquite Realty," he said, holding out a meaty hand. "I came by the other day and spoke with you. You're Heather Carpenter."

"That's right." She remembered JT had thrown his card in the trash. "Did you want breakfast? We aren't officially open but we can offer you coffee," said the ever-polite Mrs. Manners.

"Oh, no, thanks," Stanley replied. "I was actually hoping to speak with Byron McCain." He looked at the somber faces of Buddy and JT sitting in the booth and regretted his decision. "But if this isn't a good time," he added hesitantly.

"I'm Byron McCain," Buddy spoke out, without a trace of his usual smile, but managed to get up and shake his hand. "What can I do for you?"

"Well, first of all, I'm sorry to hear about your fire." Stanley's voice cracked and he flushed with embarrassment. He cleared his throat. "It wasn't serious, was it?"

"An old barn burned down that we were going to knock down anyway. Nobody was hurt. That's the important thing." Buddy tried to put a light spin on it but his voice was not convincing.

"You're right," Stanley agreed. "People are what matters. The rest is only stuff." He wished he had figured out that little fact of life earlier in the game.

271

"So what is it you wanted to see me about?" Buddy asked, eager to move on.

"Well," Stanley began, hesitancy now in his voice. "I know this isn't exactly the best time for you, but I wanted to talk with you about someone who wants to buy your property at an excellent price."

"Sit down," Buddy said with a jerk of his head toward the yellow corner booth, now empty except for JT. "Exactly who's this party interested in our property?"

Stanley grunted his hefty frame into the booth and acknowledged JT with a nod and a timid smile, clearly uncomfortable. "Ah, I think you can understand that until we have a contract, my client doesn't want to reveal his identity."

"Of course. You're right," Buddy said, moving on. "Let me ask you this. Do you happen to be acquainted with Gerald Metcalf?"

Stanley frowned. "The attorney with Metcalf and Meyers?"

"One and the same," Buddy answered. "Are you acquainted with him? Or let me put it this way. Is Gerald Metcalf also representing your client?"

"Why, no, not that I'm aware of." Stanley seemed puzzled. "My client is from out-of-state. Metcalf is a local attorney whose main office is in Phoenix. He deals mainly with agricultural matters."

Buddy shot a sideways glance at JT then continued. "Have you ever dealt with him in business?"

Stanley frowned and appeared to be frustrated at the direction the conversation was going. "Well, yes. He's represented farmers in some land sales I've handled."

"Do any of those farmers happen to be Franz Venkman?"

Stanley stared at Buddy. He swallowed and tried to adjust his collar. "Has Venkman made you an offer for your property?"

"I'm sorry," Buddy said, "but I think you understand that we can't reveal the identity of anyone we've talked to about the sale of our property."

Stanley felt like he had been punched in the gut. "Look, Mr. McCain, please don't accept any offers on your property without allowing my client to bid on it. He is willing to pay top dollar, plus."

"Plus what?"

"Plus fifty-thousand more than what Venkman will pay."

Buddy looked over at JT who had remained silent throughout the meeting, arms crossed over his chest

"Buddy," JT finally said, with a slight nod of his head. "I think we ought to consider this." He stepped out of the booth and extended his hand to Stanley. "We'll call you tomorrow."

ⓒ◌ⓒ◌

Heather stuck her head into Rachel's office. "Hey sis, Buddy and JT want us to meet with them in the Plantation Room right now."

"I'll be right there." Rachel glanced at her watch. It was four-thirty. So far, she had managed to avoid JT all afternoon. Oh, well, they were going to have to deal with each other eventually. She pushed some of her papers into a pile on her desk. There was so much more she wanted to accomplish, but it would have to wait.

The Plantation Room was aptly named. Plantation shutters lined the dining room windows that looked out over the lobby, and a

274

mural of a tropical beach covered the entire back wall. In the back corner, a narrow waterfall projected itself into the room and appeared as if volcanic rocks had fallen down the mountain and someone had built a room around it. Gurgling water flowed down the rocks to a small pool surrounded with tropical plants and lit with colorful lights.

Heather and Rachel slid into the booth next to Buddy and JT. A pitcher of iced tea sat in the middle of the table.

Buddy looked at JT and flipped over a hand. "After you, boss."

JT cleared his throat and sipped from his glass. His face, tanned and softening with age, looked weary. "As you all know, it seems like we've been under attack lately from all sides." He looked around the table. "At first, I didn't give it that much thought, because I've never taken on a job when things didn't go wrong some of the time. But with the murder right in our own parking lot and the torching of our barn, I feel that someone out there is making a real effort to intimidate us into leaving."

"I agree," Rachel said, jumping right in.

JT held up his hand to her to let him continue. "The attacks on us, whether directly or indirectly, have created a stressful situation for us, so much so that we are starting to turn on and even distrust each other."

JT looked directly at Rachel. "I am as guilty of that as anyone, and for my part in this, I apologize."

Rachel was surprised at his apology and even more relieved he didn't fire her. "I'm sorry, too, for my outbursts," she promptly said, hoping her job was still secure. "I'm just so frustrated with what I feel is our deputy's lack of ability to protect us," she added, hoping to justify past behavior. "I have to confess, I've even wondered if he was on the take."

JT held up his hand again. "Now Rachel, Dewey may not be up for any Pulitzer, but I doubt he has a sinister bone in his body."

"I think JT is right," Buddy said, pouring more tea in his glass. "But the question is, what does everyone want to do? I really love what we've been doing at the Inn, but if our lives are in danger, it's not worth it to me."

"You mean we'd drop everything and walk away?" Heather stared in disbelief. "I can't understand why anyone wants us to leave. *Everyone* I've spoken to seems to be ecstatically happy we're going to reopen the hotel."

"I know," JT said. "But *somebody* around here really wants us out." He looked around at the three of them. "Unfortunately, I don't have a clue as to why."

"Well, amazing as it sounds," Buddy continued, "we've have two offers from people who want this place and are willing to pay enough for it that JT and I could each walk away with a very healthy profit. Even Rachel could get a big bonus for her trouble."

"Two offers?" Rachel questioned. "Who was the second party?"

"Well, we think one is Venkman. If he wasn't the one who sent Metcalf to solicit me in front of the courthouse that day in Phoenix, then we'd actually have three potential buyers."

"Who was the other?"

"Oh, that's right," Buddy remembered. "You were already gone. Stanley Belinski came by representing an unknown party."

"Stanley Belinski?" Rachel blinked in surprise. "Stanley Belinski of Mesquite Realty?"

"Yes," Buddy said. "Is there a problem with that?"

Rachel gave Heather a knowing look. "Yes, there is," she said, turning back to Buddy. "I returned a call this morning to Richard

277

Markman, a Hollywood producer. His last release was *King's Ransom*, remember it? He's interested in forty-eight guest rooms, meals, box lunches, and even meeting rooms in March, for at least a week, and that would be perfect for us."

Rachel noticed JT drumming his fingers on the table so she picked up the cue and quickened her verbal pace. "The reason Markman wants to come here is that he wants to use Old Town Mesquite and Blood Mountain as locations for a movie he'll be producing and directing in the spring."

"Rachel, that's fantastic," Buddy said.

"Yes, fantastic, if it happens," JT repeated blandly, his fingers still. "And the point is?"

"The point is," Rachel continued, "Markman told me he had come out here the first of August to take a look around. He said someone told him at that time, that the hotel would be ready for occupancy in March."

Rachel paused, letting the relevance of the dates sink in.

JT looked at her thoughtfully. "You're saying someone opened the property and let Markman look around at the beginning of August, even before the property was transferred to Buddy."

"Exactly." She turned to Buddy. "At the time, your uncle still was the legal owner of the property, right?"

"Well, I had inherited it, but hadn't paid off the taxes. Not only that, the property was in shambles."

"So who let him in?" JT asked. "Only Dewey Tucker had a key to the gate."

Rachel hunched her shoulders quizzically. "All I know is that Richard Markman told me the person who showed him around, and told him the hotel would be ready for occupancy by March, was none other than Stanley Belinski."

A stunned look crossed Heather's face. "So is that the reason Stanley's buyer wants the property so badly? His buyer was planning on fixing up the hotel by March just to rent it out to some Hollywood producer to film a movie?"

"That can't be it," Buddy answered, shaking his head in disbelief. "But it does explain the strange behavior of the tax assessor. When I came in to pay off the taxes, I really had the feeling he wanted to talk me out of taking over the place."

"It doesn't make sense, and it still doesn't explain the murders," Rachel said. "No sane person is going to risk burning the barn and murdering two people for that. There's not enough incentive. There's has to be more to the story."

"Okay, people," JT said. "We can speculate on this all day. Right now we need to decide if we're going to stay and fight it out or if we should take a fast profit and sell."

He turned to Buddy. "What do you say, partner?"

Buddy looked steadily at his friend. "I say this beats crunching numbers any day. I mean, I'm still crunching numbers, but at least it's not at my desk in LA. I vote to stay."

JT looked at Heather. "What do you want to do, honey?"

Heather turned to her husband and smiled. "I never thought I'd say this, but I love it here. You're so much happier now, and that means so much to me. Plus, I have family with me." She looked at Rachel. "I vote to stay."

Finally, JT turned to Rachel. "I know you aren't a partner in this, but I also know you've had a lot of experience in the hotel industry and I value your professional opinion."

Rachel blushed at the compliment, hardly believing her good fortune. "There's something special about this place, no doubt about it. I'm really thrilled to be part of this project, being able to start something up from the beginning. Well, almost the beginning. I've seen your plans and I think, with the bar, restaurants, and meeting rooms, you'll be able to pull off a decent profit."

"Okay." JT moved his eyes from face to face around table. "I know there's a risk involved with us staying, possibly even danger to us, personally. Yet, at the same time, I have to admit I'm enjoying it here a lot more than those last few years in LA. So, I guess my vote makes it unanimous. We stay."

❧❧❧

The air still smelled of burned and blackened wood when Alex walked through the courtyard. He finally found Rachel by the pool. "I've been looking for you," he said.

"Well, you found me." Rachel didn't bother to turn her head, and looked straight at the swimming pool. The wind had died a quiet death by noon and the surface of the water looked like was a sheet of glass.

Alex walked to the front of her lounge chair so Rachel couldn't avoid seeing him.

281

His hair was slicked back from walking out of a shower, and he smelled of Polo after-shave. "We need to talk."

"So talk." She was in no mood to see him or his worthless uncle.

"No, not here. Let's take the truck. I want to go over to the old landing strip on the north side."

Rachel studied the lengthening shadows of palm trees that crossed the pool and finally looked up at Alex. He wore a knit shirt that showed off his muscular arms and chest. Neatly tucked into a pair of Wranglers, it showed off a narrow waist and the rest of his anatomy. She looked away. He was danger- ous, no doubt, but only where her self-control was concerned. She debated whether to leave with him.

"I think I know where our killer was." Alex dangled his words like a lure.

Rachel's eyes swept back to his shirt, a Henley, unbuttoned to the third button. She caught a glimpse of black curls beneath it, and she pictured her face against his chest. *He knows where the killer was?*

"That's what I want to show you."

Rachel finally looked at his face and determined he was sincere. "Give me five minutes to get my boots and jeans."

∽∾∽∾

Alex drove carefully through the rough roads on the north side of Blood Mountain, he and Rachel looking straight ahead, hardly speaking. "I know you're angry with my uncle Dewey, but I want you to know that he's doing the best he can. He's one person and has to cover his whole district alone."

He looked over at Rachel but she refused to make eye contact. "You probably think he's just some dumb redneck."

She gave him a dour look. "You're getting warmer."

"Then you tell me."

"For starters, he appears to be totally incompetent. We are the victims here and he acts like we're the perpetrators." She turned icy eyes on Alex. "Are we going to have to be picked off one by one before he stops wasting his time with Toro and actually starts looking for the murderer?"

Having arrived at his destination, Alex stopped the truck. Backing up behind an outcropping of rock, he made a visual check. He assured himself the truck was hidden from view, and parked.

"Rachel, Dewey *is* looking for the murderer, but what he can't tell you is that there's more going on than just two murders. Yes, he's sure someone murdered Juan, too, maybe the same person who killed Vicky. Only he can't prove it, not yet, anyway."

He walked around to Rachel's door and opened it. "For some reason he thinks Blood Mountain is the connection to both murders. That's why he wanted me to stay at the hotel…that, and the fact that I could offer some additional protection."

"So are you spilling state secrets here?" Rachel asked, stepping down from the truck, her hand in his.

"No, except the part about my staying at the hotel, that is." He had her eyes now, along with her hand. "And if you think about it, it's a lot less threatening to the murderer when he learns that Dewey is investigating everyone, that everyone is suspect."

Looking down at their hands, Rachel pulled away from his grasp.

"Rachel, in a case like this, you have to get everything lined up perfectly before you can make an arrest or you end up with the killer walking away in the end."

She dug the toe of her boot in the sand. "I know. You're right." She hated admitting it. "I've seen it happen."

Alex lifted a backpack out of the truck and they walked toward a small outcropping of rock. "I had Lupe fix up a little supper for us in case we got hungry."

Rachel eyed his pack. "And you assumed I'd come with you?"

He slung the pack over a shoulder. "No. But I was hoping."

The sun slipped behind the peaks to the west and cast a shadow on the cooling air. The north wall, mined of its skin and exposed to its base core, soared above them. Outcroppings of rock ledges edged them upward. Alex and Rachel climbed up the north face to a narrow ledge where they flattened their bodies against a wall, still warm from the sun. "How about a root beer?" Alex asked.

"A root beer?"

"Yeah, I thought all you Yankee girls liked root beer."

Rachel gave him a puzzled look. What else did he know about her? "Well, I wasn't born a Yankee, but I actually do like root beer. Hand me one."

Alex tried to keep from smiling when he pulled a can from the pack, knowing Lupe had tipped him off about what soft drinks Rachel preferred.

"Did Dewey's arson expert from Yuma ever find out how the fire started?" Rachel asked.

"Yeah, it was like he thought. The arsonist used a long gasoline-soaked rope leading to a gasoline-filled balloon. The guy knew what he was doing. He planned it well, and got a lot of bang for his buck."

Rachel slowly shook her head in disgust. "I'm glad whoever did it torched the barn and not the hotel."

"I suspect the reason he picked the barn was to scare you off, not kill you off."

"That does make sense when you think about it." She pulled the tab off the can of root beer and downed half of it.

"My guess is that you guys are simply in somebody's way, just not enough in the way to kill you." He turned his face away and looked out at the view. "Not yet anyway."

"That's reassuring."

"It's meant to be." Alex sat down on the rock ledge, letting his legs hang over. "I don't think the killer actually plans to murder."

"By that you mean he kills anyone who accidentally stumbles into his path at the wrong time."

"Yes, and whatever the killer was involved in was visible both from that ledge above us and the field right down there." Alex pointed to a field of lettuce. "And from the field on the south side of this peak."

Rachel sat down beside him. Her thigh brushed against his and she felt the fire. She pulled away. "So you learned all that from the diary, huh?"

"Yeah, but I had to read it through four times." He dropped his head, smiled sheepishly.

Rachel couldn't help but laugh. "So what about the ledge up there?" she asked, bending her head all the way back to see it.

"You remember when you found the telescope?" he asked. "Well, if you went about forty feet farther north, you would have been at that very ledge."

Rachel nodded. "I wondered about that." She looked around the airstrip, spotted with a few boulders and brush. "But there's nothing down here."

"Yeah, I know. *Now* there isn't."

She looked around again. "You could be right," she said. "So what about the green lights? I bet they were some kind of signal. To somebody, somewhere, even miles away." She looked at him with a puzzled expression on her face. "Like an airplane?"

"Right." Alex let his gaze rest on the mound of rock a few feet to their left. "A person could climb up that rock face and signal from there," he said, pointing. "You could see him from all the locations mentioned in the diary."

"Hmm," Rachel murmured.

"I actually drove around Venkman's farm to check the location of all the sightings." The sheepish grin was back.

Rachel's gaze flowed over him. "I'm impressed. I didn't think of doing that."

"Why would you, Rachel? You shouldn't even be involved."

"Alex, I *am* involved. Can't you see that?" Her voice bounced off the mountain. "I'm the one who found the woman's body. And Blood Mountain is my home now," she said, her voice softer. "Heather and JT are my only family." She looked down at the long slender hands in her lap, then at Alex. "I want to help you solve this case."

Alex chose his words carefully. "I can't let you do that, Rachel. If I let you help me, I'll be endangering your life or the lives of your family and Buddy. It's better that you totally disengage from this."

"I could help you, Alex." Rachel pleaded.

"Rachel, listen to me." Alex grabbed her shoulders with both hands. "These people that I am tracking tortured and beat my partner to death. Killing is nothing to them. They could have connections to people in this town who are socially elite, people that could appear to be decent, upstanding citizens. That's why it's so important that absolutely no one know about me or that you and I have a connection."

His eyes were dark pools she thought she might drown in. "Do you and I have a connection, Alex?" She felt his thigh against hers again, burning.

Alex dropped his gaze to her lips, pink and soft, and then put his mouth on hers. She responded, and then drew back. He leaned toward her again. "No," she protested. "I can't."

Suddenly leaping down the rock face to the next level, she continued downward until she reached the old airfield and walked east. She struggled with conflicting emotions, ones that had been simmering in her for days, and kicked at a pile of debris in frustration. A plastic sack meshed in a sagebrush skeleton and a tin can wedged in between two rocks stood in her path and she had expected to see them fly away. Nothing moved except tiny, brittle pieces of sagebrush. Again, she kicked at the trash; but a dull, hollow thud from the rock was the only response. Puzzled, she knelt down and dug around in the debris.

"Well, well, well," she said, intrigued. "Alex, come take a look at this."

Alex, already walking toward her, came and knelt beside her. "It's all wired together and there's some kind of hook holding it to the ground," he said, after completing his inspection. He tapped the rock. It sounded hollow.

Rachel walked to a three-foot boulder in the center of the airstrip and banged it with a stone. The boulder responded with a dull thud. "It's a prop," she exclaimed, and walked over to a second boulder. It responded with same hollow sound. "They're all props. My brother-in-law made stuff like this for our swimming pool."

"Someone put these props on the airstrip to make it look like it hadn't been used for years." Alex said as he continued walking. "Whoever uses this area, pulls the props aside when they need the strip, and then puts everything back when they're done. They even brush out tire marks and footprints." He stopped walking when he arrived at the edge and looked around. "But there are no landing lights."

Rachel sat on a boulder at the end of the airstrip while Alex poked around the rocks and detritus. "What are you looking for?" she asked.

"Anything. Everything." He bent over and picked something up. "This."

Rachel stood up to look at his find. "What is it?"

"It's a piece of cigarette that didn't get totally mashed. See?" he asked, holding it up between his thumb and forefinger.

Rachel looked but couldn't see the significance of it. "Lots of people smoke."

"But this hasn't been here long, and if you read some of the little letters that are still legible, you can see it's actually part of an expensive, imported cigarette. A Nat Sherman."

Rachel's eyes popped wide open. "Alex, I know someone who smokes those. Weezer Chaffee."

Alex's eyes turned dark. "Rachel, listen to me." Alex brought his face so close to hers she could feel his breath on her lips. "You need to stay away from him. If he's involved in this, he could be very dangerous. Do you understand me?"

"I understand, Alex. I promise I will be very careful."

"That isn't the answer I wanted."

"Alex, I'm not going to lie to you. It's the only answer I can give you."

Chapter 13

The parking lot of Southwest Chemical was empty when Rachel pulled up by the sun-bleached door. She stuck her head into the office, greatly relieved her greeting was met with silence. Her Bottega Veneta heels tapped on the vinyl tiles when she walked through the reception area headed directly toward the office in the back. An old metal desk, heaped with files and papers, held a nameplate engraved with William "Weezer" Chaffee, Manager.

"Can I help you?" a voice called out.

Rachel turned to see a young man in a tan uniform, stepping through the back door. His eyes widened at the sight of the long-legged blonde standing in front of him.

"Hi, Sergio," Rachel said with a slow smile, reading the name embroidered over his pocket. "I'm looking for Weezer. Is he here?"

"No," Sergio answered, focusing his gaze on her breasts where her push-up bra was inviting attention. "He went to the post office," he said, finally drawing his eyes back to her eyes. "He'll be right back."

"Oh," Rachel said breathlessly, "Is it okay if I wait here for him?" She hopped up on the corner of the desk, allowing her short skirt to reveal creamy, slender legs. *Shameless hussy,* she thought to herself.

"Yeah. No problem." Sergio stared at her legs. "That your ride out there?"

"Sure is. Newest model and it's loaded." Rachel held up a ring of keys and looked at him from underneath thick mascara-covered lashes. "Want to check it out? Go ahead, drive it around the block."

"Yeah, thanks." Sergio slowly reached for the keys, scanning her body for a last look.

When the door clicked behind him, Rachel jumped down and quickly yanked open the top center drawer and dug around in the jumble of keys, paper clips, and other office paraphernalia, but nothing interested her. Rifling through the two left drawers, Rachel found only recent bills-of-lading and customer invoices. The bottom right drawer seemed to be stuck, but she opened it with a yank. *Interesting,* she thought, looking down at the stacks of travel literature and maps. A small, fat book about Costa Rica lay on top.

Rachel rummaged through the pile, careful not to disturb the order. She pulled out an envelope with the return address of the Grand Cayman Islands Reserve Bank. The postmark was blurry but Rachel could make out the abbreviation "Sept."

"Now we're talking," she thought, as she scanned the recent statement. The slam of a truck door suddenly caught her attention and she quickly put the papers back in the envelope. She managed to put the envelope back and close the drawer at the same time the door opened. She looked up as Weezer walked in. Rachel turned and greeted him brightly from her seat on the corner of the desk.

"Well, hello, darlin'. What are you doing back here?" Weezer's voice was light but his eyes were guarded while he scanned the top of his desk.

"Sergio let me in and I was just admiring your yacht," Rachel answered, turning her attention to the bulletin board behind the desk.

Dozens of photos of his seventy-five-foot Hatteras completely covered it. "I can see why you never married again. She is one beautiful boat."

"She's even better looking in person, darlin'." Weezer walked steadily toward her while his eyes dropped to her cleavage. "Maybe you'd like to come out and spend the weekend with me sometime." Throaty and seductive, his voice sent a rush through her. "We could cruise over to Catalina Island and have dinner."

"Spend the weekend?"

"Not to worry, darlin'." The corners of his mustache turned up. "She's equipped with three bedrooms and two baths."

"That does sound very tempting," Rachel said, her eyes locking on his. "If we ever get the hotel finished and things running smoothly, I might be able to take a weekend off to go."

"I'd like that." Weezer removed his Stetson, spun it toward the rack in the corner, and watched it land squarely on an empty hook. "But what about your boyfriend, Buddy? Won't he mind?"

"Buddy? He's not my boyfriend, he's JT's partner." Rachel's mouth turned into a pout and she noticed Weezer inching closer to her. "Aren't you going to ask me why I came to see you?"

"Okay, darlin'. Why did you come to see me?"

"I wanted to thank you for the beautiful roses."

Weezer looked down at Rachel's breasts again. "And I want to thank you for the beautiful pink blouse," he said, closing in on her.

Blood raced to Rachel's face. She suddenly realized her plan was overkill. What had she done? The diversion was now becoming a problem in itself.

Leaning over her, Weezer gently brushed her long, silky hair back from her face. His gaze rose to her lips and he was about to kiss her when the side door opened.

They both jerked back when Sergio stepped in and sensed the awkwardness of his intrusion. "Pretty cool ride," he said, turning his head away. He dropped the keys on the corner of the desk and quickly left.

Rachel slid off the desk out of Weezer's reach. "Well, I guess that's my cue. I better get back to work and let you do the same." She picked up her keys and glanced around the office.

"Wait, I'll walk you out." Weezer put his arm around her and led her toward the side door. A poster on the office wall caught her eye and Rachel quickly scanned the names on the work roster before she stepped out.

The afternoon sun was a sharp, dazzling reflection on the body of the Hummer when Rachel climbed up into the cab. Looking back at Weezer, her eyes drifted to the auburn mustache feathered over his lip.

"Did you know we had a fire on the property?" Rachel asked him, her eyes still on his lips.

"I heard an old shed burned down."

"It was a barn *and* a shed, actually. It singed a couple mesquite trees, too. Deputy Tucker said it looked like arson." She looked for a flicker of something to register in Weezer's eyes, but nothing did.

"Arson?" Weezer scratched the back of his head.

"Yes. Arson. Like we haven't had enough trouble." Rachel turned on the ignition and three hundred and twenty-five horses under the hood came to life. She flipped the air conditioner to maximum and flashed Weezer a smile. "See ya, cowboy," she said and put the Hummer in gear.

When Rachel arrived back at the hotel, she spotted an Infinity sedan she had never seen before, parked near the front entrance of the main building. Once inside the coffee shop, she followed the sound of voices to the kitchen.

Buddy and Heather were talking with a small, wiry man who was wearing dreadlocks and a very wide smile.

"Henri," Rachel squealed. "I'm so glad you could make it." She walked over to shake the hand of the chef she and Buddy had interviewed in Phoenix. "What do you think of the property?"

"Oooo, I like it, Miss Rachel. The island look makes me feel right at home." He turned to Buddy and Heather. "I was born in Jamaica, you know." His broad smile was dazzling against skin the color of cola.

"That must have been fun growing up there," Heather said. "JT and I went there once and I can't wait to go back." She turned to Rachel and informed her she had already shown Henri around the main building. "He said he could start in time to prepare for the open house. Isn't that great?"

"It's more than great. It'll save my butt." Rachel turned to Henri. "It's a done deal, then?"

"Well, I do have a couple little questions when you have the time," Henri replied.

"Okay, swing by my office at the end of the lobby when you're done with the tour. I'd like you to go over the menu with me and make sure it meets with your approval. You'll want to add some of your specialties, too."

Turning her attention to Heather, Rachel handed her the stack of mail she had picked up from the post office box. "I see you're quite popular today."

"Hmm," Heather murmured, already rifling through the mass of envelopes. "Bills, bills, and more bills."

Rachel's mood was light when she walked through the lobby, the tapping of her designer shoes echoing against the warm mustard walls. *If Henri comes on board, things will be heading in the right direction again,* she thought, wishing she could jump up and click her heels. JT had just finished the remodeling of the main building, so hiring Henri would be the last major item that needed to be accomplished before the open house. *Then I can spend more time on trying to find the strangler.*

Continuing on, Rachel picked up the delicate fragrance of papaya and mango that drifted through the building. She could always count on Heather to put something in the air that smelled wonderful. A tequila and lime scent had been Rachel's first request, but not a single manufacturer thought of that idea. Too bad.

Rachel reached the french doors of her office and saw Alex sitting inside. He did not look happy.

Her mood plummeted. "Am I in trouble?"

"Big time." Alex's drew his lips into a thin, tight line. Even his eyes were cold.

"For what?"

"For having your Hummer parked in front of Southwest Chemical."

Rachel grimaced. "I knew I should have parked in the back."

Alex glared at her, trying to keep from raising his voice. "Rachel, this is not a joke. You could have put yourself in jeopardy and possibly screwed up our whole investigation." He looked at her blouse. "And you wore that outfit?"

Picking up his attitude, she snapped back at him. "Yes, I wore this outfit. You got a problem with that?"

"Not if you were going to a costume party dressed as a hooker."

"Thanks a lot." Rachel glared at him. "Just so you know, I wore it for a particular reason. I used it as a diversion."

"A diversion?" Alex snorted and nervously pulled out a cigarette before he noticed the thank-you-for-not-smoking sign. He put the cigarette back and softened a little. "Rachel, you don't need to dress like that to create a diversion. You especially don't need to be creating any diversions. It could complicate things."

"Is that *so*? Well, at least I'm doing *something*." She flicked her hair back as if to dismiss him, and sat at her desk. "Then I guess you're not interested that I found out a few things."

Alex's eyes shifted in her direction. "What things?"

"Things you couldn't have found out."

"Like what?"

"Like mail from the Cayman Islands Reserve Bank. Like a whole drawer full of literature and maps from Costa Rica. Like the name Quintero on the employee roster."

"Quintero?" Alex asked. "What's that supposed to mean?"

"Well, if the Quintero on the roster is married to the Lupe Quintero that works for us, then I think I know who the bad man was who paid Quintero five hundred dollars to make Lupe Quintero put the tarantula in my room."

Alex stared at Rachel. "What in the world are you talking about?"

"It's a very long story that you will have to wait until tonight to hear, and only after you ply me with a big fat margarita."

Alex's voice sounded edged with exasperation. "This isn't funny, Rachel."

"I'm not trying to be funny, Alex." They stared each other down. "Look," Rachel said, finally looking away, "the truth is I'm beginning to have a bad feeling about Weezer. Something bothers me about him, but I can't quite get a handle on it."

"Wouldn't that somehow be a clue that you might want to stay away from him?"

"Not if I want to get at the bottom of what's going on around Blood Mountain."

Alex grunted in frustration, and then asked quietly, "So you think Weezer is our killer?"

"Killer, arsonist, tarantula keeper?" Rachel pondered, staring off. "All I know is that as handsome and charming as Weezer is, I'm beginning to suspect he's connected to some of the weird stuff that's been going on around here."

Alex gazed at her steadily. "If that's the case, then promise me that you won't go to see him again."

Rachel's eyes danced around the room, and then finally came back to him. "I promise," she finally agreed with a sigh. "But what if he comes here?"

"Oh, he will. No doubt about that," Alex answered with a quick glance at her revealing blouse. "Just try to act busy."

෬෬෬

Stanley Belinski waited in his real estate office all day for the phone call. Too stressed to work, he had been sitting at his mahogany desk for hours, hiding behind a stack of papers, looking around his office, thinking.

Framed certificates of his achievements lined the wall behind his desk. Plush carpeting, Spanish antiques, and ample upholstered

304

chairs added a rich and comfortable feel. Only today, Belinski wasn't feeling too comfortable.

Usually in cases like this, he always had a back-up plan, something he could offer to close the deal. But if McCain and Carpenter didn't want to sell for any amount of money, he had no other options.

Things had gone exceptionally well for him for a while, he remembered. Buying the hill on the east end of the mesa and convincing the town to build a golf course on it was a stroke of genius, even if he did donate some of the land. When the house lots started selling and his brother started building spec homes, his income exploded like a shaken bottle of Coke.

Belinski had used his new wealth to buy a house on the golf course, a new car every year, and started traveling. People treated him with respect, even admiration. He was flying high and never once considered that his income stream would stop. He, like many others, never guessed real estate in Arizona would take a dive.

Even then, he would have been okay if he hadn't developed a weakness for blackjack and pretty girls. He knew Stella suspected, but she was definitely of the old school, content to raise their son, clean her own home, and ask no questions.

When Belinski found the money well had gone dry and he was in debt, it felt like the earth had crumbled under his feet. He wasn't just *in debt*. Besides the credit cards and his twice-mortgaged home, he owed the owner of his favorite casino more than he could ever repay.

Nobody else knew, not Stella, not his brother. Even if they suspected things weren't going that well with him, he still managed to put on a good front.

At one point Belinski thought he had found the solution to his problems when the casino owner wanted to buy Blood Mountain. He actually agreed to delete Belinski's entire debt if Belinski completed the deal without the name of Cyrus Templeton ever being mentioned.

Belinski had it all figured out. He would buy the property at the tax sale with Templeton's money and then get a kickback from his brother to have the place renovated. With Richard Markman lined up to rent the place in March, he'd even get a percentage of that transaction; maybe even get to run the whole place. There was also the action he might get in on with that very special piece of property on the north side.

Three days, that's what killed it. Three days before the tax sale when the nephew showed up to pay off the lien.

Sweat was already forming on the back of Belinski's neck when the phone rang. He picked up the receiver. The number showing on caller I.D. was the one he had been waiting for.

Buddy McCain's voice was pleasant, but firm. He and JT definitely decided not to sell. Not to him, not to Venkman, not to anyone.

Belinski stared at the receiver after Buddy disconnected. After twenty years in real estate, he could sniff a sale better than anyone could, and deep down, he had feared this was a no-go from the beginning. He mentally added up his future commissions already on the books. He looked around his office and wondered what everything he owned would bring at a yard sale. No way near enough. Even if he could come up with the money to pay his debt plus the vig, Templeton might not accept it.

Cyrus Templeton wanted Blood Mountain, Belinski had promised him Blood Mountain, and Templeton had a reputation for the way he took care of people who didn't deliver what they promised.

When Belinski finally hung up the receiver, he was soaked with sweat. It dripped off the little tuft of hair he had at the back of his head, down his back, and pooled up in the roll of fat above his waist, soaking his shirt. He needed a shower and decided he might as well go home.

⌘

Stanley could smell the cabbage cooking before he walked into the kitchen. Stella was preparing *golabki* for dinner. Tender cabbage leaves stuffed with a mixture of seasoned ground pork and rice was one of his favorites that Stella didn't have the energy to prepare often. She hated the smell, too.

Belinski watched her for a moment. Standing over the boiling pot, Stella carefully lifted the cabbage leaves and set them aside.

"Stanley, what are you doing?" she asked, her face flushed with steam.

"Just watching you," he answered.

Stella looked at him, puzzled. She was even more puzzled when he bent over and

308

kissed her on the cheek. "Did you have a bad day?" she asked.

"Did I have a bad day?" Belinski repeated. He wanted to scream that he had experienced the worse day in his entire life but he barely had the energy to speak. "Not so hot," he finally admitted. "I lost a sale."

"Oh, I'm sorry." Stella's eyes were wide and sympathetic.

Belinski made a face as if to say it wasn't that big of a deal. "I'm going to take a shower and then I'll be in the office," he said, and left the room.

Stella had hoped a traditional meal of his favorite Polish foods would improve her husband's mood and the three of them could sit around the table and pretend to be a normal, happy family. She watched her husband slog out of the room.

Giving her attention back to her cooking, she carefully wrapped each cabbage leaf around a short log of pork mixture. She sautéed each little packet, and placed them in a square glass dish and poured some broth over the top. When she finally put the dish in the oven and cleaned up the kitchen, she realized how tired she was.

Belinski had closed his office door, then sat in front of his computer and tried to calm the anxiety that nearly overwhelmed him. He resisted reaching for the bottle of Grey Goose hidden in the bottom drawer because he knew of all times, this was the time he needed a clear head. When he pulled up the word processing document, he typed in the date and salutation: To Whom It May Concern.

⌀⌀⌀

Later that evening, Stella studied her husband from the kitchen, the way his chest rose up and down when he slept, all stretched out and relaxed on the sofa. She was happy the way the dinner had gone. Their boy was cordial for once, and Stanley voiced his appreciation of the meal she had prepared. She wiped her hands on the towel and decided not to wake her husband. This was the first time in weeks she had seen him at peace.

As she headed toward the bathroom, Stella spotted Stanley's clothes lying in a heap in front of the door. She looked at them and her mood quickly changed to one of suspicion. Lately there had been too many changes of clothes, too many trips to Las Vegas, too many phone calls she wasn't allowed to hear.

Stella picked up her husband's pants and smelled them for sex and his shirt for the scent of another woman. Well, at least no woman this time, she thought. She emptied the pockets, put the contents on the dresser, and hung up his suit. As an afterthought, she slipped her hand inside his jacket pocket.

She pulled out some papers and quickly realized they were overdue credit card bills. Her heart sank. She carefully folded them up and put them back, still feeling uneasy. They had been broke before; but Stanley had never acted like this before.

She put the rest of the clothes in the hamper, feeling certain she was missing something. Stanley hadn't been himself for months and wouldn't talk about it, either. Whenever she tried to question him, he just raised a ruckus. Whatever the problem was, Stanley was keeping it to himself. Stella pulled a clean nightgown out of the drawer. One of these days, she thought to herself, she'd stop caring.

❧❦❧

Alex had spent the last hour in a near-mindless state of highway hypnosis before he finally reached the city limits of Yuma. He checked his watch. Even with the road crews fixing the highway over telegraph pass and the hold up at the border patrol inspection, he wouldn't be late by much. He turned off the freeway at Exit 2 and followed Marty Griswald's directions to the Mexican restaurant. Once inside, he spotted his boss sitting in a private booth against the back wall wearing one of his famous pink shirts.

"I'm glad you could meet me, Chief," Alex said, joining him.

"No problem. I had to come to El Centro anyway, and it took less time to get here than my morning commute," Griswald said with a grin. "Besides, I hear they have world-famous nachos here."

"Sounds good," Alex said, scanning the room, his eyes resting on a large mural of a man with a big sombrero on his head, mounted on a black horse. A middle-aged woman dressed in a peasant blouse and colorful skirt came over and quickly took their order. When she left, Marty leaned back in the booth. "Well, how is it going?"

"I've made some progress," Alex said. He lowered his voice and hunched forward. "The cocaine originates in Bogotá, just like I thought. It's one hundred percent pure, but they cut it in Mexico City. Next they fly it into an area outside Alixta, about forty miles from the border, then cut it again and repackage it, and finally truck it to a farm close to the border."

Griswald rubbed his jaw. "I suppose now you're gonna tell me a crop duster flies it across the border into Mesquite."

Alex smiled his crooked smile. "Just skimming over the wall." He pulled out his cell phone and tapped up a photo. "Here's a picture of the pilot, not too clear, but he's untouchable."

"How's that?"

"He's the brother-in-law of the chief of police," Alex stated matter-of-factly.

"Huh," Marty grunted. "So what else is new? Well, at least Mesquite's a small town. It shouldn't be that hard to locate all the landing strips."

"Actually, I think I've found it. What I can't figure out is how they land in the dark on the side of a mountain, unload, and get the stuff to LA right under our noses."

They both stopped talking when the waitress brought two Dos Equis to the table with a pair of frosted mugs in one hand. Alex poured his beer into one of the mugs and took a long sip. "Did you get that information on William Chaffee, aka Weezer?"

Griswald just looked at him. "I can't believe that name. He sounds like a complete nerd."

"You'd never convince the ladies of that. He's very good looking and as smooth as the top of your big black head."

"Very funny, Alex."

A picture of Weezer putting the moves on Rachel suddenly popped into Alex's mind and he drummed his fingers nervously. "So, what have you got on him?"

Griswald pushed a folder over to him. "He lives in an apartment but owns a used seventy-five foot yacht that he keeps in LA, with no banknote on it. Goes there nearly every weekend to work on it. Parties with the locals on occasion but is pretty private about his life. No big bank accounts. Looks like he puts all his money in the boat."

"What about off-shore?"

"That's anybody's guess. But he registered for a passport two years ago and took a trip to the Cayman Islands."

Alex leaned back and folded his arms in front of his chest. "I find it hard to believe an entomologist can afford a seventy-five -foot yacht. Even if it was an old tub, retrofitted, it has to run a million, at least."

"Yeah, and no record of time payments. No big cash deposits or withdrawals." Both men stopped talking and waited while the waitress set a large plate of nachos on the table. Marty glanced at her nametag. "Those look great, Delores, thanks."

"Another beer?" she asked.

Alex nodded and held up two fingers, then picked up a nacho that had a long tail of melted cheese stuck to the plate. He swirled the cheese around with a finger from his other hand and plopped the whole thing into his mouth. "Oh, man, this is good."

Griswald picked the jalapenos off the top of one of the nachos and noticed Alex watching him. "My ulcer is kicking up." He downed the nacho in one bite and turned back to Alex. "So, any more on the murders?"

"Dewey thinks, and I happen to agree with him, both victims were in the wrong place at the wrong time." Alex let his gaze wander back to the large mural on the wall. "Both on the night of the new moon, a lunar month apart. Everything was pitch-black and both victims had a view of the landing strip."

"Any leads?"

"They found a trace bit of tissue from underneath the fingernails of the woman who was killed. It looks like she put up a fight. The results aren't back from the lab, but with any luck, we should know in a few days."

"So I assume you'll be setting up on the...what night is it?"

"The twelfth of November, if they're running true to schedule. But we're checking the area every night, just in case."

"Well, when you need us, let me know." Griswald leaned forward and Alex could see the scars on Marty's skin left from a bout of teen-age acne. "You know everybody in the whole precinct wants in on this one," he said.

Chapter 14

Alex drove back to the Mesquite Mountain Inn and pulled into a parking place close to the front of the cafe. Coming inside, he noticed the commotion and asked Heather what was going on.

"We're having a trial run on our desert tours and open house party, all at the same time," she answered, without stopping her work.

Rachel walked in on them from the kitchen and turned to Alex. "Hi, stranger. I haven't seen you around for a while. We have room for one more guest if you want to come out to the landing strip with us."

"What?" Alex was stunned by Rachel's choice of location. He gently took her elbow and steered her out to the hallway. "What are you doing?" he whispered. "Are you insane?"

"Listen, the airstrip is the perfect place to set up our gourmet meals for the Hummer desert trips" she replied calmly. "It's flat, it's in the shade of the mountain, and it's a fun ride there."

"That's not what I mean, Rachel, and you know it." Alex struggled to keep his voice low.

Rachel talked on, ignoring Alex's rising stress level. "Alex, we are simply a group from the hotel going out for a picnic. We don't know anything. We don't suspect anything. We're just a group having a party. If anyone happens to see us out there, and it makes him a little nervous, so be it. We might rattle enough nerves to get a reaction from someone."

"I don't like it, Rachel."

"We will have two women and three men. If you come, it will be four men. I think we'll be safe enough. Besides," Rachel said, looking him over, "you look like you could use a drink."

Heather appeared in the doorway. "Hey kids, we're ready to go."

The Hummer and JT's pickup rolled out of the parking lot about four o'clock, carrying the two women, four men and two vehicles packed full with supplies.

After they had driven the twisted, undulating trails up the mountain and arrived at the old airstrip, the men unloaded the trucks near a large table already set up with six chairs. The women dressed the table with a damask tablecloth, china, and stemware.

"What a perfect place." Heather walked around, surveying the area. "It's flat; we have shade and an incredible view. We're even protected here if there's any wind."

Rachel shot an I-told-you-so look at Alex, who was helping JT set up the grill. Then she and Heather started working with Henri to set up preparations for the meal.

When everyone seated themselves, Buddy opened a bottle of Artadi Roija and a California Pinot Noir while Henri served the first round of tapas.

The group discussed ways in which they could set up with less time and effort, and by the time they were into the second bottle of wine and another course of tapas, they had already agreed on some improvements.

Buddy stood up and walked to the wall of mountain behind them. "Look, this area has a nice, flat, straight surface. We could bolt in some brackets right along this edge to hold a portable work space." He had started pacing off the back edge when he tripped and fell.

Rachel jumped up to help him, but by then he was already up and brushing the sand off himself. "That's interesting," he said, crouching down again, feeling around at his feet. "I know I tripped over something…here."

Rachel knelt on one knee and felt what appeared to be a sand-colored pipe sticking out of the ground about an inch. She helped brush away the sand around it and tapped on it with her ring. "It's metal."

Alex came over and inspected the pipe, then walked slowly in a direct line until he found another pipe about fifty feet away. Buddy found the next one, and then Alex walked to the opposite side and found the same kind of pipes, also laid out in a straight line.

"What are they?" Heather asked when they returned to the table.

"My first thought is that they are a base that held some kind of light system to guide in the planes when the landing field was in use," Alex said, "but of course there's no electricity."

"What about reflectors?" Buddy asked. "I heard about this guy who manufactured a type of reflector that could be set up for a temporary landing strip in places that didn't have electricity. The plane's own landing lights would create enough reflection to guide it in."

Alex slapped his head. "Of course."

JT turned to Buddy. "Are you thinking you would use this strip to bring in your Bonanza?"

"Are you kidding? I wouldn't even try it here in the daylight."

"Well, that's a relief."

Henri interrupted their discussion with a call for dessert.

When the group came back to the table, they found their chef had set up two fondue pots filled with chocolate, blended with liqueur. Bowls of strawberries, banana chunks, and small squares of pound cake were available for dipping. He had also arranged a vintage port, along with coffee, on the table.

After dessert, Henri started packing up what was left from their party while Alex, Rachel, and Heather started walking toward the large outcropping of rocks at the end of the airstrip. "What a wonderful idea for a party,

Rachel," Heather gushed. "It should be a big hit with our guests."

"Thanks. We'll have to charge plenty to make it work, but I think enough people would be willing to pay to have such a wonderful experience."

When they arrived at the end of the airstrip, Alex began to climb up the rocks that led to the peak. He turned and helped Rachel up, but Heather said she was going to go back to the table. "You go on ahead," she told Rachel.

Rachel started up the hill but stopped partway, wondering if she should go any farther. She started forward again and when she pulled herself up, a couple of chunks of rock by her feet dislodged themselves and tumbled down the hill. One skipped down the hill making a metallic sound, then suddenly and silently disappeared. The one right behind it tumbled and bounced, then hit the bottom boulder with a hollow-sounding thud before it fell to the landing strip.

"Hey," Rachel turned toward Alex. "Did you hear that?"

Alex was already on his way toward her. When they reached the bottom, they began removing the pile of debris stacked against the boulder.

"What are you doing?" Heather asked, walking back.

"Looking for secrets," Alex replied, and asked Heather to bring JT and Buddy over. A few minutes later, with JT and Buddy helping, Alex and Rachel had removed all the rocks and debris from the rock wall.

"If I'm right, we might find something of interest here," Alex said.

The three men pushed the large boulder, amazed at how easily it moved for its size. "Pretty good job, for a man-made boulder," JT said, running his large hands over it. "But why on earth would someone go through the kind of time and effort it would take to make it?"

"One more push," Alex said, "and we'll know."

The rock moved and Heather gasped. "It's a cave."

The group stepped inside and waited while their eyes adjusted to the semi-darkness.

Rachel pointed to two large lanterns near the entrance, each fitted with a green lens around its circumference. "Look. There's our UFOs."

"Well, I'll be." JT stood at the entrance, shaking his head.

"What's that awful smell?" Heather asked.

"What's that thing?" Buddy pointed to the hopper in the middle of the room. "It looks like a giant funnel."

"I think it might be something close to that," Alex said. He walked over to a container behind the lanterns and lifted the lid, looked inside, and put the lid back before anyone else could see the Tyvek suits inside.

"What was in there?" Rachel asked.

"Nothing important," Alex lied. "You know, I think we need to get out of here. Heather is right about the smell. It's bad and could even be poisonous."

When they arrived outside, everyone was glad to breathe the fresh air.

"So you think we found the old gold mine?" Buddy grinned.

"Looks that way," Alex agreed, "But someone's used it for another purpose recently."

"You mean recently, as in the last few weeks?"

"It's possible. I think Dewey needs to come out and look at this."

"Do you think this could have anything to do with the murders?" JT asked.

"Anything's possible. That's why we need to put everything back exactly the way we found it and let the law handle it." He looked around. "Everyone, please stay out of this area until Deputy Tucker can check it out, and, don't say a word to anyone." He looked directly at Rachel. "That means you, too, blondie."

∽∾∽

Night breezes flowed down the mountain through Rachel's window and into her bedroom. She turned over in bed, flipping her pillow around, looking for a cool spot. In the last three hours, she had twisted and tossed the bedding into a mess while she pondered the discovery of the cave and what it meant. She checked the clock again. It was two-thirty and she was no closer to sleep, nor to the answers to the questions the cave presented.

She finally slipped out of bed, felt her way to the refrigerator, and poured out a glass of milk in front of the night light, knowing she was out of anything else that would help her sleep. Then she dug around the cupboard for a cookie and came up empty handed.

Wandering over toward the veranda, she unscrewed the safety lock on the glass door and opened it with a pop. Below her, colored lights had turned the gardens into a fairyland, and the fragrance of white honeysuckle swirled in the air.

Rachel stood, leaning against the wrought iron railing, hidden by the shadows and savoring the breeze that flowed against her. She gazed mindlessly at the gardens, letting her eyes wander along the vines that lined the sidewalks.

She blinked. A moving shadow had caught her eye. She blinked again, scanning the darkness in front of the guest rooms on the east side, her adrenaline kicking in. The shadow moved again.

Slipping back into her room, she grabbed her cell phone. "Where are you?" she whispered.

Toro picked up. "Behind the main building, toward the west side."

"I think I saw something move in front of the east side guest rooms."

"I'll go check it out," he said, already moving in that direction.

Rachel pondered a moment then punched in another number. "Did I wake you?"

"No," Alex answered. "I'm actually in my truck on the way back from the landing strip, heading up the hill."

"I just called Toro and told him I thought I saw something move over by the eastside guest rooms. I'm going over there."

"No, Rachel, stay where you are," Alex said. "Wait, what's this?" Alex slammed on his brakes, fishtailing in the dirt.

"What? What's going on?"

"Nothing. There's a car parked out here, off to the side of the road, down from the entrance. An old beater." He glanced inside. "But it's empty. Rachel...Rachel?"

Rachel was already out the door, skimming down the stairs, racing down the sidewalk by the time Alex was back in his car. She saw Toro running across the parking lot, the light from his flashlight bobbing up and down in the shadows. Then she spotted the intruder as he tore down the hill, sprinting through the parking lot that fronted the guest rooms.

He's headed for the road, she thought. *The car Alex found has to be his.* She raced toward the road herself, hoping to intercept the man.

Glancing in Toro's direction, her heart sank when she saw he was trailing too far behind to do much good. She cut through the courtyard, jumping over plants and rocks. *Faster*! Her mind screamed. She noticed the intruder in the light, already approaching the corner. She had gained on him. She pushed herself to run even faster, her long legs an advantage over the heavily dressed man.

The man in black reached the corner and Rachel was just a few feet away when the lights on Alex's truck flashed on them. The intruder, clearly visible now, wore a black ski mask covering his head.

Alex stomped on his brakes and Rachel lunged for the masked man. She caught the hood of his sweatshirt and jerked him back and he suddenly turned and blocked her with his body weight and with his beefy arms knocked her hard to the ground. She landed with a thud and skidded on the gravel shoulder first, the breath knocked out of her.

Toro charged forward, having gained a few seconds on the intruder. He tackled the man's legs, knocking him face first into the gravel. The man appeared stunned for a moment then suddenly twisted over on his back and raised a gloved hand gripping a knife.

Alex jumped out of his truck and yelled, "Hold it! Police!" followed by a click of his revolver. Both men on the ground froze. Toro grabbed the man's wrist and tossed the knife.

Rachel brushed the loose gravel off her arms and legs and hobbled forward. Toro was lying across the fallen man, both of them prostrate, both breathing rapidly.

Alex snapped a pair of handcuffs on the masked man. Toro rolled to his feet and yanked the intruder upright.

"Wait. Please allow me." Rachel insisted. She reached for the intruder's mask, grabbed it, and yanked it off his head. Her face registered shock and she was speechless when she recognized the man.

∾◌∾

Eddie Porcini cracked his knuckles while he waited for Marino to get off the phone. He thought about how his mother always told him his knuckles would get big and ugly if he cracked them. She was wrong. His knuckles were big, all right, and why not? He was a big man, but his knuckles weren't ugly and they were very, very strong. He could knock out a guy with one punch or knock out four teeth with his bare fist and hardly feel it.

Not only was Eddie tough, he also was smart. He got where he was in the organization because he could think on his feet and knew how to follow orders, Vittorio Marino's orders. He had taken out eight men during his lifetime; three of them had been cops.

The last one, Angelo, was a mistake, that was true. Angelo, or whatever the cop's real name was, just wouldn't talk. Eddie knew he had worked him over pretty bad, but he hadn't meant to kill him. Sometimes he underestimated his own strength, especially when it came to undercover cops.

Eddie knew Marino was mad about Angelo's death. Their operation had been doing good in Arizona for at least a couple years and if that Angelo had not infiltrated the organization, it still would have been good. Now they weren't so sure.

They didn't know how much LAPD knew, how much Angelo had been able to pass on before they found him out. Eddie knew it was his fault the cop died, but figured Marino was over it already. He also knew Marino needed him and trusted him.

He guessed this meeting was about the little problem with their two guys in Arizona. First, they killed a wetback and made it look like a suicide. No big deal. Then they kill some old schoolteacher and all hell breaks loose. Now the little twerp wants to quit before the November shipment. No way was that gonna fly.

Eddie figured it was obvious why Marino called him to come in for a meeting in the middle of the night.

He was a fixer; and Marino had a problem that needed to be fixed. After fifteen years of working for Marino, Eddie was practically a mind reader. When his boss made a decision, it didn't matter what day it was, what time it was. He acted.

Marino hung up the phone, leaned back in the leather chair. "I need you to go to Mesquite, Eddie." He looked past Eddie and drummed his fingers on the arm of the chair, as if he were considering something one last time. His fingers stopped. "You gotta fix our little problem down there before those morons screw up something else."

Eddie rubbed the calluses on his knuckles. "Yeah, boss," he said, standing. "I'm already

on it." He nodded, and accepted the large envelope Marino handed to him.

Chapter 15

Rachel stood staring at the intruder. "Stanley? Stanley Belinski?" was all she could say, too dumbfounded to say another word. Stanley hung his head and silently stared at the ground.

Within seconds, Deputy Tucker pulled up in his truck, lights flashing and siren wailing. Just as he stepped out the door, an explosion rocked the ground and a fireball blew out of room 307. Tucker fell against his truck and hung on.

Window glass showered the sidewalk and the ear-splitting shriek of a smoke alarm wailed through the night. Smoke and fire burst outward and upward.

Alex and Rachel ran back to the guest rooms and grabbed the extinguishers mounted on the exterior wall. They raced toward the fire as flames shot out of the window, licking upwards at the roof. The newly installed sprinkler system spewed water everywhere.

Rachel emptied the contents of her extinguisher at the place the window had been just moments before. Alex sprayed the open door and wooden frame while Toro arrived behind them with another extinguisher.

JT was jolted awake by the explosion and came running.

Within minutes, a fire truck shrieked to a noisy stop in front of them and four men leaped out, dragging hoses, and Alex and Rachel stood back.

Heather raced over, her nightgown flapping at her legs. She took a good look at her sister. "Are you okay?"

Black soot mixed with water covered Rachel, streaking her hair and blotching her face. Blood oozed from abrasions on her arm and legs, and the nightgown that fell just below her hips was ripped, blackened, and totally soaked.

Rachel grinned, green eyes glowing from her soot-covered face. "Never been better."

෨෬෭

Morning sunshine peeked through the bamboo shades of the Hibiscus Cafe, glazing the booth in the corner with a warm glow. Fabric in a tropical design now covered wide cornices and hung in long drapes between the windows, softening the light.

Buddy blew on his coffee and took a cautious sip. "JT, I have to admit you were right about Toro, and you know I had my doubts when you hired him." He pulled an ice cube out of his water glass and plopped it into his coffee. "I hate to think of what would have happened if he hadn't been there."

"I know." JT turned to Rachel with warmth and gratitude in his eyes. "If you hadn't been up at the right time and seen Stanley's movement..." he said, letting his voice trail off, shaking his head.

Rachel blushed. She had been nervously folding her paper napkin into a fan and now pushed it aside. "Thanks, JT. I'm glad my insomnia has finally found a useful purpose." More than the praise, she was happy to be off JT's list of delinquent adults.

Heather sat cheerfully, just grateful for the peace between the two of them.

A gust of wind blew inside when the front door opened, sprinkling the floor with sand.

"Hey, look what just blew in," Buddy joked, and waved at their unexpected guest. "I thought you said you were going to sleep through lunch."

Alex walked toward the group, dragging himself along as if he were towing a ton of rocks. A day-old beard covered the bottom half of his face. "Yeah, that was just a happy thought, I guess." He sank down into the seat next to Buddy.

"You look like you could mainline some caffeine," Buddy said, pouring him coffee from the carafe on the table. "What's going on?"

Alex quickly swallowed a half cup of coffee and refilled the mug. "Our friend, Mr. Belinski, is currently a guest of the county of Yuma and is conferring with his attorney. But he doesn't seem to be particularly eager to get bail."

"Really? Isn't that interesting?" Rachel scanned the surprised faces of the group. "For whatever reason, I'm glad. At least we don't have to stay up nights watching the hotel, wondering if we're going to get torched."

"Oh, I wouldn't be too quick to drop the security." Alex took another long swig from his cup, leaned against the booth, and closed his eyes.

"Why?" Buddy looked puzzled. "Don't we have our man?"

Alex opened his eyes. "For starters, Stanley's not talking. We don't know who else is involved, or even if there is anyone else."

"What about the murders?" JT asked.

"Stanley absolutely denies having anything to do with that. His alibis are airtight; and frankly, even if they weren't, I don't think he's our man. It just doesn't feel right."

"He's big and strong enough to be," Rachel said, tracing her finger around the rim of her glass. "But the motive to kill…" She pondered that thought. "I can't believe he'd murder two people simply for a commission. Surely, he has other places he can sell. There are only two real estate agencies in town, for Pete's sake."

"I think we need to find out a lot more about Mr. Belinski and his dealings before we can draw any accurate conclusions," Alex said, refilling his cup again. "It's possible he didn't have anything to do with the murders. Maybe he just set the fires in a desperate attempt to scare you off."

"Well, we did have at least one other offer for the property," Buddy offered. "I was approached right after I paid off the taxes at the assessor's office. Didn't even make it to my car." He pulled out his wallet and dug around in it until he found the card. "Here you go. Gerald Metcalf, attorney-at-law. I understand he has a lot of farmers as clients."

Alex looked the card over and put it in his pocket. "I'll give Mr. Metcalf a call and see what he has to say."

Heather looked at Alex with concern. "Maybe you just need to get some sleep, Alex."

"Well, I don't know about you, but I'm taking the rest of the day off." Rachel pushed her plate aside. "I think I've had enough excitement for a while." She looked at Alex when she stepped out of the booth. "Come on, you can walk me home."

The wind whipped at their clothes and sand stung their faces when they stepped outside. Rachel kept her head down and mouth shut while they navigated the sidewalk past the guest rooms.

When she reached the stairs to her casita, she turned to Alex. "You can tell me the rest of the story now."

Alex turned his back to the wind and lit a cigarette. "Stanley's still in jail, I just told you."

"I believe you. But I know there's more." Rachel started up the steps. "You can either keep me in the loop or I can poke around myself."

Alex followed her up. "Okay, okay," he said, giving up. "Stanley claims he's being blackmailed, threatened by someone who wants to buy Blood Mountain. He expected to pick up the property cheap at the tax sale, but as you know, that didn't happen. So then, he tried to buy it. That didn't work out either."

Rachel stopped, glanced down at the sand that swirled in the wind around her feet. "Maybe that's why the tax assessor was reluctant to take Buddy's money. He could have had some kind of deal going with Stanley Belinski."

"Could be. It sounds like the assessor made a deal with *some*body. In addition to that, the assessor asked Dewey for the key to the padlock early in August so he could reassess the value, which he did, and loaned the key to Stanley Belinski. Belinski then showed the property to Richard Markman, without the owner's permission, as you well know," he added. He and Rachel continued up the stairs to the sound of wind whirring through palm fronds.

"But why would Belinski try to torch the place?" she asked. "What could anyone have on Stanley that would cause a successful real estate broker to become an arsonist? And why would anyone want Blood Mountain so badly they'd risk so much to get it? Hotels don't make *that* much money."

She stood at the top of the landing, next to her door, and looked around. Her suite blocked the wind and her tangled hair fell back to her shoulders. "There has to be something else here, something somebody else knows about and we don't."

Alex stubbed out his cigarette in the sand-filled ashtray in the corner of the landing. When he turned back, Rachel leaned suggestively against the metal door. Alex stepped up close. "Well, when you figure that out, Sherlock, you let me know."

He kissed her softly on the lips and Rachel felt a twinge deep down inside. They looked at each other for a long moment, and then Alex walked back down the stairs.

The next morning, the hotel kitchen smelled of caramel and freshly ground Saigon cinnamon. Heather leaned through the doorway.

"Hey, sis. You have a visitor."

Rachel wiped her hands on her chef's apron, blotted the steam off her face, and walked into the cafe, immediately spotting the cowboy in the tight Wranglers. "Weezer, nice to see you. What's going on?"

Weezer noticed the strands of hair falling out of the chef's hat on Rachel's head and his eyes twinkled, amused by her appearance. "I was in this end of town so I thought I'd stop by and see if I could take you to lunch." He took a lock of her hair with a finger and gently pushed it back. "But it looks like you're busy."

"Henri is trying to teach me a few things about making French pastry, but I suspect I'm not that good of a student." Rachel laughed and scratched her nose, leaving a spot of flour on it. "And I'd love to have lunch but Rosario's coming in for a dress rehearsal of the open house party. You're still coming, aren't you?"

Weezer reached over and wiped the flour spot off her nose. "I wouldn't miss it for the world, darlin'."

"Good, because I've lined up 'El Banditos' for dancing, and I expect a dance with you."

"Only one?"

"You haven't seen me dance yet."

Weezer laughed. "Show me the new bar," he said, linking his arm through hers and steering her out the door to the lobby. "Are you really going to be ready to open for business on Monday?"

"You bet. Take a look." Rachel keyed on the lights at the entrance and Weezer walked in beside the elegant mahogany bar. The room was decorated in a contemporary style, with dark woodwork and taupe walls and still had that new-paint smell. A parquet dance floor occupied the middle of the room, opposite the bar, and small tables surrounded the open space.

"Pretty classy place," Weezer said, taking it all in. "I like it."

Rachel walked over to one of the booths lining the perimeter of the room and sat down. A swirling red globe of blown glass hung down over the table, casting a sensuous glow. "Heather did the decorating. I'll tell her she impressed you."

"You impress me," Weezer said, his gaze washing over her as he moved into the booth next to her. He looked around. "I can smoke here, right?" and flipped out the last cigarette from a pack of Nat Sherman's.

"Well, not really, but I won't tell."

Weezer took a deep drag before he spoke. "I heard you had another fire."

"What else did you hear?"

"That Stanley Belinski started it."

"Does anything ever get past you?"

Weezer took her fingers and pulled them to his lips for a tender kiss. "It better not, darlin'."

"Well, you heard right. It was Stanley. If Toro hadn't caught him…" Rachel said, her voice trailing off as her gaze flowed past him. "Even so, the inside of the room he torched is completely destroyed. If we didn't have a tile roof and metal beams," she said, looking back at him, her words hanging in the air. She shivered. "But I really don't want to talk about it."

"Okay, I'll change the subject…unless you want more roses." Weezer kept a straight face but his eyes smiled. "I came by to see you yesterday around four o'clock. The place was locked up."

"Oh, we had a practice run on our Hummer desert tours. Henri made a great spread and we set up our fancy china out on the old airstrip on the north side."

Weezer looked away, taking another drag off his cigarette. "How was it out there?" he asked, knocking the ash into the palm of his hand.

"It was beautiful, Weezer." Rachel's eyes lit up as she spoke. "It's the perfect stopping off place for the tours."

At that moment, Buddy came into the bar. He greeted Weezer then happily announced that Rosario had arrived.

"Uh-oh. Time's up," Rachel said.

When they all reached the lobby, Buddy stood with Weezer and Rachel until it became awkward. Finally, Rachel reached out her hand to Weezer. Buddy put his arm on Rachel's shoulder when she shook the other man's hand. "Thanks for coming by," she said in farewell.

"Yes, thanks for coming by," Buddy seconded, but his blue eyes were mocking and his arm was glued to Rachel's shoulder.

"I'll call you, Rachel," Weezer said, totally ignoring Buddy, and walked out.

After the doors closed behind Weezer, Rachel turned to Buddy. "What was that all about?" she demanded.

"What?"

"You know what."

"No. What?" Buddy's eyebrows arched up in innocence.

Rachel looked skeptical.

Buddy grinned and walked her back into the kitchen.

❧❧❧

Eddie Porcini carefully attached the black mustache to his upper lip and smoothed it out. He stepped back a bit and examined his face. The beard he had put on earlier, short and heavily streaked with gray, was so natural looking, no one would have suspected he hadn't grown it. It also aged him a good ten years. He slipped a small gold hoop onto one ear, and studied his reflection and laughed. He was getting good at this.

Leaning closer to the mirror, Eddie spied the gray hairs sprinkled through his sideburns.

He was a big, broad man with massive hands and large, coarse features. Even with the gray in his hair, his appearance alone was usually enough to intimidate. Still, he thought, weaving his hair through his fingers, what would it hurt to touch it up a bit?

On the bed nearby lay the rest of his disguise: a padded vest, a Panama hat with a red band, polyester pants, and a day-glow print shirt designed by someone appearing to be suffering from drug withdrawal. The outfit was perfect. It was garish, it was ugly, and it would definitely draw attention away from his face.

Putting on the fat vest first, Eddie dressed, and then memorized the information he needed from his new ID and credit cards. He counted his cash and put everything in his wallet. A pair of non-prescription glasses, lightly tinted, with thick black frames went on last. After one final check in the mirror, he walked out of his apartment to the rental car that would take him to the location of his new assignment with his new identity of Paul Costanza, tourist from Nebraska.

ငာၒၒ

Several hours later, Rachel stood behind the front desk and gave the man walking toward her a gracious smile. "Welcome to Mesquite Mountain Inn," she said and tried not to laugh at the outfit he was wearing.

"I need a smoking room for tonight." The man cheerfully placed his wallet on the front desk.

Rachel looked at the portly tourist in the gaudy shirt. "You're in luck. It's our grand opening weekend and you get a deluxe suite for the price of a single room."

"Great. What a deal," he said. Too bad I'm checking out early tomorrow. I thought I'd head out to the Organ Pipe National Monument." He slid his driver's license and credit card over. "I'd like to pay cash."

Rachel nodded and punched in the keys on the computer. "Perhaps you can stop back on your return trip," she said, completing the transaction. Within seconds, the receipt popped up. Rachel handed it to him along with a key card, map to the room, and a smile that masked her desire to ask where he found the shirt.

"You're also invited to our grand opening party," she added, giving him a bright orange card. It starts this afternoon at five, right here in the lobby. Please enjoy your stay, Mr. Costanza."

When Eddie walked away, Heather slipped in behind the desk. "Go take a break," she told Rachel. "The party will be starting before you know it."

Rachel thought about the long evening ahead of them. "I think I will get off my feet for a while. Everything is pretty much set up anyway. When is Lupe's daughter coming in to take over the front desk?"

Heather looked at her watch. "Ten minutes. I told her to page one of us if she ran into a problem."

A tape of contemporary western music played softly through the lobby while Rachel wandered by the refreshment tables decorated with bright, striped Mexican blankets and crepe paper flowers. She studied the set-up for one last, compulsive check.

Outside the back door, a warm breeze greeted Rachel. She walked by the pool, making sure the freshly planted chrysanthemums were still intact and stopped to inspect the new stainless-steel grill, gleaming in the sun.

When her casita came into view, Rachel noticed the man who had just registered, entering the suite next door to hers. Our first customer, she reflected, and like people who save their first dollar, she saved the memory of the barrel-chested tourist in the hideous shirt.

❦❦❦

After bolting his doors and closing the drapes, Eddie Porcini opened the black bag he had brought and pulled out his Glock and knife and laid them on the nightstand. He pulled out three pairs of surgical gloves and stuffed them into the pocket of his pants, saving the other pocket for the length of cord he always carried with him.

Pulling back the covers on the bed, he sprawled out on the clean sheet to plot his evening and plumped up the pillows behind his head. Finding the house would be easy. No problem getting there, and it wouldn't take much gas, either. He glanced at his Rolex. He'd have time for a nap, maybe watch a little TV, and leave just before dark.

❦❦❦

Rachel felt wired like a bag of Mexican jumping beans by the time she walked back into the lobby and nervously rechecked the buffet table. She took a deep breath and let it out slowly, trying to calm herself. The result of all her work would soon be evident...if anyone showed up for the party, that is.

Henri arrived, pushing a steel cart from the kitchen. On it was the ice carving, a bust of a man wearing a large sombrero filled with sparkling sugared fruit. Rachel checked her watch and paced until Henri finished putting it in place.

"Did you see the flowers?" Heather asked, appearing by her side. Together they walked to the lobby entrance and admired the huge, tropical arrangement that graced the center table. "They're a congratulatory gift from Claudia Camarino, the owner of the flower shop on Main Street." Heather looked knowingly at her sister. "I don't suppose you had anything to do with that."

"I did suggest a theme," Rachel admitted, "but it was Claudia's idea to send the flowers. She's no dummy. She knows that little gift will come back twenty times over."

No sooner had Rachel smelled the luscious flowers than Claudia arrived, greeting the sisters warmly, her petite figure dazzling in a lipstick-red dress. She quickly checked over the arrangement to make sure none of the flowers had been damaged in transit and made a minor adjustment. *Not only smart, Claudia was elegant, too,* Heather thought, noticing her perfectly manicured hands.

Rachel drifted back toward the entrance and caught her reflection in the glass wall next to the lounge. Her hair flowed past her shoulders and she nervously fluffed it, untangling it from the triple strand of turquoise beads that hung around her throat. The simple black silk slacks and top she wore clearly contrasted with her skin, and Rachel's face took on the look of a delicately crafted porcelain doll.

Buddy walked up to her and looked at their reflection. "You look absolutely stunning," he murmured, his voice smooth and calming, without his usual hint of humor.

The door swung open and the mayor and his wife walked in. The party was starting. The couple was followed by a long string of visitors who lined up at the door waiting to shake hands with the new owners. After introductions, Rachel quickly spirited guests away to the hors d'oeuvre table and offered them a choice of sangria, ice tea, or if they chose to go in the bar, a frozen margarita a la Rosario.

Rachel was quick to point out the remodeled cafe and adjacent dining room. Guests walked up to brass stanchions that allowed full views of the décor and voiced their approval. Even the ballroom, simply set up with round tables and a portable dance floor, elicited excitement.

Rachel glanced at Henri who was presiding over the buffet table. He grinned widely at her, white teeth flashing against skin the color of coffee beans. She gave him a wink and a thumb up.

Signs advertising beer and *carne asada* tacos by the pool appeared in several places in the lobby and many of the younger people headed out that way. Eddie Porcini headed out, too, throwing his bag into the trunk of his car, carefully backing out of his space and avoiding the partygoers.

Once at the bottom of the mountain, Eddie Porcini noticed the sun was setting, but he still had plenty of light to navigate the grid of roads to the home designated on his map. He easily found the fifties ranch. It was low and long, mid-century style, and it was out in the middle of nowhere.

When he slowed down to check out the house, a small group of people emerged from the front door and stopped to stare at his approach. Eddie cursed his luck and made an instant decision. He stopped the car and rolled down the window. "Hi, folks," he jovially called out. "I'm afraid I'm lost and I need to find the Mesquite Mountain Inn. Can you point me in the right direction?"

One of the men eyed him with suspicion, having noticed that Eddie was far out of his way. "We're headed there ourselves," he called out. "Better just follow us."

Chapter 16

Heather was flushed with excitement as she stood near the entrance with Rachel, having their first turn together at greeting duty. She wore a long, colorful, western skirt covering the tops of her cowgirl boots. A blue corset-style blouse, laced up the front, topped the skirt and matched her blue eyes perfectly.

"You look adorable," Rachel told her during a lull in the line of guests. "You always manage to put together the perfect outfit, just like you decorate a room." She touched the western hat that hung down behind Heather's neck. "Even your accessories are perfect."

"Thanks, sweetie." Heather held out her skirt and did a little curtsy. "And speaking of perfect, so is your party."

In response, Rachel brought her hand up to her face, covering most of her mouth, and pretended to rub a spot under her eye.

"Shall we knock on wood? The Venkmans are here."

Looking ravishing, Katerina Venkman strode in like a model in a stunning, long, violet gown, covered with sequins. Tips of platform heels peeked out from under it. She towered over Franz, who wore a dark, custom-made suit.

"I simply love what you did with the lobby," Katerina enthused, pointing with an elegantly jeweled hand. She engaged the sisters in conversation while Franz stood by her quietly, occasionally stealing a glance at Heather's cleavage.

Rachel led the Venkmans into the lobby and invited them to look around and partake of the buffet table. When she returned to the entrance, Heather softly recited her critique of Katerina's looks to her sister: expensive new dye job with hair extensions, Botox on the forehead and cheeks, top quality boob job, and a full face-lift about five years ago. "But the jewels are real," she added.

"Oooh, that's cold." Rachel said, making a face. "But you didn't mention her eyes. That ol' gal has been partying since noon."

A few more people arrived, and after directing them to the buffet, Heather asked Rachel where her handsome cowboy was.

"I don't know, and I'm beginning to worry." When Rachel turned back to watch the doors, Otto Venkman strutted in, accompanied by a tiny but stunning oriental woman. She had dark, almond eyes, gleaming black hair that hung halfway down her back, and a neckline that dipped a lot farther than that.

Nanci Lee smiled shyly when Otto introduced her. When Rachel took her hand, she found it to be light and delicate, like a bird's wing. She caught the way Otto looked at Nanci, and it put to rest her question about Otto's sexual preference. Yet, another took its place. How did two rather homely men manage to land such beautiful women?

Anna, the Venkmans' daughter, was the biggest surprise of all. She had the height of her mother, plus large bones that appeared to have come from a sperm donor. She carried an extra forty pounds of weight and wore no makeup. Blonde hair cut short, along with a tailored pantsuit fully buttoned over her chest, made her look like a Gestapo henchman out of a WWII movie, and not necessarily a female one.

Before the first hour passed, nearly two hundred people had filed into the lobby, overflowed the lounge, and settled out by the pool. JT escaped outdoors and took his turn holding court by the keg of beer. Buddy took JT's place inside.

As guests filtered outdoors, the outdoor host invited them to tour room 306, which was located on the east side of the courtyard, directly across from the pool. The room, a standard guest room, also provided a quick retreat for those needing a nearby restroom.

When Rachel began to wonder if Weezer was ever going to come, he walked through the door. "Sorry I'm late, darlin," he said with a smile and a look that Rachel felt down to her toes. "You don't have your dance card filled up, do you, Miss Ryan?"

"Why, certainly not, Mr. Chaffee. I deliberately left one dance open for you."

"Then, shall we?" He held out his arm to lead her to the lounge.

"Not until you taste one of Rosario's margaritas," Rachel said, steering Weezer to the bar. She picked up the next drink Rosario made and handed it to Weezer.

"I see you have a packed house," he said, taking a sip and scanning the crowd.

"Yes, it's amazing what free food and booze will do to fill up a party."

Weezer laughed and took another sip of his drink just as the band started up a new number. "I believe this is our dance."

Everyone turned to watch the striking couple two-step around the floor. Rachel had suspected that Weezer would have a sense of rhythm and smooth style when it came to dancing, and she was not disappointed.

He held Rachel close and whispered in her ear. That worked perfectly for Rosario who carefully picked up Weezer's glass from the bar, emptied its contents, and placed it in a plastic bag that had his name on it.

Meanwhile, Heather worked her way over to the Venkmans' table. Katerina was on the dance floor with a Matt Damon look-alike while the rest of the family watched her. After chatting a minute, Heather offered to refresh everyone's drinks and reached for Kat's empty glass. "She's had enough," Franz snapped. "And no more for me," he added, more softly. "I'm going outside for a while."

When the music ended, Weezer walked Rachel back to the end of the bar where Rosario had replaced his margarita with a fresh one.

"Wish I could stay longer," Rachel said, "but I need to get back to work. I'll talk to you later."

Rachel caught Heather's eye, pointed to her watch and gave her the signal for five minutes. Once in the lobby, she stopped to check with Henri to see if he needed anything, then moved with ease through the crowd on her way to the restroom. When she finally met up with Heather in the kitchen, she looked shaken.

"Are you okay?" Heather asked, noticing Rachel's face. "You look upset."

"I *am* upset. I just saw a woman doing a line of coke in the restroom."

"You're kidding. Out in the open?"

"No, not hardly. She was in a stall, and you know how when you open the door and there's that little gap between stalls? I couldn't help but see."

Heather's eyes grew wide. "Could you see who it was?"

Rachel dropped her head. "I went into the next stall and looked down. I saw her shoes.

359

Tiny black heels with sequins. I knew right then there was only one person who could have feet that small."

Heather's eyes grew wide. "Otto's date, Nanci Lee?"

"I waited until she came out, to make sure." Rachel nodded. "I was so shocked, I could hardly speak, but I'm not sure she noticed the difference."

"No. I can't believe it." Heather was stunned. "She is so sweet. Do you think Otto knows?"

Rachel gave Heather a look. "You can't be serious. Otto is probably the one who buys it for her."

At that moment, the band in the lounge finished a set, and Rachel's voice bounced across the quiet kitchen. She slapped her hand over her mouth, and she and Heather looked at each other.

"I can't believe this," Heather whispered. "This is such a small town in the middle of nowhere, and people use cocaine?"

"Geez, Heather. Where have you been the last ten years? It's everywhere. I just didn't expect to see it tonight, here at the hotel."

"I suppose you're right. But something else happened, too. I walked in on Otto and

Weezer having a terrible argument in the ballroom."

"Really? How interesting. Did you pick up anything?"

"No." Heather shook her head. "As soon as I stepped into the room, they saw me and stopped cold. I turned around and walked back out."

"Well, I wonder what that was all about." Rachel said, mulling over their discoveries while the music from the lounge seemed to get louder by the minute. "The Venkmans are the strangest family. It may not mean anything, but I will tell Alex when I see him." She checked her watch. "Which should be in about five minutes."

Rachel could hear the laughter before she arrived at the pool area and guessed Buddy was up to his usual antics. She was right. She could hear him telling a joke, complete with authentic Irish brogue, surrounded by a large group of listeners.

A little father on, Lupe was busy cooking on the new grill and handing soft tacos to guests who were lined up in front of her.

What a perfect party, Rachel thought. *I haven't lost my touch.* She spotted Alex beside the waterfall and was about to motion to him when a sudden increase of voices by the beer keg distracted her. A new guest had joined Buddy's fan club. The pompous Deputy Sheriff Dewey Tucker had finally arrived.

"What's going on?" Rachel asked, poking her head into the inner circle.

"I finally got the call from Phoenix I been waitin' for," Tucker replied in a voice loud enough to be overheard. "They completed the DNA work on the skin sample from under Vicky Donovan's fingernails."

Rachel's eyes lit up. "That means they can positively ID the killer as soon as they get a match."

"That's right," Tucker said, with his walrus-style smile. "And it also means yours truly is done for the night. He grabbed an empty lounge chair and sank down into it with great emphasis. "So I'm just gonna sit down right here and have myself a beer." He looked around, quite happy to be the center of attention. "Hey, Lupe," he called. "You got any of them tacos left?"

Rachel slipped away from the pool area and noticed some others doing the same, no doubt wanting to be the first in their group to spread the update about the Donovan murder. She had to concede Tucker did have a good idea about blabbing about the DNA they found on Vicky. Even if he had to make it up.

She walked through the back entrance of the main building at the same moment a man rushed out and bumped into her, spilling his drink, and knocking his glasses to the floor.

"Oh, I'm so sorry." Rachel said, beating the man to the glasses. "Are you okay?" She straightened up and recognized the man as Mr. Costanza, their only paying guest.

"I'm fine," he snapped at her, snatching the glasses from her hand. He quickly put them on and rushed off toward the pool before she could say another word.

Puzzled, she realized Mr. Costanza had a sudden change of personality. His eyes were downright scary and it wasn't his thick, bushy eyebrows, either. She shook off the uncomfortable feeling and entered the lobby in search of something to wipe the spill.

Back on the patio, Otto Venkman set his beer and tacos down on a table. His stomach churned, and he rushed toward room 306, fearing he was going to be sick. Slamming the bathroom door behind him, he vomited until everything he had eaten that evening was gone.

A knock on the door startled him. "I'll be right out," he yelled and quickly finished washing his face. When he opened the door, he found himself staring at the large frame of Eddie Porcini/Paul Costanza.

"Remember me? I was the lost guy." The fat man stood grinning, blocking the doorway.

"Oh, yes, I remember." Otto felt a ping in his gut and tried to step around him. "Please excuse me."

The big man had no intention of moving. Instead, he shoved Otto back into the bathroom, stepped in behind him, and locked the door.

ᏣᏍᏣ

Bits and pieces of conversation floated like butterflies through the lobby. Rachel picked up news of Deputy Tucker's announcement that was rapidly circulating through the crowd. She suspected Dewey's news was more rumor than fact, but it didn't matter. The effect was what he was after, and she reluctantly gave him credit for that.

She looked at her watch. Fifteen more minutes before the band shut down. She glanced over at Lupe's daughter, Amelia, who stood at the front desk. Looking attentive and professional, Amelia signaled Rachel that everything was okay. Chef Henri had artfully rearranged the food that had remained on the buffet table, removing the empty platters, and making sure the hors d'oeuvres still looked fresh and attractive.

Even though Toro and the rest of the help stayed pretty much in the background, they kept the party areas clean and the pitchers of tea and sangria filled.

With everything secure, Rachel decided to sneak a quick break. She needed to take off her killer heels and rub her feet. Picturing those pointy-toed demons going directly in the trash bin after the party, she quietly slipped behind the stanchion that guarded the entrance to the dining room. She headed for the first booth, but when she turned, she jumped back, startled. So did Claudia Camarino and Franz Venkman, who had been sitting in the booth with their arms entwined.

"Excuse me," she said, thoroughly embarrassed, and immediately exited the room. *This evening is playing out like the Venkmans' personal soap opera.* Rachel hobbled back to the lounge and scanned the crowd. The dance floor was now crowded with loud, mostly younger people dancing to a rock song, and she couldn't see Weezer anywhere.

Rosario seemed to be thriving on the laughter and excitement around the bar. A large tip jar was stuffed with bills. It was definitely not Pablo's.

"Have you seen Weezer or Otto lately?" Rachel asked her.

"They both left about fifteen minutes ago," Rosario replied. "And I haven't seen Franz for a half hour."

"Oh, don't worry about him. He's quite happily occupied."

After glancing again at her watch, Rachel signaled to the band to wrap it up. Back in the lobby Henri was removing decimated platters from the buffet, and Toro was picking up the trash left from the guests. Rachel caught a glimpse of Franz Venkman as he slipped out of the dining room to join a group at the far end of the lobby. She shook her head in amazement. *What in the world does that ugly little man have?*

She headed for the lounge, but Nanci intercepted her, looking for Otto. Rachel admitted she hadn't seen him for a while.

"I've looked everywhere for him, even in the car," Nanci confided, obviously worried. "Do you think someone could check the men's room?"

"Certainly." Rachel waved Toro over, left the problem in his hands, and walked out, remembering she was supposed to meet Alex.

❧❧❧

At the pool area, only a few couples remained sitting at tables, sipping drinks in the moonlight. The majority of guests were walking toward the main building with Buddy, laughing and talking. Lupe had already shut down the grill and was busy gathering up all the left behind plates.

JT had just placed an "EMPTY" sign over the beer tap when a clean-shaven, cleaned up, but drunken Jesse Ray Greever staggered up to him and bellowed, "Ya nearly killed me, ya know."

JT looked at the old man as if he had flown in from outer space. "Excuse me? I think you're confusing me with someone else."

367

"Nope," Jesse Ray said, teetering. "Ya shot my plane and nearly killed me. I coulda crashed and killed us all, ya know."

JT was astonished. This man was the crazy pilot. He led Jesse Ray to a chair and sat him down. "Listen, old man," he said quietly, "if I had wanted to kill you, I could have hit you right between the eyes. But all I wanted to do was keep you from buzzing my home and scaring my sick wife."

Jesse Ray reeled back as though JT had stuck him. "You got a sick wife?" He looked confused. His mouth twisted around as he tried to keep from crying. "I had a sick wife, too," he moaned, remembering the woman he had been married to for thirty-five years and the suffering she went through before the cancer took her. "That little weasel never said nothin' about a sick wife."

In spite of his anger, JT felt a surge of pity and gripped the older man's shoulder. "What little weasel?" JT asked. "Was it Franz Venkman?"

"Franz Venkman?" Jesse Ray contorted his face and a tear leaked out. "That tightwad? Heck no, it weren't Franz."

"Then who? Who was it?" JT's grip tightened and Jesse Ray tried to squirm free. "Tell me," JT demanded, leaning right in his face.

Frightened, Jesse Ray's eyes bulged open. "It was Otto. Otto, the kid," he blurted out.

It was Otto Venkman? Shocked, JT loosened his grip. Otto? Why, he had even given that phony little creep and his girlfriend a tour earlier that evening.

JT spotted Toro quietly picking up trash and called him over. He put the keys to the Hummer in Toro's hand and told him to take Jesse Ray home.

Rachel spotted Alex by the pool. "Sorry I'm late. Did I miss anything exciting?"

Alex dropped the cigarette he had been smoking into a paper cup with an inch of beer left in it. "Well, I broke up one drunken brawl, confiscated a few fireworks, and removed one naked lady from the Jacuzzi."

"Oh, that must have been interesting."

Before Alex could explain, Nanci ran up to Rachel, nearly crying. "We still haven't found Otto."

"Did you check the restaurant and dining room? He could be sleeping in one of the booths.

"Good idea," Nanci said. "I'll go do that. I'll check the ballroom, too."

The lounge was emptying out like Noah's ark when it finally hit dry land. Rachel squeezed her way in and came face to face with Weezer. He looked anxious and grabbed her arm. "Walk me to my truck, Rachel."

The force of his grip startled Rachel. "I can't, Weezer. I have a hundred things to do right now." She pulled away from him, and moved along with the flood of people who were leaving the lounge. "I'll see you tomorrow."

"I have to cancel tomorrow. I'm leaving town for a couple days. I'll call you when I get back," he called out, as the crowd pushed them out the door.

"Rachel," a feminine voice cried out.

She turned to see Nanci in tears, her make-up smeared around her eyes. Anna Venkman stood right behind her, with hefty arms folded over her chest. "I'm really worried," Nanci cried. "Anna wants me to go home with the family, but I'm afraid to leave without Otto. What if something happened to him?"

Deputy Tucker stopped when he caught the last of Nanci's words. "What's going on?"

"Otto is missing," Rachel explained.

Tucker handed Nanci his handkerchief. "Aw, Nanci, he's probably sleeping it off behind a bush. Let's go look by the pool. That's where I seen him last."

Rachel glanced at Anna who stood frowning, a steely gaze in her eyes.

"Anna, go ahead and leave if you want," Rachel told her. "We'll get Nanci a ride home if Otto doesn't show up sober."

By the time they met the others by the pool, Rachel was worried. Otto had been gone a long time. It was always a possibility Otto had met some other woman and had taken off with her for a little interlude, but Rachel's gut feeling told her that didn't happen. In fact, she couldn't shake the feeling that something was terribly wrong.

"Did you happen to check the men's room again?" Rachel asked Tucker. "Yep," he said. "Even had a woman check the ladies' room."

Rachel gave him an odd look.

"You never know," he said, making a face.

Heather strode up to them and reported making a thorough inspection of the main building.

"I'm going with the men to look around the area in back," Tucker said, and started walking toward the suites.

Rachel looked at her sister. "You okay, Heather? You look a little peaked."

"I'm okay. Just a little tired. It's been a pretty wild evening."

"I'll say," Rachel agreed. "Did anyone happen to check room 306 for Otto?"

"I tried to, earlier," Nanci said, "but the door was locked. I figured the tours were over."

"Well, let's take another look," Heather said, reaching in her skirt pocket for her key card. "Just to be sure."

From where they stood, the door appeared closed. When they arrived at room 306, they found someone had locked the door from the inside. "He may be asleep in there," Heather said, as she unlocked the door.

He wasn't. The room looked untouched, the bed perfectly made. Rachel opened the closet. "He's not in here," she said.

Heather tried the bathroom door, but someone had locked that, too. Hearing the hum of the exhaust fan, she knocked, and called out, "Anybody in there?" After she knocked and called out a second time, her answer was still the low hum of the fan inside. She prayed there was no one in there sick or unconscious. Hesitantly, she unlocked the door, called again, and finally looked inside.

She saw blood smeared on the floor, wet and blood-strained towels in a heap by the toilet. For a moment, she was puzzled. She reached for the shower curtain, flung it open, and stood rooted to the spot. Someone was screaming.

When Rachel pulled her out of the room, Heather realized it was her own voice piercing the night.

છ૭ છ૭

"Don't go in!" Rachel screamed at Nanci.

She was too late. Nanci bent over the body of her boyfriend with her hands over her face, sobbing.

Deputy Tucker rushed into the room and halted in front of the tub. Otto was sprawled awkwardly; his eyes open, staring at nothing. Blood covered the front of his starched white shirt and had flowed down into the tub.

So much for the night off, Dewey thought, pulling Nanci away from the body. *Good thing I only had one beer.*

It was past ten. Lupe stayed on past her shift, working through the evening and making coffee for everyone still on the premises.

JT sat crouched over, statue-like, in the corner booth. He cupped the mug in front of him with both hands and stared into it, the fragrance of the dark Swedish roast slowly twisting upward in a vortex of steam.

Remaining motionless, he ignored the slow slapping of sandals when Rachel walked in. Not bothering to look up, he acknowledged her presence with a slight wave of the hand.

Rachel poured herself a coffee and stared at a spot on the wall above JT's head, not wanting eye contact either. "Is Heather okay?" she finally asked, knowing JT had already given Heather a sedative and put her to bed.

"No, she's sick," JT answered simply and without lifting his head. "Not only did she exhaust herself working the party, but the stress from finding Otto dead has about put her over the edge."

"I was afraid of that," Rachel said, her voice full of dread. "You need to tell me what I can do to help."

JT slowly lifted his head. His eyes were bitter and his face had the look of a man who hadn't slept in days. "I think you've done enough."

Rachel felt his words like a knife in her heart. "That's not fair," she protested, her voice quavering. "You know I couldn't keep her away from the party. She was having a wonderful time until..." She looked down at her mug.

JT straightened up and leaned back against the booth. "I'm sorry, Rachel," he said. You're right. I can't blame you for this mess."

Without speaking, Lupe appeared and set a bowl of scrambled eggs and flour tortillas on the table. JT and Rachel each took a plate from the stack in the center.

"We might as well eat." JT's voice sounded weighted down with fatigue. "I don't think this nightmare is ever going to end."

Rachel put a thimbleful of food on her plate and took a bite. "I know it seems that way, but don't be discouraged."

JT turned and gave her an incredulous look. "We've had two arson fires and two murders in less than two months and you're telling me not to be discouraged?"

"That isn't what I mean," Rachel answered softly. "You're our strength, JT. You're our leader. You can't give up." She poured more coffee into her cup. "I don't think you realize how much we all look up to you."

"Okay, okay. Save the sermon. I get the picture."

Lupe returned to the booth with a plate piled with home fries. "These eggs are so good, Lupe. What's in them?" Rachel reached for the potatoes.

"*Chorizo,* Miss Rachel, Mexican sausage," she said cheerfully, and departed toward the kitchen.

"You really mean that?" JT studied her thoughtfully against the sounds of dishes clinking in the kitchen.

"What? About the eggs?"

"No. The other part."

Rachel fixed her eyes on him. "Of course, I meant it." She handed the platter to JT, suppressing a smile. "But don't let it go to your head."

℘℘

On Sunday, Rachel checked the main entrance to the lobby, making sure the "Grand Opening" sign hadn't blown away. She wandered through the lobby. It was silent and

376

clean. Rosario sat at the front desk doing the paperwork from the bar, alert for any potential guests.

Rachel ambled out the back door and noticed clouds gathering in the east. They were red as the morning sun approached the horizon. A breeze out of the south blew against the side of her face. "An ill wind that does no good," popped into her head, and she tried to remember the genesis of the line, but couldn't. Her mind was a jumble of memories like the scrambled eggs she had eaten the night before.

She sat at a poolside table and stared at room 306. She wanted a cigarette, badly. If this were the old days, she suspected she would get stinking drunk.

Bright yellow police tape flapped in the breeze, marking off the crime scene. Sheriff Tucker had taped off the area around room 306, marking the door with a big X, and had attached a large sign tacked to it warning all the curious, in both English and Spanish, to keep out.

"Did you sleep?" Alex was walking toward her, smelling of something sensuous.

She pictured herself falling into his muscular arms and him comforting her, and then she averted her eyes, putting the thought out of her mind. "Hardly. You?"

"No, not much." He sat down beside her.

"You smell good. Calvin Klein?

"Thanks. It's Polo."

They both sat and stared at the crime scene. Rachel turned, studied his face, and fought down the urge to ask for a cigarette. "Is this a good time to tell you my theory?"

"Oh, man."

"Hey, be nice. I didn't say I was going to do anything about it."

"Okay, pardon the pun, but fire away."

"It was the Weezer in the guest room with a knife."

He looked at her. "Okay. I'll bite. Why him?"

"Number one, Heather heard him and Otto having a big argument in the ballroom earlier. Number two, I tried to keep my eye on him during the evening, but he completely disappeared at least twice. Number three, I saw him when everyone was leaving and he seemed very stressed, told me he was leaving for LA and therefore couldn't see me. That last little bit of news, by the way, was revealed to me about an hour after he whispered in my ear that he had a surprise for me the next day."

Alex pressed his lips together and turned his head away in frustration.

Rachel leaned over and put her hand on his knee. "Listen, Alex," she whispered. "I think Weezer is getting ready to run. His desk drawer is full of information on Costa Rica. He owns a yacht that's ocean worthy and I found a bank statement showing a transfer of funds from the Cayman Islands to Costa Rica."

From the look on his face, Rachel realized Alex felt aroused from the pressure of her hand that was now on his thigh. She jerked it back and brushed a strand of hair behind her ear. "You know Weezer has expensive tastes so he has to have money coming from somewhere. I'm guessing it's drugs, gold, guns, or some other thing that gets smuggled into the country by plane. Okay, so don't tell me what it is. But whatever he's smuggling, according to Juan's diary, he's been doing it for a couple of years. Very successfully."

"I know," he agreed, looking away.

"You know?" Rachel asked. "You know? Then why hasn't anything been done about it?"

"You're asking me to tell you things I *can't* tell you."

"You're asking me to sit here and watch while he gets away with murder."

Alex looked up at her. "We have no proof he committed any murder. There were nearly two hundred people here last night. Any one of them could have killed Otto. Besides that," he added, trying to think of another reason.

Rachel stubbornly sat back in her chair and glared at him. "Besides what?"

"Besides, I need to ask you again about that Mr. Costanza who checked in at two-ten."

"I already told you everything I know." She turned her gaze to the horizon.

"We ran through Costanza's credit card. He's been dead two years."

Rachel snapped her head back. "What? What are you talking about?"

"The card was stolen. His rental car was also under the name of Costanza. He turned the car in at ten forty-five last night with only enough mileage on it to account for the trip from LA to Mesquite and back. So he never did go look at the cactus."

Rachel moaned, and bent over clutching her stomach, feeling like someone had punched her. "So he could have killed Otto, jumped in his car, gone back to LA, dropped off the car, and disappeared."

"Right, but don't beat yourself up over it, Rachel. It was my job to watch the pool area. I never saw him go into the room. I never saw him, period."

"It seems nobody else did, either."

Alex took her hands. "I know it's possible, actually quite probable, that Mr. Costanza used his ridiculous costume to distract. A fake goatee is easy to apply. However, you did say that when he bumped into you, his glasses fell off, so you saw his eyes. Do you think you could identify him if you saw a mug shot?"

"I'm not sure. Are you saying that I'm the only witness?"

"So far we've found only one other person who even saw the man, but she's not exactly credible." Alex dropped his eyes.

Rachel frowned at him. "Let me guess. She wouldn't happen to be Lady Godiva, would she?"

Embarrassed, Alex avoided her eyes. "Well, she did admit that a large man with a goatee and a loud shirt paid her five hundred dollars to jump naked into the pool. But she was under the influence at the time, and now she says she can't remember what he looked like."

"Oh, that's just great," Rachel bristled. "So am I the only witness to what the so-called Paul Costanza looked like?"

Alex glanced down and nervously rubbed his jaw. "Well, um…" He looked up with a hangdog expression on his face. "Actually, yes."

Chapter 17

It was like the most overused cliché, but it actually rained the day of Otto's funeral. Mesquite hadn't seen a drop of moisture for over a year, but a front from the south blew in for three days, blocking the sun and setting everyone's nerves on edge until the long drought ended. Franz and Katerina Venkman just happened to have picked that day for Otto's funeral.

It seemed like the whole town turned out for the "celebration of his life." Not that everyone loved Otto so much. Politics and curiosity brought in some, and others came for the catered lunch and drinks. The Mesquite Mountain Inn was not asked to do the catering, however. Even though the owners of the inn were not responsible for Otto's death, Kat and Franz blamed them anyway.

Heather paid Claudia's Flowers to send a large bouquet of roses to the funeral parlor but felt it would be in everyone's best interest if her family didn't attend the funeral. JT and Rachel heartily agreed.

The day after the funeral, the rain slowed to intermittent showers while black-bottomed thunderheads moved rapidly across open patches of sky. Whatever the reason, business was nearly dead at the Mesquite Mountain Inn.

When the western sky cleared by mid-afternoon, Heather flew back with Buddy to LA. She figured there was nothing a few days with Justin and Joseph couldn't fix, and there was nothing going on at the hotel that Rachel couldn't handle.

By Tuesday, business had picked up, and the lounge served enough customers to pay for Rosario's salary and the band, but crowds weren't exactly breaking down the door. Revenues from the restaurant were good, however. Breakfast burritos flew out the kitchen to hungry customers, and everyone raved about the rich Swedish coffee.

By that time, of course, everyone in town knew Otto had been murdered in room 306, so it was only the few travelers lured in by the

Internet or the billboard along the highway who actually spent the night. Rachel upgraded them to suites, and those who stayed were extremely pleased.

Secretly, Rachel was glad Heather had a chance to get away. Her extra workload was the perfect excuse to turn down invitations from Weezer, but by Friday night, she didn't need an excuse. The place was jumping.

੭�`੭ჼ੭

"Where's your boss?" The gravelly voice of Dewey Tucker greeted Rachel. She looked up from the front desk. The deputy and Alex stood across the counter looking tired and disheveled. "He's not in bed, is he?"

Rachel gave him a sour look. "Hardly." She picked up the phone and paged JT, then kept her eye on the front desk while she ushered the two men into the manager's office. "So do you have the results?" she asked without preamble.

"Nice office you got here," Tucker said, ignoring her query. He sat down and studied the oil painting that hung behind the desk. "I always liked paintings of the desert even though I see the real thing every day."

"That's very interesting, Dewey," Rachel said, standing in the doorway, "but what about the DNA test results from Vicky Donovan? I don't know if you noticed, but we have a little problem here. People are already referring to Vicky's killer as the Mesquite Mountain Murderer. It's bad for business. People are worried he'll strike again."

"Humph," Tucker grunted. "Don't look to me like they're worried enough to stop drinkin' and dancin'."

Before Rachel could reply, JT came around the corner. "They're inside," she told him with a toss of her head.

JT noticed the sad shape his visitors were in. "You guys look exhausted," he commiserated. "You must have important news or you'd be home in bed."

"Yep, we sure have news, and you're right about the bein'-in-bed part, too," Tucker agreed.

Rachel stuck her head back into the room. "So stop with the blah-blah and just tell us."

"Now just calm down," Tucker said. "We know who killed Ms. Donovan. It was Otto."

Rachel looked at him blankly. "What?"

"It was Otto," Tucker repeated. "Otto Venkman killed Vicky Donovan. It was his skin that was underneath her fingernails."

Rachel stared openmouthed at him. *It was Otto? Otto Venkman? How could that possibly be?* Then she remembered seeing the bandage on the back of his hand when she met him. She toyed with the beads around her neck, thinking. *But he was so small.*

"Are you sure?"

"One hundred percent sure." Tucker stated.

"Do the Venkmans know?"

"They do now."

"They refused to believe it," Alex added. "They said they were going to sue the county, get another test run."

"And?"

"I told 'em to have at it," the deputy said. "I even gave 'em the name of the person their lawyer can call."

"Wow," Rachel exclaimed. "This is incredible. I can hardly believe it myself."

"Same here," JT admitted. He rubbed his hairline, pondering the new information. "Otto didn't look strong enough to kill a cat, never mind a strong, athletic woman like Vicky."

"I suspect he weren't alone," Tucker said. "We ain't done with this."

"So that means there's another problem." Rachel glanced out at the front desk and back at the men. "We have no idea who killed Otto. Or why."

"True," Alex agreed. "But we do have a couple of suspects."

"Speaking of suspects," Rachel said, remembering, "Weezer came by yesterday. He said he had just come back from LA and had heard the news about Otto's murder."

"What did he say?" Tucker asked.

"It isn't what he said, it was how he looked," Rachel answered gravely.

"Which was?"

"Terrified."

Rachel turned her head to check the front desk again and noticed a woman teetering on platform shoes apparently on the way to the restroom. She was singing along, rather badly, with the music seeping out of the lounge.

When the woman was out of earshot, Rachel continued. "Weezer wanted to know all kinds of details, everything." The others were listening to her with rapt attention. "I played dumb, of course."

The deputy squinted at her and scratched his head. "That weren't too hard to do, now was it, Miss Rachel?"

Rachel ignored him and continued. "He looked sick, actually. White. You could see every freckle on his face." She dropped her eyes. "I kind of felt sorry for him."

"Humph." Tucker gave Alex a sidelong glance.

"Think whatever you want," Rachel snapped. "Nobody can act that well. He was scared to death." She dropped her eyes again, a little embarrassed. "I don't think he killed Otto after all."

"Well, that's just great, Miss Sherlock, but he's still on our list."

Rachel bristled. "And what about our cave? Did you manage to get it checked out before you left?"

"Yes, we did," Alex answered softly, hoping to smooth things over.

"And?"

Alex looked at Dewey, letting him be the bearer of bad news. "We can't say," the deputy said.

"You can't say?" Rachel looked from Dewey to Alex and back to Dewey. "You can't say?" She felt a strong urge to smack his stupid face.

"Sorry about that."

"Fine," she snapped. She turned on the heel of her sassy red shoes and stomped back to her place at the front desk.

Alex walked over to her a couple minutes later, hoping to make peace. Rachel whipped around to face him. "At least tell me this. What was that awful smell in the cave?"

Alex looked back at Dewey, but ignored his frown and the minute shake of his head. "It was Parathion," he mumbled, hoping Rachel wouldn't know what that was.

"Parathion? Ah-ha. I knew it." Rachel beamed.

"Knew what?" Alex glanced at Dewey who was shaking his head back and forth.

"I knew I recognized the smell from somewhere," Rachel announced gleefully. "It's the same stuff Weezer gave me in a little baggie to kill the bugs on our bougainvillea bushes."

છરછ

Stella Belinski signed the visitor's log and showed her ID. She waited patiently to be processed, and then sat quietly with her hands in her lap, watching the clock. The waiting room in the jail filled with people of all ages, sizes, and colors, but Stella had never expected to be sitting among them.

At seven o'clock sharp, a large, uniformed officer opened the door. He had the look of someone who had been on the job too many hours for too long a time, and announced visiting hours were open. Stella stood and was immediately swept up in the rush down the corridor. Two young Hispanic women in revealing tops and four-inch heels pushed past her, rushing to see their men.

When Stella finally saw her husband, his appearance shocked her. Unshaven, with dark circles under his eyes, Belinski motioned to her to pick up the phone. Tears began to well up in her eyes when she studied her husband through the reinforced glass that separated them.

"Don't cry, Stella. I'm not worth it," Stanley begged, spreading his hand out on the glass.

"Don't say that." Tears flowed down Stella's face and she stifled a sob.

Stanley watched in agony while his wife tried to compose herself. "We don't have much time and I have a lot of things to tell you."

Stella looked up and leaned toward him. She placed her hand on the glass, matching her fingers to her husband's.

"I'm so sorry, Stella," Stanley moaned. "I was so stupid. I've done so many stupid things."

She saw the raw pain in his eyes. Gone was the pretense, the anger, the vanity.

"You must leave town," he urged, "right away. Take the kid and go stay with one of your sisters. Just leave everything, and don't tell anyone where you go."

Stella heard the fear in his voice and sensed his panic. She finally understood and pulled back, staring directly into his eyes. "You're in big trouble, aren't you," she stated, watching the last puzzle piece fall into place. "Bigger trouble, even, than starting those fires."

Stanley nodded sadly. "There's a letter in our safety deposit box explaining everything. Find Dewey Tucker and give the letter to him."

Her eyes widened. The drone of voices in the room bounced off the concrete walls, the noise a swirling wind inside her head. Bright dots of light passed in front of her and she felt faint.

"There's also a life insurance policy in there for you. It's for a half a million dollars."

"What?" Stella's jaw dropped. She took slow, deep breaths, still gripping the phone tightly.

"It's the only thing I did right the last three years." Belinski's face softened. "If anything happens to me, you and the boy will be okay."

Stella's eyes filled with fear. "What? What do you mean, if anything happens to you?"

Belinski looked at his wife, not able to say the words. He tried to remember the last time he *really* had looked at her, touched her face, cherished her, but he couldn't. All those years, she had been such a good wife, a faithful wife. Stanley shook his head and realized he had been a fool.

ભગભ

The slow rain that fell the day of Otto's funeral soaked into the desert floor, giving it a temporary rebirth. Ocotillos sprouted tiny leaves on tall, thorny spikes, and tuffs of vegetation perked back to life. Even the creosote bushes took on a greener hue.

"One or two more good rains and we'll see desert flowers in the spring, Miss Rachel," Toro promised.

"Any chance of that happening?" Rachel asked, gazing out at the landscape, trying to imagine how flowers could grow out of a bunch of rocks.

Toro shrugged his massive shoulders. "Maybe."

Rachel drove the Hummer up a hill while the words, "Desert Flower Tours" repeated themselves in her head. She imagined herself pointing out various examples of desert flora to the tourists she drove around. It was a fitting name for the gourmet tours she wanted to promote. If Mother Nature failed to cooperate, she'd drop the "flower" part and learn the names of a few rocks instead.

Rachel looked at her watch. They had been out nearly two hours, driving the trails, and were heading northeast toward the airstrip. Stomping on the brake, she ground the Hummer to a stop and jumped out. "Hold it one second. I see something."

Rachel came around to Toro's side of the Hummer with a large potshard in her hands. "Look what I found," she said, showing him her prize. "It looks old."

Toro took the piece of broken bowl from her hands and examined it. "It *is* old. It's a piece of ceremonial pottery," he said almost reverently. "It has spiritual significance. You need to put it back exactly where you found it."

Crestfallen, and clearly not wanting to part with her treasure, Rachel debated what to do.

"If you don't put it back, you will have bad luck."

"Okay," Rachel sighed. "You just said the magic word. I don't need any more bad luck right now. She walked back to the spot where she found the shard and carefully placed it between two rocks, giving it a gentle love pat before leaving it.

Heading down the north face, it wasn't long before Rachel came to a flat area surrounded by boulders. It was the perfect place to hide the Hummer. "Toro, I want to show you something," she said and parked.

She led Toro down a steep footpath that led to the airstrip and was surprised at his surefootedness. Near the base of the hidden cave, they found a flat rock that overlooked the north valley, sat down, and opened bottles of water.

Rachel downed half her drink. "This is my very favorite place on the entire mountain. I could sit here all day and look at that little village down there."

"I was born in that village," Toro said, not taking his eyes off it. "See that big building next to the river? The one with the red tile roof? It's the medical center for the reservation and Council Headquarters."

Rachel turned to look at him. "You're a Native American?" As soon as she said that, she felt stupid. Of course he was. She had so much to learn. "I didn't even know there was a reservation there."

"It don't look different than anything else, 'cept maybe a little poorer." He turned to look at her. "But we call ourselves Indians. Anyone that's born here is a Native American."

Her gaze turned back to the view. "I'll try to remember that." She thought about the time she drove Toro home from work when his car failed to start. "But you don't live there now."

"I lived there until I was seven. My birth father was a descendant of the Hohokams, and my mother is half Mexican and half Co-copah."

A sudden burst of dry wind came from the west, blowing through the boulders with a low, eerie hum. Rachel looked around nervously, almost as if she expected something to jump out of the rocks.

Toro continued in his slow, halting speech. "When my father died, my mother moved into town. She married a Mexican-American who raised me. I think of him as my real father. I even took his name."

"Is he still alive?"

"No."

"Oh, I'm so sorry." Rachel felt a sudden sadness. "I lost my father, too," she said. "And my mother." She looked away, pushing the thoughts of her parents to the back of her mind. "Is all that area down there the reservation?" she asked, wanting to change the subject.

"No, only the area along the river, before it bends. The other side is Old Town Mesquite."

"Oh, yes. We went there the other day. It was interesting and fun." She tipped her head back and looked at the rock wall behind them. "You know, Toro, there's something I'd like to check out. But I need your help and I need you to keep it a secret."

"No problem, Miss Rachel." He looked at her solemnly. "I owe you. I know you stood up to the sheriff for me."

Rachel felt the flush creep all the way up to the top of her head. "You don't owe me anything, Toro. Come on, let's go."

They both worked to remove the debris from the rock wall entrance. Toro felt around the huge manmade boulder that secured the entrance, then easily moved it back by himself while Rachel watched, amazed. They gazed into the interior of the cave and she pulled out a couple of pairs of goggles and respirator masks from her bag. After warning Toro to be very careful not to disturb anything, she entered with Toro a step behind her.

Rachel first checked out the container near the entrance, the one Alex said held nothing of importance. It contained several white jumpsuits sealed in plastic bags. She set them back down and closed the lid. *Why did Alex lie?*

Walking over to the funnel-shaped piece of equipment, she eyed the white powdery residue clinging to the inside and covering the floor around it. Yes, it definitely looked and stank like the bag of insecticide Weezer gave her. But then the whole cave smelled that way.

Rachel walked toward the back of the underground chamber and pulled a flashlight from her bag. She advanced a few more steps and waved the light against the back wall. Quartz crystals and mica chips imbedded in the rock flickered in the sweep of light as Rachel wended her way toward the rear of the cave. A dark tunnel opened up before her, no doubt the entrance to the old mine. Even there, the offensive powder covered everything with a thin film of white. Rachel took another step and heard a click. She spun around at the same moment someone shouted, "FREEZE!" and she found herself staring down the barrel of a Smith & Wesson.

ༀༀༀ

Happy Hour at the lounge was packed. Henri brought out hors d'oeuvres, and people were staying longer and buying more drinks. When JT walked into the lounge, he spotted Weezer surrounded by three young women.

He waved at him and Weezer promptly walked over, leaving his fan club.

"Have you seen Rachel?" Weezer asked, looking around.

"No, she's out with Toro in the Hummer, scoping out the desert trails."

Weezer frowned. "She is?" He began to look around as if she might have walked back into the room.

"Don't worry. She'll be fine," JT insisted. "She can't get into too much trouble with Toro watching out for her."

Weezer didn't look reassured.

"Come on, Weezer," JT said. "Sit down. I'll buy you a beer. Bud okay?"

Weezer nodded, and they headed toward a table near the middle of the room, which was the only one available. Mostly younger people filled the tables, but there were a few older farmers sitting at the bar slinging back icy bottles of Coors. JT waved at the cocktail waitress and held up two fingers. After they seated themselves, JT leaned in close.

"I'm really sorry about Otto," he said. "Rachel said he was an old friend of yours."

"Yeah, we went all the way through high school together. It's hard to believe he's gone." From force of habit, Weezer pulled out a cigarette, and then put it back. JT noticed his hand shaking.

"It's hard for me to believe he was killed right under our very noses," JT mused. "He was right out there with us that night, drinking beer, remember? You were there." He leaned back in his chair and studied Weezer carefully.

"Yeah, I guess I was. I mean, I don't really remember seeing him." Weezer avoided JT's eyes and looked around the room. "There were so many people milling around...and then that girl..." He seemed to be at a loss for words and began to tap the table with his fingers.

"I'm sure you've heard about his connection to Vicky Donovan."

Weezer's face turned pale and his freckles popped out in bold relief. "Yeah, they said he killed her."

"It's pretty hard to believe isn't it?" JT pressed. "I mean, he was such a little guy, kind of delicate looking, you know what I mean?"

Weezer nervously looked around the room again, as if he was searching for an excuse to leave the table. "Yeah, he was small, but he was pretty tough."

Finally, Weezer caught the eye of a petite woman with straight black hair that hung down to the small of her back. He raised his hand and she returned his wave. "Would you excuse me a minute, JT? I need to talk to Nanci Lee."

After Weezer left, JT looked at his watch. *What in the world was keeping Rachel? Why didn't she answer her cell phone?* He was beginning to get a bad feeling like he did years ago when she was always getting into trouble. He chided himself. Rachel was an adult now and she could take care of herself. Yet, he reached over, punched the redial button on his cell phone, and waited. She still didn't answer.

When he clicked off, his pager beeped. "JT here."

Heather's voice sounded nervous."Can you come to the front desk? There's a really mad Indian here looking for you."

When JT arrived at the front desk, he saw the tall, barrel-chested man walking toward him at a brisk pace. Western jeans fit snuggly over his thin legs, and he wore a leather belt boasting a large silver buckle decorated with turquoise and coral.

"You Mr. Carpenter?" the man asked, his weathered face revealing nothing.

JT sensed the anger in his voice. "Yes, and you are?"

"Running Deer," the man said, taking off his black felt Stetson. His long black hair fell past his shoulders. "I'm a tribal elder from the Hoco-Chin Reservation. I'm here to tell you something very important."

The visitor puzzled JT. He sensed the old man was angry under his stiff façade and didn't want a scene in the middle of the lobby. "Would you—"

"Stop." Running Deer raised his hand to silence him. He took a step closer that brought him within inches of JT's face.

"You are making our Creator angry. If you continue with your plans for Blood Mountain you will desecrate our ancestral land and many of our people will die."

Chapter 18

Rachel thought she would faint. No one had ever pulled a gun on her before. From the corner of her eye, she saw Toro with his hands up in the air. He looked terrified.

"What the hell are you doing here?" Deputy Tucker demanded, still aiming the Smith & Wesson at her. He took a step closer, his eyes narrowed and his face glowing red with anger.

"And just what are *you* doing here, Deputy?" Rachel demanded, yanking off her safety mask and goggles. "The last I knew, this was my family's property."

Alex suddenly appeared with his gun drawn. "What the—" he began, spotting Toro and Rachel. His face contorted and he let out a few profanities. Toro looked from Alex to Dewey and back again, hands straight up, still as a statue, the whites of his eyes in sharp contrast to his black eyes and dark skin.

Deputy Tucker lowered his gun and shook his head in disgust. "*You* deal with her." He turned on the heel of his boot and stomped out.

"Let's go," Alex said, with a harsh edge to his voice. He pointed to the entrance with the barrel of his pistol. Rachel walked out first, head held high, nose up. Toro followed closely with his eyes downcast.

Alex holstered his weapon and slumped against the boulder. He drew in a breath of fresh air. "Exactly what are you doing, Rachel?" His voice was tired, as if the proverbial last straw had just fallen on his back.

Rachel arched her neck. "I just happen to be on my own family's property, inspecting some of the land they own."

"Cut the crap, Rachel. I'm not in the mood for that today."

Rachel silently stole a glance at Toro, whose color was slowly coming back. He had even dropped his arms.

Alex glanced at Toro. "I suppose she dragged you into this."

"Leave him out of it," Rachel burst in. "You know it was my idea."

Alex studied her a moment, then sighed in defeat. "Okay, let's get this place put back together. We can talk later." Alex turned and tried to push the entrance boulder back in place.

Toro nudged him out of the way and slid the boulder back with one easy motion. Alex stared at him. Toro held up an arm and flexed his muscles. "Spinach," he said, straight-faced.

Alex had to smile, in spite of himself.

When they finished pilling up the brush and debris against the boulder, he turned to Toro and nodded in the direction of the cave. "Do you know what this is all about?"

"No." Toro squinted at him, still as a woodcarving.

"Okay," Alex said, resigned. "Two people have been murdered, possibly three, and Deputy Tucker believes that this cave is somehow involved. We have asked Miss Rachel to stay away from here for her own protection." He turned his head and glared at her.

Toro made no response.

"We didn't want Miss Ryan anywhere near this area," Alex continued, "for the one, single reason that we didn't want her name on the growing list of dead people in this town."

Alex waited for some kind of response from Toro. "Do you understand what I'm saying?"

Toro thought a while before replying. "I will tell no one there is a cave here. As long as I'm around, no one will ever hurt Miss Rachel."

"I appreciate that, Toro, but you see, now that you know about the cave, your life could be in danger, too."

Rachel looked down, humiliated, realizing she put Toro's life at risk and perhaps those of her family and Buddy. When she looked up, Alex was staring at her, still angry.

"Do I need to say anything else, Miss Ryan?" he asked.

"No." She shook her head. "I'm really sorry." She meant it.

CJCJ

JT stood rooted to the lobby floor. He was speechless, alarmed by the emotion in Running Deer's eyes. He wondered if the old Indian was mentally ill and looked for any sign of a weapon. He was sure he could take down the old man if he attacked, but not if he had a gun. Relieved to see the old Indian wasn't carrying, JT tried to calm him.

"I certainly don't want any of your people to die, sir. I can see you are very upset and would appreciate it if you would sit down." JT's voice was calm and he extended his arm toward the sofa and chairs on the side of the lobby. "I want very much to hear what you have to say."

Running Deer gave him a quick, silent nod, and walked, slightly bowlegged, to one of the chairs and sat down. JT sat across from the old man, giving him his full attention. Close up, JT could see Running Deer's face was dark and wrinkled from many years in the sun, and his glossy black hair was streaked liberally with long strands of gray.

"Why don't you just start from the beginning," he asked gently, hoping to calm his accuser.

The old man settled back in his chair, the overhead lights glinting off his silver and turquoise beads. "I am an elder of my tribe and I am dedicated to protecting the ancient ways and wisdom," Running Deer began in a smooth, tenor voice. "Our tribal council keeps saying these are modern times, but have not asked direction from the elders regarding the land exchange with you."

"Hold it right there," JT said raising his hand, very confused. "What land exchange?"

Running Deer aimed a look of astonishment at JT. "Mr. Carpenter, I do not appreciate disrespect."

Before JT could speak, Toro approached them and did a double take.

The old Indian looked up and squinted at him. "Little Feather?"

"Yes?" Toro asked, staring at the old Indian. "Running Deer? Is that you, my father?"

"Little Feather?" Running Deer arose with slow dignity and embraced Toro. "My son, it's been so long." He held him at arms' length. "I heard you were back. You have not come to see me."

"I'm sorry, my father." Toro looked at his feet. "I was ashamed."

"Do not be. I will always be your father," Running Deer said, an arm still across Toro's shoulder.

Suddenly reminded of JT's presence, Running Deer asked, "What are you doing here, Little Feather?"

"I work here. I have a good job," Toro replied. "And these are good people."

JT stood up. "If it's okay with Running Deer, perhaps you'd like to join us, Toro. There seems to be some confusion about a land swap I'm not aware of."

The old Indian nodded and they all sat down.

Toro turned to Running Deer. "Is this about the new casino?"

The old Indian answered with a slight nod.

"New casino?" JT asked, shaking his head. "What new casino?"

Toro spoke. "First let me tell you, Mr. Carpenter, Running Deer is thought of with much respect on the reservation. What he has to say is true and worthy of your consideration. I have heard some rumors that the tribal council is considering building a casino."

"What exactly does that have to do with me?" JT asked.

"Our tribal council has been negotiating with someone to build a casino on our land," Running Deer began. "Our only available land borders your property north of Blood Mountain where the shadow of the sun falls on it most of the year. We cannot farm the land for lack of sun."

JT nodded, following Running Deer's words closely.

"Many years ago, the red mountain belonged to the ancestors of both the Hohokams and the Cocopahs. It was a sacred place of our religious rituals. The bones of many of our people rest there."

The old Indian stopped speaking as a young couple walked by them and headed out the back door.

"Would you prefer to go to my office?" JT asked.

"No, it is not necessary." Running Deer demurred, and continued. "The problem we elders are concerned with is this: our reservation is now small, both in land size and in people. There are only two hundred and sixty of us left. Mostly we are farmers like our fathers before us. But the men on the council who want to build a casino plan to take our good farming land and trade it for some of the land from Blood Mountain."

JT held the eyes of the old Indian. They were as black as obsidian, the skin around them deeply lined. "Are you saying the tribe doesn't have enough land to build the casino without using some of the land from Blood Mountain?"

"Yes, it is so. We elders object. The red mountain land is sacred land. It should not be

411

disturbed. There can be no building there, no digging on the land, not even for a parking lot."

The lobby had turned quiet. Someone had unplugged the jukebox in the lounge while the band was setting up for the evening, and the silence was welcome.

JT still looked puzzled. "So why has all this gone on with no one contacting Mr. McCain or me about it?"

Toro and Joe Running Deer exchanged glances. "Mr. Carpenter, are you saying you know nothing about this?" Toro asked.

"That's exactly what I'm saying. This is the first I've heard about any of this."

Running Deer looked steadily at JT. "Mr. Carpenter, have you had any contact with Stanley Belinski?"

"Stanley Belinski?" JT's jaw dropped. "You mean the Stanley Belinski who's now sitting in the county jail because he tried to burn down my hotel?"

It was Running Deer's turn to be surprised.

JT leaned back in the chair and clasped his hands behind his head. "Well, for the first time, this whole thing is beginning to make some sense."

The next morning Alex sat on the corner of Deputy Tucker's desk and looked at the calendar for November. There were only seven more days until the new moon, only seven more days until they expected new shipment of cocaine to come in. Alex could hardly wait to get his chance to avenge the torture and murder of his former partner and friend.

He looked down at Rachel who was studying a book of mug shots spread open on the desk. She had her head propped up on one hand, her pale hair flowing down onto the pages of the book. "No. Nope. No," she muttered and slowly turned the pages over. She looked up. "I'm done." She rolled herself backwards in the high-backed chair and put her feet up on the desk.

"I don't think so." Alex picked up the three albums Rachel had already examined and carried them over to a credenza covered with papers and laid them on top of the mess.

A small brown spider scooted out of the way and dropped to the floor. Alex quickly stomped him and turned back to Rachel who witnessed the assassination.

"My hero," she said.

"Now you owe me. That reminds me," Alex recalled, lugging over three more large books. "Did you ever find out the owner of the tarantula, the one someone left in your room?" He dropped the books on the desk next to Rachel's boots.

Rachel took her feet off the desk. "I did ask Lupe who her husband worked for, and she said it was Southwest Chemical."

"The one Weezer manages."

"Yes, just as I suspected."

Alex shrugged. "It doesn't prove any-thing."

"I know, but it's *something*. I'm not sure what, though." She looked down at the stack of books and whined, "Suppose I do find whatever-his-name-is. Then what? Will he come back and try to kill me?"

"Not if we find him first."

"Oh, that makes me feel real confident."

"Never mind that." Alex pointed to the book in front of her. "Keep looking."

With resignation, Rachel began flipping through the pages. Alex walked to one of the windows and stared out through a layer of dirt. A large mesquite tree sat in front of the window, partially blocking the sun, its long branches flowing like lace in the breeze. A gust of wind pushed against the glass with a deep hum and rattled the window. The mesquite thrashed briefly.

"What's going on out there? Are we having a storm?" Rachel asked, lifting her head from the book.

Alex watched the American and Arizona flags snap in the wind, their cords banging against the metal pole. "No, and don't worry about it. Just find our Mr. Costanza."

Rachel muttered and went back to flipping pages. "Can we photocopy any of these pictures?" she asked, after a bit.

"Why? Does someone look familiar?" His eyes lit up.

"I'm not sure. Can you enlarge the top right photo?"

Alex picked up the book and quickly made a copy. Handing it to Rachel, he asked, "Is this the guy?"

Rachel studied it, and then laid it on the desk. She took a pencil and began shading in a mustache and beard like the one on the man who had checked into the hotel. Leaning back in her chair she held up the photocopy. "This is it. It's him. It's Mr. Costanza."

"Are you sure?"

"Yes, I'm sure." Rachel answered. "Who is he?"

Alex was smiling. "His name is Eddie Porcini, and he works for a guy by the name of Vittorio Marino."

"And?"

"Marino runs a big crime organization out of LA. We've never been able to get anything solid on him. But he could be responsible for the murder of my partner, and there's a good chance he sent Eddie to kill Otto."

"Someone in LA sent Eddie to kill Otto?" Rachel's face registered surprise. "But why?"

"I wish I knew the answer to that question." Alex shook his head. "My guess is that he was working for Marino and fell out of grace. Maybe the new moon murders hit too close to home, and Marino needed to distance himself from his people down here.

"Wow," Rachel said softly, letting it all sink in. "But what about Weezer? Where does he fit in?"

Alex took her hands and pulled her up out of the chair. "Remember I told you how there were some things I couldn't share with you because I was afraid you could be hurt?"

"That's kind of a moot point, isn't it? If I pick out Eddie from a line up, he'll know it's me and I'll be the next person in a body bag."

"You aren't going to be in a line up."

"Alex—"

Rachel's cell phone rang, jarring her. Heather's number showed on the screen. "It's me," she said, answering. "What do you need?"

"I need you to come back right away. JT just called an emergency meeting in the Ocotillo Room," Heather said, her voice anxious. "And Rachel, JT said Alex might want to come and hear what he has to say."

The Saguaro and Ocotillo meeting rooms sat side-by-side along the front of the main building. They were divided by an accordion partition, and both rooms shared access to the kitchen. Heather did a temporary, bare bones decorating job on the rooms, which left them acceptable for meetings, but rather lacking in flair. She seemed puzzled when Rachel and Alex met her.

"I noticed another group has taken over our usual meeting room," she said.

"Yes, The Sunshine Club meets there on alternate Tuesdays now," Rachel replied, "and I'm working on the Rotary and the Valley

417

Quilters for some of the other days. Sorry I didn't keep you up to date on that."

Before Heather could comment, Buddy rushed in from the outside entrance. "Sorry I'm a little late," he said, tugging in his brief-case. "Another plane was actually landing when I flew in. Imagine that."

After everyone exchanged greetings, JT started the meeting with little introduction. "I met with the elders and council members at the Hoco-Chin Reservation earlier today about a couple of matters concerning the ho-tel. I also stopped by Deputy Tucker's office to fill him in on what had transpired, and he passed on some information to me that he re-cently learned."

Everyone was watching him intently, and after a quick sip of water, JT continued.

"A few months ago Stanley Belinski ap-proached the president and council of the Hoco-Chin Reservation about the possibility of someone building and operating a casino on their land. As most of you know, the reser-vation borders our property on the north side of Blood Mountain."

Rachel's thoughts immediately went to the day she and Toro had sat on the ledge of the mountain, and he pointed out the Hoco-Chin council headquarters and medical center.

"According to Deputy Tucker," JT continued, "our friend Stanley Belinski was the front man for Cyrus Templeton, who was lined up to finance the operation. Templeton's plan was to build a casino similar to the one he owns in Las Vegas right at the base of the mountain. Although the Hoco-Chin council loved the idea of a casino for the money and jobs it could bring in, the reservation didn't contain enough land to accommodate the casino and parking lot within the boundaries of the reservation itself."

JT reached up and nervously rubbed his hand over his hairline. "According to the deputy, Belinski left a letter with his wife that indicated he had a serious financial obligation to purchase our property for Templeton. That's why he was desperate enough to set fires to try to drive us out."

Rachel nodded. *It makes perfect sense now.*

JT pointed behind him. "Back there, at the base of the mountain, there's an area of about forty acres of nearly level ground. Templeton wanted and needed that piece of land as an adjunct to the property the Indians already own to build the casino on. You see, the only available land the Hoco-Chins own that's wide enough to hold a building of that size is bordering our property, but it's only large enough for the casino itself, not the parking lot and other buildings that are needed to go along with it.

Heather nodded in understanding. "So you're saying Templeton *had* to have our land in order to build the casino. It really must have fouled Stanley up because we refused to sell."

"Exactly. In addition, I found out that Blood Mountain used to belong to the ancestors of the Hoco-Chin reservation several generations back. The land is of great historical and spiritual significance, especially to the elders of the reservation."

"But we'll have bad luck if we disturb any of that land," Rachel blurted out.

JT paused to look at Rachel. "Like we've had nothing but good luck since we started here, right?"

Rachel hunched down in her chair, trying to disappear.

Buddy, who had been carefully listening to everyone's comments, finally spoke, quoting one of JT's favorite phrases: "So the bottom line is?"

JT tried not to smile at his little joke. "I told them we were not interested in getting involved in the casino business in any capacity. I also told them we would not trade or sell any of our property."

Heather breathed a sigh of relief. "Thank goodness. So this mess is all over and done with?"

"Not exactly." Deputy Tucker shuffled into the room, head down, Stetson in hand, and all heads turned to watch him. "I hate to break into your meeting, but I have some news."

JT read his face. "What happened?"

Tucker paused at the end of the table. His voice broke when he tried to speak.

"I–I'm sorry. I just found out s–someone murdered Belinski in his jail cell. He stabbed him to death with a homemade knife."

❦❦❦

The next day Heather carried an open folder into Rachel's office. "Take a look at these numbers, sis," she said, spreading out a computer printout on Rachel's desk. "I'm thrilled we're doing as well as we are, in spite of the murders."

Rachel scanned the sheets until she found the bottom line. "This is excellent. Much better than I expected."

"You and me both," Heather said, sitting down in one of the chairs in front of Rachel's desk. "A little bit here and a little bit there. It all adds up." She glanced at the bulletin board behind the desk. "So how's the sales and catering department coming?"

Rachel beamed. "Well, I booked our first wedding reception for the ballroom in December and have three people coming out next week to look us over for their association conferences two years from now, in November. In addition to that, I'm waiting for confirmation on a large church retreat in March of next year." She leaned back in her chair and asked nonchalantly, "Have you seen Weezer lately?"

"No, and I take it you haven't either."

"He usually lets me know if he's going to be gone for the weekend," Rachel replied, "but he's acted so strange since Otto was murdered."

"Well, I'd be a little strange if *my* friend was murdered."

Rachel sighed deeply. "True, but I don't know what's bothering me about it. I just have a bad feeling."

"Maybe it's your guilt feelings for suspecting the poor boy of murder."

"Go ahead. Rub it in." She began to twirl a strand of her hair around a finger. "Maybe I should go by his office and check." Rachel looked out the office door that led directly to the lobby to avoid Heather's eyes.

"No. Absolutely not." Heather stared at her sister. "Rachel, look at me."

"What?"

"Promise me you won't go to see Weezer."

Rachel rolled her eyes to the ceiling. "Really, Heather."

"Don't 'really Heather' me, Rachel. Just promise me you won't go to see Weezer."

"All right," Rachel agreed. "But I need to go to the drug store and I think I'll just swing by his office and check to see if his truck is there or if he left for the weekend."

Heather narrowed her eyes at Rachel. She knew that was the closest she'd get to a promise. "Okay...but if you aren't back in an hour, I'm calling Alex. I mean it."

Rachel looked down at her watch. "Fair enough."

❧❧❧

Southwest Chemical looked deserted when Rachel drove up. *I wonder if they close up early on Fridays,* Rachel thought, coasting down the driveway. *Weezer might want an early start to LA.*

I'll just check to see if his truck is here, Rachel told herself, continuing to pull around back. Weezer's truck wasn't there; neither was Sergio's, for that matter. *Maybe I should take a quick check of the office.* Rachel parked the Hummer where no one could see it from the road and walked to the back door. The knob turned easily, surprising her, and the door swung open. She hesitated a moment, then glanced to the right and left before she stepped inside.

She saw no one. *Well, I'm in this far. Perhaps he left a note.*

Rachel tentatively walked over to Weezer's desk. No note. *Oh well,* she sighed. *Whatever.* She pulled open the middle drawer, and saw it was filled with the usual office junk, but no papers. She opened the bottom right-hand drawer. It was completely empty. She heard the back door open, and quickly shut the drawer. Too late.

"Did you find what you were looking for?" Weezer glared at her, his voice icy cold.

Rachel's face turned as bright as the coral top she wore. Even worse, she could not think of a single clever answer. "I-I'm sorry," she finally managed, not daring to look him in the eye. "I came by to see you, to see if you were okay. I didn't know if you were leaving town. I just got nosey." Her shoulders slumped and her voice faded away.

Weezer glared at her again for a few moments, and then paced back and forth in front of his desk, as if he were trying to make up his mind about something. "Actually, I *am* leaving town," he finally said, stopping. "And you're coming with me."

"What?" Rachel looked up, puzzled.

"You heard me. Let's go." Weezer grabbed her arm and pulled her.

"No." She pulled back.

"I hate to do this the hard way, but you are now my insurance policy, darlin'." Weezer put his other hand in his jacket pocket and pulled out a small revolver. He pointed it at her face. "You will do exactly what I say or I will shoot you, and before anyone ever finds you, you'll be half eaten by spiders and roaches."

Rachel's eyes and mouth snapped open. "You. It *was* you who had the spider put in my room."

"Just shut up and turn around." Weezer grabbed her shoulder and spun her around with one hand while he held the gun in the other. He flipped the gun over and hit her hard on the back of the head. She fell against him, unconscious, and slowly sank to the floor.

Chapter 19

"Heather?" JT stood over his wife and looked quizzically at her. She was sitting quietly on the sofa with a magazine in her lap, staring out into space. "You haven't heard a word I've said."

"Oh, I'm sorry, sweetie." Heather shifted her gaze to his eyes. "What did you say?"

"I said— Oh, never mind. You've been in la-la land since I came in."

Heather glanced down at her watch.

"Am I keeping you from something?"

"No, but I think, well, I'm *hoping* there isn't, a problem." She looked down at the magazine, her forehead knotted up into a frown.

JT was suddenly alert. "What kind of a problem?"

Heather grimaced. "Well, Rachel took the Hummer into town because she had to go to the drug store. She was worried about Weezer so she was going to go by his office and see if his truck was there or if he left town."

Warning bells went off in JT's mind. "How long ago was that?"

"An hour and a half."

JT calculated the time the trip would take. "Did she have anything else to do?" he asked, knowing she should have returned long ago.

"Only pick up the mail." Heather finally looked at him. "I told her not to go see Weezer and that if she wasn't back in an hour that I would call Alex."

JT immediately began to pace, waving his arm. "You know, she's worse than a ten year old. Sometimes she acts like she doesn't have a brain in her head."

"Now, honey, don't get excited," Heather said calmly. "That won't help. Do you think I should go look for her?"

JT stood still. "No. I think you should call Alex, just like you said."

Heather studied JT's face. "I hate to get Rachel in trouble."

"Call," JT said, pointing to the phone on the table beside her. "Knowing your sister, she's probably already in trouble."

‹›‹›

Rachel moaned. The clanging in her head softened as she slowly regained consciousness. "What happened?" She opened her eyes and realized she was riding in a vehicle, buckled into a seat belt, with a view of the desert flying past her window. She moaned again and turned her head. Weezer was next to her, behind the wheel.

"Go back to sleep," he ordered dispassionately.

Rachel closed her eyes and turned her head away, softly moaning at each bump in the roadway. She could feel the tape that held her hands together, and as she shifted her body, she realized Weezer had also tied her feet. Thoughts bounced around in her mind like ping pong balls moving in slow motion. In a brief moment of clarity, she remembered going to Weezer's office, his walking in on her...the anger in his eyes, the gun. When she opened her eyes again, she tried to focus, tried to concentrate. A blue Interstate 8 shield flashed by. She was headed west; the lowering sun was shining directly on her face. Painfully, she turned her head slightly toward the side window. Shadows were beginning to stretch across the desert. *I must have been unconscious at least a couple of hours.* Rachel closed her eyes again. Better for now to pretend she was still asleep. *Where in the world am I?* She wondered. Nothing had looked familiar, and she had a headache like she'd never had before.

The truck slowed down and Rachel felt it move to the right, heard the turn signal clicking. Shortly, the truck pulled to a stop and made a sharp right turn. Rachel opened her eyes barely enough to see she was on the outskirts of a city. Signs for restaurants and motels flew by and soon the humming of the tires against the highway lulled her back to sleep.

In a little while, the truck slowed, turned, and Rachel's body strained against the seat belt, waking her. She could feel the change when the truck bounced to a more rutted and winding road. She tried opening her eyes again and caught a state road marker with the number 111 on it. She was in California. Of course. Weezer was taking her to his yacht.

By the direction of the sun on the left side, she knew the truck headed north.

It wasn't long before she felt the truck slow, pull into a gravel driveway, and come to a halt. She caught a glimpse of a farmyard but didn't move, and instead, maintained the pretense of sleep.

Weezer looked over at Rachel. Her eyes were closed. Her mouth hung open and he could hear her breathing slowly and deeply. Satisfied, he took his keys with him and walked over to a man sitting on a hay bale.

Rachel opened her eyes in time to see the man, dressed in jeans and a western shirt, hand Weezer a wad of bills. After counting the money, Weezer and the other man walked to the back of the truck. Rachel felt someone jump onto the bed of the truck and felt movement for a short time, then nothing. Through her eyelashes, she watched Weezer and the man walk toward his barn, each carrying a bag of Parathion. Weezer climbed back into the vehicle, looked at Rachel, and started the engine.

Before Rachel stole another look, the truck was already nearing the Salton Sea. Weezer pulled into a small settlement of travel trailers parked in a grove of lush date palms. Once more Weezer accepted a large wad of cash, but this time dropped off one bag of Parathion.

Rachel tried to memorize the route signs they passed and the stops they made, but it was impossible. Her brain was fuzzy and everything kept jumbling together. What had happened to her?

Finally, the truck pulled to a stop and Rachel opened her eyes, fully awake. She saw they were at a gas station, one that was old, run down, and had no other customers.

"Please, let me use the rest room," she begged, her voice dry and cracking. "And I need water."

Weezer thought a moment before deciding. "Let me get gas first."

When he finished, Weezer went into the building, picked up his change, and came out with two bottles of water and a restroom key. He pulled the truck around to the side of the building in front of a dirty-looking door marked with the universal sign for women.

After he opened the passenger side door, he pulled a switchblade from his boot, and cut the tape that bound Rachel's ankles and hands. Trying to restore the circulation in them, she rubbed and massaged them.

"I'll help you get down." Weezer said. "And remember, Rachel," he added menacingly, "don't try anything. The spiders and cockroaches around here are awfully hungry."

He pulled Rachel out. She crumpled against him like a paper bag, nearly slipping from his grasp. "Just take it slow. I'll walk with you."

"You drugged me," she cried, the realization finally hitting her. She looked up at him with hurt and accusation in her eyes. "With what?"

"Roofies. Rope. You know, Mexican valium."

She squinted at him and anger surged through her. "You mean Rohypnol? You gave me Rohypnol, the date rape drug?" Rachel mind spun with the implications of it. "Why?"

"So I wouldn't have to kill you." His voice was curt and cold as his eyes. "But don't worry, your virginity is still intact," he added sarcastically. "Now, walk."

Rachel hobbled over to the restroom, leaning on Weezer, still weak from the drug and stiff from being immobilized for so long. While Weezer unlocked the door, Rachel took a quick glance around. They were in the middle of a bunch of dry California hills and they were totally alone. Even if she could run, where would she go? She couldn't even *think*.

After flipping on the light and shutting the door, Rachel looked around the restroom. The small space was unadorned and none too clean. Even worse, there was absolutely nothing available she could use to help herself escape.

In due course, she zipped up her jeans. When she started to buckle her belt, she had an idea. She quickly pulled off the belt, and with the buckle, began scratching into the old green paint on the back wall behind the door. She flushed the toilet and continued scratching letters as quickly as she could.

"Rachel," Weezer called, banging on the door.

"Just a minute," Rachel answered, then flushed the toilet again, turned on the faucets full blast, and made as much noise as she could while still scratching the wall with her belt buckle. Then she left the belt behind on the floor.

"Took you long enough," Weezer grumbled, when she came out.

"Yeah, men definitely get the breaks in that deal," she answered dryly, and shuffled back to the truck. When she clicked on her seat belt, Weezer ripped out a long piece of duct tape and secured her feet, leaving her hands free for the bottle of water. *If I'm good, maybe I can get him to trust me,* she thought, and began to search her mind for a plan.

೮ာ೮ာ

When Alex walked into JT's office, JT and Buddy were already waiting for him.

"Did you find anything?" Buddy asked, looking anxiously at Alex.

"The Hummer was parked behind Weezer's office, with Rachel's purse still sitting on the front seat," Alex responded, handing the leather Coach bag to JT.

"Well, that explains why she didn't answer her cell phone," Buddy said. "But where could she be?"

"She wasn't in the office. It was locked, but Dewey had Sergio come down and open it. All Weezer's personal stuff was gone. So, we had the landlord check his apartment. All his personal stuff was gone from there, too, plus most of his clothes." A worried look spread across Alex's face. "I hate to say it, but Rachel was right. He's running."

"But what about Rachel?" JT nervously reached for his hair.

"He could have taken her with him as a hostage, or left her somewhere or..." Alex couldn't finish the sentence. "Dewey's already put out an APB on his Ford, and he's checking the space at Long Beach where Weezer docks his yacht. Rachel was convinced he was planning to go to Costa Rica."

"Can you find out if he applied for a visa?" Buddy asked.

"He already had one."

The cell phone on Alex's belt began to vibrate. JT and Buddy listened to Alex's responses, and the call didn't sound positive. When he snapped his phone shut, he said, "Weezer's yacht is gone. He apparently moved it out a couple days ago."

"Where?" Buddy looked frantic. "He must have docked it somewhere else on the coast. There aren't that many marinas that can take a boat that size," he said.

"Right. My office in LA is checking that out right now," Alex said.

"You mean the LAPD?" Buddy asked, looking at Alex squarely.

"Yeah," Alex answered, dropping his eyes. "I'm really sorry I had to keep you guys in the dark. It was for your own protection. We suspected Weezer and Otto had been smuggling cocaine and using the north side of Blood Mountain to expedite it. We wanted to follow it up the line and apprehend everyone involved. But I think he might have been scared off by Otto's murder and decided to run before they gave him the axe, too."

JT ran his fingers through his hair and began rubbing his forehead, assimilating what he'd just heard. "So what do we do now?"

"My guess is that Weezer moved his yacht to San Diego. It's the closest to international waters." Alex's phone began to vibrate again. He flipped it open and looked at the caller ID with a puzzled expression. "Alex Tucker here," he said, and listened attentively to the caller on the other end of the line. There was a long pause, then, "Yes. Where did you say you were located? Is there any kind of airstrip nearby?" Alex's voice and face became animated while he continued the conversation and began to jot notes on a small pad.

Finally, he snapped the phone shut and looked at JT and Buddy. "Do you know if Rachel has a leather belt with a silver buckle that had a sun design on it with a round turquoise stone?"

"Yes, she does," Buddy said. "I remember it because I was with her the day she bought it in Phoenix."

"Then it's possible Rachel is alive. She may have left us a message in a gas station restroom in Thermal, California, and left her belt for identification." He looked at Buddy. "Is your plane available right now?"

"You bet it is. Let's go." Buddy was already getting to his feet.

☙☙

Rachel greedily sucked on the bottle of water. When she was finished, she screwed the cap back on. "Thank you for not tying my hands."

Weezer glanced over at her without saying anything, and then back at the road.

"You know I had feelings for you, Weezer," she said softly, laying her head against the seat, her eyes toward him.

"Forget it, darlin', that ain't gonna work."

"I didn't say I loved you," she chided him. "I just said I had feelings, that's all."

He turned and studied her. "What kind of feelings?"

"You must be pretty dense if you couldn't tell." She turned her face to the window.

"Oh." He paused, almost softening. "Well, it doesn't matter much now, does it? I'm getting out of here."

"You mean, before they kill you, too?" Rachel had a look of genuine concern on her face.

Weezer looked at her out of the corner of his eye. "Yeah, something like that."

They drove on for a few minutes in silence.

"So what was it?" Rachel asked casually. "Diamonds? Guns? Plutonium?"

Weezer remained silent.

"Cocaine?" She looked at Weezer and laughed. "Just ordinary cocaine?"

Weezer turned his head to glare at her. "That ordinary cocaine has made me a lot of money in the last couple years," he snapped back. "Enough to buy my yacht and retire to Costa Rica at a young age."

"A lot of good that will do you if they kill you."

"They have to find me first, and I don't think they're gonna waste their time."

Rachel turned her head to watch him. "Well, I hope you make it, Weezer," she lied.

"I have to admit, it was a very clever plan. I mean with the cocaine inside the Parathion and all. I'll bet even the drug dogs couldn't find it."

Weezer finally smiled at her. "I never took the chance. I always took the farm roads and avoided the Border Patrol wherever I could."

Rachel pretended to have admiration in her eyes. "I'm impressed." She took another quick sip of water. "Too bad Otto had to screw up."

"It wasn't Otto, darlin', it was you and your stupid family." He scowled. "Once you moved in, it was pretty much over."

"Unless you convinced us to move out."

"Right."

Rachel laid her head back against the seat and looked up at him. "So that's why you had the spider put in my room and had Otto pay Jesse Ray to buzz our place."

"Jesse Ray was Otto's idea."

"He didn't seem smart enough to me to think of that."

"Actually, he was. He had a lot of brains." Weezer looked over at her, his eyes two narrow slits. "Just no backbone."

Rachel felt a sudden chill and turned her head away. The glint in his eyes sent a wave of nausea over her. She rubbed her scalp and felt the painful lump on the back of her head. *It may have been Weezer, after all, who killed Juan and Vicky*, she thought, and shivered. *If that's true, he's probably going to kill me, too.*

Chapter 20

The police cruiser pulled up in front of the old gas station in Thermal, California, and idled. Alex and Buddy stepped out. The officer who had given them a lift from the airfield rolled down the window. "I'll be back in fifteen minutes," he said. Alex was surprised at the brush-off but was grateful for the ride. "Thanks, Jack," he said, and the cruiser sped off.

Buddy walked to the building first and held the door open. The glass was smudged with fingerprints and covered with outdated flyers that filled in whatever space the dirt did not.

The wood floor sagged and creaked when Buddy and Alex headed toward the woman sitting behind the counter. She weighed over three hundred pounds and looked meaner than a Doberman. "Are you Mavis?" Alex asked after they introduced themselves.

"Yep," the woman said, snapping her gum. "You got IDs?"

Alex flashed his badge and Buddy dug out his driver's license.

Mavis grunted her acceptance and retrieved a bag from behind the counter. She made a big production of slowly removing the belt.

"It looks like Rachel's." Buddy picked it up for a closer look. "Notice the turquoise stone?" He showed it to Alex. "It's green, rather than the more typical blue. That's what she really liked about it."

"Pretty nice belt," Mavis said in a monotone. "Silver buckle an' all." A large strand of hair, now maroon from a dye job gone bad, fell across her face.

"Yes, it's beautiful."

"I figured it must be worth a pretty penny with that turquoise stone." She stared at Buddy with the eyes of a dead fish.

Buddy turned to Alex and raised his eyebrows. He looked back at Mavis. "It cost sixty-nine, ninety-nine new but I think it's worth a hundred dollar reward." He pulled out his wallet and laid a hundred dollar bill on the counter.

Mavis picked up the bill and held it up to the light before she stuffed it in her bosom, which was straining against her dress. She snapped her gum again and looked from Buddy to Alex. "Ya wanna see the writing?"

"Yes, we definitely do." Alex stepped aside and Mavis waddled out from behind the counter. The wood floor complained loudly as they followed her out of the building to where the restrooms were located. When she unlocked the door, Alex and Buddy stepped in, greeted by the smell of sewer gas.

Scratched into the paint on the back wall was a message in uppercase letters. "HELP" it read. "CALL ALEX LAPD" with his phone number following, had been scratched in below that. "TAKEN BY W" was near the bottom, next to "LOOK IN P," just before her initials.

"Is this where she left her belt?" Alex asked.

"Against the wall under the letters," Mavis pointed.

"What about the guy who picked up the key?" Alex stepped back into the night air. "Do you remember what he looked like?"

"Tall. Real tall. Good lookin'. Red beard and mustache." Mavis's face was still completely expressionless, as if it had been Botoxed.

"Were you able to see the girl?"

"Blonde. Skinny. Looked anemic."

"What about the vehicle? Do you remember the make or model?"

"Do I look like a mechanic?" Mavis didn't take her dead fish eyes off him. "It was a truck. A white one."

Buddy snapped a couple of photos of the wall before he joined Alex. "Thank you very much," he said, turning to Mavis. "You've been a very big help and we really appreciate it."

She turned to Alex without as much as a flicker of her eye. "Who's gonna pay for the damage to the wall?" She popped her gum. "I gotta buy me some new paint and get somebody in here to paint it."

It was Alex's turn to raise his eyebrows and look at Buddy. If anything, Rachel's scratch marks actually improved the look of the room. Nonetheless, Alex pulled out his wallet and handed Mavis two fifties.

The two men stood at the curb waiting for their ride, staring at the view on the other side of the road. Buddy spoke without turning his head. "As a respected member of the LAPD, are you familiar with the term 'shake-down'?"

"You don't have to rub it in," Alex said, rubbing his jaw. "If we ever get Rachel home alive, she's gonna owe us big time."

Just then, Jack appeared and pulled the cruiser to a screeching stop in front of them. Buddy and Alex climbed in, and Jack sprouted a grin from ear to ear. "Well, boys, how much did it cost ya?"

The trip back to the airfield, with lights flashing and siren blaring, was quick. Once they were back in the air, Buddy leveled the Bonanza off at 7000 feet. "What if the yacht's not in San Diego?" he asked, heading for Banning Pass.

"It has to be in San Diego," Alex replied. "Can't be anywhere else."

"What if he's already out to sea?" Buddy turned his head toward Alex, looking for more reassurance.

"If he is, then it means he took the freeway and completely slipped through all the check points. It could have happened, I suppose, but I have a feeling he took the back roads. He may have dropped off some cocaine along the way."

"Inside the Parathion bags? Is that what the "*P*" in Rachel's note meant?"

"That's my take on it." Alex pointed to the windshield. "But I'd appreciate it if you'd watch the air or whatever you do to keep the plane on track." He looked down at his belt. His phone was vibrating again.

"Okay if I use the phone in here?"

"No problem."

Alex put the phone to his ear. "Heather?"

On the other end of the airwaves, Heather was crying and talking at the same time. "Rachel called. She's with Weezer."

"Now calm down," Alex said with quiet in his own voice. "We know she's with him."

"But she said she was okay. That everything was fine. She said she decided to go for a ride with him." Heather began to cry again.

"Heather, please stop crying. Was there anything else?"

"Yes." Heather took a breath. "She was lying."

"Did you happen to get a phone number from where she was calling?"

"Yes," she sniffed, and read the number back to him from the scrap of paper in her hand.

"Heather, that's excellent." Alex quickly scribbled the phone number on his wrist. "You've been a tremendous help."

After disconnecting, Alex made a quick call. While he waited on hold for an answer to a question, Buddy anxiously looked back and forth between him and his instrument panel. Then Alex flipped off his phone and turned to Buddy. "Rachel just called Heather from a phone with a San Diego County area code."

"And?"

"She said she was with Weezer voluntarily. He probably thinks we can't go after him with a kidnapping charge that way."

"So are you saying he's not worried about us tracking him down?"

"Exactly." Alex nodded. "Right now we don't have anything we can charge him with other than kidnapping and he probably knows it."

"But he doesn't know Rachel left us a message at the gas station."

"Right. So, we know Rachel is alive, and we know they're headed to one of the marinas around San Diego. Now get us as close to the coast as you can. I'm going to call the chief and see if they've found the yacht."

A blanket of fog hovered over the waterfront. Rolling waves rhythmically slapped against the pilings and a briny smell saturated the air. Rachel stumbled along the wharf ahead of Weezer, shivering in the damp night, fear reaching into the marrow of her bones.

The drug haze had worn off, and Rachel contemplated her plight. She doubted Alex would get her message in time, if ever, which she had left in that pathetic excuse of a restroom. If only Heather realized her phone message was a lie. *Good luck with that*, she thought. She'd just have to figure out a way to save her own life, she decided, as her gaze slid down to the murky water on either side of her. She was hauling a large trunk on wheels that Weezer had attached to her wrist with a cord, and pictured herself jumping over the edge of the pier, the large trunk pulling her down to the depth of the bay. *Not a good idea.*

"Keep moving," Weezer ordered, walking a step behind her. He toted a handcart stacked with boxes, its wheels rumbling and clacking over the uneven boards of the dock, the noise of it reverberating over the water.

Rachel listened for voices, hoping someone might be nearby, someone close enough to hear her scream. *No such luck.* She heard only sounds of distant horns and bells punctuating an otherwise quiet night.

"Turn right here," Weezer demanded. Rachel stopped and looked up at the yacht moored in front of them. She caught her breath at the sight of it, glowing white under the lights of the marina.

"Wow. She's beautiful," Rachel said, her gaze flowing down the full length of the ship, momentarily forgetting why she was there.

"Keep moving." Weezer's voice was harsh, and he jabbed a finger, hard, at her back. Rachel flinched, back to reality, and trudged ahead to the slip, guessing he was eager to board and get rid of her. The wheels of the trunk caught on one the boards when she turned, and she had to yank the cord with both hands to free it.

When they arrived at the gangplank, Weezer made Rachel stand on the walkway while he loaded his boxes into the yacht and dropped them just inside the door. Rachel looked down at her wrist. It was raw from rope burns. She looked around. Even if she could free herself from the albatross Weezer had attached her to, she had nowhere to run.

The two of them managed to move her trunk up the gangplank and into the ship, and once inside, Weezer detached Rachel from the trunk and simply bound her hands together.

She looked around the salon. A second pile of boxes had been stacked in the middle. "Is that your life?" she asked.

"Pretty much." He turned and studied her as if he were debating what to do with her.

Rachel sensed her time was running out. "Take me with you, Weezer," she said softly, almost in a whisper, and looked up at him with as much longing as she could rally. It was a cheap trick, but it was the only thing she could think of to stall for time.

Weezer drew her close and put his lips on hers. He kissed her deeply for a long time, his tongue reaching for hers. Rachel shamelessly kissed him back.

When he let her go, she had tears in her eyes. "I can't believe you finally got around to kissing me," she said, hoping to convince him the tears were for him.

"Whose fault was that?" He cut her wrists free and reached for her again.

She pulled away slightly and looked up at him from beneath her lashes. "I'm a little road weary. Do you think I could I freshen up a bit?"

"I don't think so," a woman's voice barked.

Rachel and Weezer spun around to face the woman walking toward them. She held a .22 automatic, the barrel pointed at Weezer's heart.

"Kat! What are you doing here?" Weezer gasped.

"You killed my son," she said flatly, not taking her eyes off her target.

"That's not true," Weezer cried, but Rachel saw the panic in his eyes. "I tried to protect Otto," he whined.

Katerina's eyes narrowed into snakelike slits. "You killed him as surely as if you put the knife in his heart."

"Kat, listen to me," Weezer said calmly, taking a step forward. "Otto—"

"Stop. You move one more inch and I'll shoot."

Weezer froze, just six feet away from the point of her gun. "Okay, okay. I won't move," Weezer assured her, raising his hands in surrender. "Just tell me what you want."

"I want my son." She spit out the words.

"Listen, Kat, you know how sorry I am. I loved Otto." His eyes pleaded with her. "He was my best friend, the brother I never had."

She appeared to accept none of it, and took another step closer, the gun still pointed at Weezer's heart. "You killed that woman and he took the blame for it. You ruined Otto's name, our family's reputation."

Rachel jerked her head around and glared at the man.

Katerina's eyes picked it up and she sneered. "Apparently your girlfriend didn't know you were the Blood Mountain strangler. My, my, Weezer," Kat said, maliciously. "I guess I've given away your little secret." She clicked back the safety on the gun.

"Look, Kat," Weezer began to plead. "You know I've always taken care of you."

"Sure you have."

"Even now, I've got a package you need. I kept one back for you."

"Sure you did." Kat laughed. "That's why you're leaving town. But don't worry, Weezer, I'll find your little present after I kill you."

A shot rang out and Rachel instinctively squeezed her eyes shut. When she opened them, she watched Katerina's face take on a strange, puzzled look. A bright red spot blossomed on her chest and spread across her sweater as she slumped to the ground.

When Rachel tore her gaze away, she saw Eddie Porcini coming toward them with his gun still smoking.

He pointed it at Weezer. "Going on a cruise, are we?"

Weezer swallowed, tried to sound calm. "We were going to Mexico for the weekend."

"Yeah, right. I can tell," Porcini said, waving his gun toward the pile of boxes. His demeanor changed to anger. "Where's the money?"

"What money?"

"The money from the cocaine you just dropped off. While you're at it, you can hand over the money you been skimming the last couple years."

Weezer stared at him, mute.

"You know, you make a pretty lousy thief, Chaffee. Then you want to bail out before you even finish the job." Porcini turned his head and spit on the floor without taking his eyes off Weezer. "Now it's time to pay up."

❧❦❧

Buddy lowered the landing gear on the Bonanza when they started the descent into Lindbergh Field. He hit the brakes hard the moment the wheels touched the runway and pulled off at the first taxiway. He and Alex quickly transferred to one of the three cruisers waiting at the executive terminal, and they raced through the city with lights flashing and sirens screaming. Buddy anxiously looked at his watch at five-second intervals.

"Don't worry about it," Alex said, interrupting his thoughts. "It takes about forty-five minutes to get a boat that size ready to shove off."

"I wasn't worried about that. It's Rachel," Buddy said, his voice trailing off.

"Try not to think about it. She's smart. She'll figure out some way to stay alive." Alex spoke with a confidence he really didn't feel. "Besides, Chaffee doesn't have to be in any hurry to take off. He thinks we're not a threat to him."

"I suppose." Buddy nervously twisted his hands and he didn't sound very convinced. The wail of the sirens stopped; Alex understood they were getting close to the marina. "It won't be long now."

Porcini held his Glock in one burly hand, finger on the trigger, and pulled out a two-way radio with the other hand. "I found our friend," he said and clicked off. "Okay, move it, Chaffee." He cocked his head toward the stairs. Weezer walked ramrod straight in that direction. "You, too, Miss America." Rachel complied without uttering a word. At the bottom of the stairs, she found herself in the stateroom. Porcini pulled a length of cord and a pair of handcuffs out of his pocket and threw them at Weezer. "Cuff her. Then tie her legs."

Rachel felt the pain when Weezer pulled her arms back and snapped on the handcuffs, but she bit her lip and refused to cry out. He threw her down on the bed. More pain shot through her shoulders and she squeezed her eyes shut to keep from crying. Finally, he tied her legs with the cord, cinching it tight against her skin.

Porcini moved to the door that led to the deck and pulled a small flashlight from his belt and shined a beam of light at the top of the stairs.

A man with a large Roman nose and slicked back hair stepped down into the stateroom. He wore an expensive Italian suit and had a lit cigarette in one hand. "Who's she?" he asked, pointing the cigarette toward Rachel.

"This here's Chaffee's girlfriend," Eddie answered.

"I am *not* his girlfriend," Rachel burst out. Filled with anger, she yanked herself upright on the bed. "My name is Rachel Ryan and I happen to be the Sales and Catering Director of the Mesquite Mountain Inn. I was abducted and drugged by this man," she accused bitterly, cocking her head toward Weezer, "and forced to come here by gunpoint. Furthermore, I happen to know the LAPD is looking for me right this minute and if you have any brains in your head at all, and it looks like you do, you'll—"

"Shut up!" the man yelled and slapped her face hard. It knocked Rachel back and brought tears to her eyes. She put her head down against the bedspread and kept it there. The man looked her over slowly, taking a deep drag from his cigarette, its smoke slowly curling up in the damp air. "Gag her and put her in the closet."

Porcini took a small bottle out of a jacket pocket and dumped a little of the liquid on a rag. Rachel jerked her head back and forth when Eddie tried to tie the rag over her mouth. He slapped her hard on the other side of her the face, stunning her into compliance.

Rachel held her breath as long as she could, and then the thug tossed her into the closet like a rag doll. When he shut the door, she scraped her head against the carpet trying to dislodge the gag around her nose and mouth, and finally gulped for breath only a moment before the chloroform began sending black spirals careening across her field of vision. She felt herself losing consciousness even when the rag slipped down below her nose.

When Rachel opened her eyes again, everything was black and everything was quiet. She panicked for a moment, and then remembered where she was. Her face throbbed from the brutal slaps and her shoulders ached from being handcuffed so tightly. Her legs felt numb. By rolling and moving her head, she managed to work the gag down past her chin, and when she opened her mouth, pain flashed across her jaw. Her cheeks felt hot and swollen.

A volley of gunshots suddenly echoed from somewhere outside the yacht. Rachel flinched at every blast, then shook, terrified, wondering if the next bullet would be for her. *If not—if they don't come back to kill me—will anyone ever find me alive?*

A period of quiet followed, and Rachel lay in the dark, tears finally flowing from her eyes, wetting the carpet beneath her face. *Boy, I've really done it this time. All those times I've thought of killing myself...and now, here I am, thrown away in the bottom of a closet, desperately wanting to live. What irony.*

Rachel lost track of the time she spent examining her life, but eventually she heard a noise, a thud, a thump. She heard muffled voices. People were coming closer. She heard and felt movement inside the yacht, doors slamming. *But who? The killers?* Panic swept over her again and she lay frozen with fear.

Within minutes footsteps led to the stateroom. The closet doors were jerked open and light flooded in, momentarily blinding her. She held her breath as she felt someone's arms pulling her out, cutting the cord on her legs.

When she saw Alex's face, it took a few moments before she could speak. "I see you found my note," she mumbled through swollen lips.

Alex smiled at her, snapping open the metal bracelets. "Yeah, and such terrible penmanship for a graduate of Catholic school, too," he said, and then gathered her up in his arms.

✑✑

Alex strode into Rachel's hospital room, carrying a bouquet of white roses. He set the vase down on the table next to the pink ones Buddy had brought earlier.

Rachel gazed at the roses. "Thank you, Alex. They're just beautiful." She turned toward him. "You're so thoughtful."

He leaned in close and kissed her on the forehead, the only spot on her face that wasn't swollen or discolored, and took her hand. "How's the concussion?"

Rachel was sitting partway up in bed, with an intravenous drip going in her left arm. "It still hurts, but it doesn't look like my brain separated or anything horrible like that." She tried smiling, but it felt like her face was frozen. "I just have to be careful not to get whacked again. Then I could have a real problem." She looked him over from head to toe. "But what about you? Are you okay?"

"I'm doing great." His eyes reflected a calmness she had never seen there before.

"Tell me again what happened. I was so out of it last night."

"We had the parking lot surrounded and— well, you heard the shoot-out. That's when Eddie Porcini and Vittorio Marino, the big boss, were both killed. The other two surrendered."

"Marino was the one with the big nose and expensive suit?"

Alex nodded. "He had my former partner killed. One of the other men confessed he actually saw Porcini do it on Marino's order."

She nodded, not bothering to mention Marino was the one who blackened her face. What she suffered was minor in the whole scheme of things. "What about Weezer?"

"He died early this morning, Rachel."

She looked quickly away. She hadn't wanted that. She wasn't even sure why.

"Marino used Otto and Weezer to distribute the cocaine they had flown in from Mexico, to dealers all the way into LA."

"Wow." Rachel said the word softly and exhaled deeply. Like a video on fast forward, the events of the last two months flashed through her mind. "And you're not mad at me?" She looked up at Alex with a face so childlike, eyes so wide and innocent, Alex had to laugh and shake his head.

"You rescued me for the second time, Mr. Tucker," she said in mock formality, her eyes twinkling. "And for that I'll be eternally grateful."

He glanced down to gather his thoughts and then looked at her in a torn kind of way. "And I'm grateful to you, Rachel. You were instrumental in allowing us, not only to take down the organization, but to solve a case we've been working on for a long time." He leaned over her and kissed her softly on the lips.

"So this is goodbye." Rachel locked her eyes on his, searching, her face inches from his. A wave of emotion welled up in her.

Alex straightened up, not able to say it. "You never know," he whispered and left the room.

Epilogue

November's dry, cool air blew in on schedule. Though not bone rattling, the night was cold enough for Buddy and Rachel to enjoy the fire by the pool. They sat there alone, nursing steaming mugs of hot chocolate.

The fire popped, spitting out an ember that landed near Rachel's feet, and she jumped off her chair, sloshing some of the cocoa out of her cup.

"It's okay, it's okay," Buddy said, catching her arm and pulling her toward him. Rachel settled back down and stared at the fire. "You know, it's funny what happens to your mind when you think you're about to die."

"You mean when your whole life flashes before your eyes?"

Rachel's eyes searched Buddy's face. "No. I mean when you finally realize what's important to you."

He leaned in closer to her. "As in *who* is important to you?"

She smiled, teasing. "Maybe."

"Does that mean you'll marry me?"

"Oh, Buddy. You know I can't marry you." She picked up the poke stick and stuck it in the fire.

"Really? Now why is that?"

"You know why."

"No. Why?"

She wouldn't look at him. "I have issues."

"So what? I have some issues myself."

"Yes, but my issues…"

"You mean because you're bi-polar?"

Rachel jerked her head up. "Where did you hear that?" Then an instant later, "Never mind. I know where you heard it, and so help me, I may brain my sister and there will be two of us with concussions."

Buddy laughed. "Rachel, don't you know I don't *care* that you've got problems? I can deal with it. Besides, I have a real good friend back in LA that I think can help you."

Another ember popped, and Rachel flinched, nearly falling off her chair. "Dang!

You know, I wonder how long it's going to take before I stop jumping at every spark and loud noise. Frankly, I'm getting pretty sick and tired of it."

"Rachel, you have to give yourself some time to recover." Buddy reached up and stroked her cheek. "Your face is nearly healed, but the emotional part always takes longer."

Rachel turned her face away. "So they say, but I'm getting tired of lying low, being careful so I don't hit my head. Then there's my life, which is now about as exciting as watching concrete set up."

"Whoa, what are you, some kind of adrenalin junkie? It's only been two weeks." Buddy moved another log to the top of the fire.

"Right. Two whole weeks off the job. Meanwhile, the vultures of boredom are slowly pecking me to death."

Before Buddy could respond, JT and Heather strolled over and greeted them.

"How are you feeling, Heather?" Buddy asked.

"I'm feeling great," Heather said, her face flushed. "I haven't had a fibromyalgia attack since Rachel came home, business gets better every day, and I've even started painting again."

"That's wonderful," Buddy exclaimed, and motioned for them to sit down. "Join us."

Rachel peered at her sister. "Okay, Heather, now you can tell us the whole truth."

Heather blinked. "What do you mean?"

"Just look at your face. It's glowing." She looked at JT. "I'll bet Justin and Joseph are coming for Thanksgiving."

JT looked at his wife and she laughed. "Well, there goes our surprise."

"That's okay," Rachel said. "I think I've had enough surprises for a while."

Heather handed her sister an envelope. "This is for you. Fed-Ex just dropped it off."

Rachel looked at the return address, then at Heather.

"Open it, girl," Heather insisted. "It's from Richard Markman, the movie producer," she said, turning to Buddy. "Remember, I told you? He's the movie producer Stanley Belinski showed the property to last summer."

Rachel tore open the envelope and pulled out the letter. When she finished reading it, her face was beaming. "He said he was very impressed with the package I sent him," she said, glancing at the letter again. "He liked our brochure and our prices and our menus and our private meeting rooms." She looked up at everyone. "So he's coming here, in person, to check out our lovely hotel. So, unless there's a problem, he'll sign on the dotted line and film part of his next movie right here on Blood Mountain." She stood up and raised both her arms. "Hallelujah! I have been saved from a life of tedium and dreariness."

"Spare me," JT said dryly. "Casting calls aren't 'til later."

"But imagine, JT," Heather said, looking off dreamily. "A hotel filled with Hollywood celebrities."

"Oh, I'm so impressed," Buddy said with a high-pitched voice and a bend of his wrist. "Maybe I'll get a job as an extra." He batted his eyelashes and smiled coyly.

Rachel whacked him on the shoulder. "This is not funny, Mr. McCain. This means a lot of money for us." She pounded on him again.

He laughed, hunching over and covering his head. "Ow, ow, ow. Okay you win."

"Okay, kids, enough. Rachel is right," JT said. "If she nails this deal, we might even end up in the black next year." He took the poke stick and pushed one of the logs toward the center of the fire. "So, Rachel, exactly when do we have to have the hotel ready for Mr. Hollywood Producer's inspection?"

Rachel looked blank, and then quickly scanned the letter. She lifted her head and looked around at everyone. "Tomorrow," she said with a wry smile. "He'll be here tomor-row."

About the Author

Joanne Taylor Moore was born in Massachusetts and enjoyed life on a small, family farm where she learned to love nature and develop her imagination. She has published some of her poems and has written a column for a weekly newspaper, but mystery novels are her favorite genre.

Blood Mountain is the first of her series of mysteries about life and murder in the Arizona desert. Joanne lives in Yuma, Arizona, with her husband, Larry, and loves to spend her free time reading, designing jewelry, and visiting with their four children and eleven grandchildren.

www.ingramcontent.com/pod-product-compliance
Lightning Source LLC
Chambersburg PA
CBHW050020030726
47506CB00001B/37